Also by Ellen Crosby

Moscow Nights
The Merlot Murders
The Chardonnay Charade
The Bordeaux Betrayal
The Riesling Retribution
The Viognier Vendetta

THE SAUVIGNON SECRET

SECRET

A Wine Country Mystery

ELLEN CROSBY

SCRIBNER

New York London Toronto Sydney

SCRIBNER

A Division of Simon & Schuster, Inc.
1230 Avenue of the Americas
New York, NY 10020

First Scribner hardcover edition August 2011

SCRIBNER and design are registered trademarks of The Gale Group, Inc., used
under license by Simon & Schuster, Inc., the publisher of this work.

For information about special discounts for bulk purchases, please contact
Simon & Schuster Special Sales at 1-866-506-1949 or
business@simonandschuster.com.

The Simon & Schuster Speakers Bureau can bring authors to your live event.
For more information or to book an event, contact the Simon & Schuster
Speakers Bureau at 1-866-248-3049 or visit our website at
www.simonspeakers.com.

Manufactured in the United States of America

1   3   5   7   9   10   8   6   4   2

Library of Congress Cataloging-in-Publication Data

Crosby, Ellen.
The sauvignon secret : a wine country mystery / Ellen Crosby.
—1st Scribner hardcover ed.
p.   cm. —(Wine Country Mysteries.)
1. Montgomery, Lucie (Fictitious character)—Fiction. 2. Vintners—
Virginia—Fiction. 3. Cold cases (Criminal investigation)—California—
Fiction. 4. Vineyards—California—Fiction. I. Title. II. Series: Crosby, Ellen.
Wine Country Mysteries.
PS3603.R668S28 2011
813'.6—dc22   2011012425

ISBN 978-1-5011-8840-4
ISBN 978-1-4516-2841-8 (ebook)

For Tom Snyder

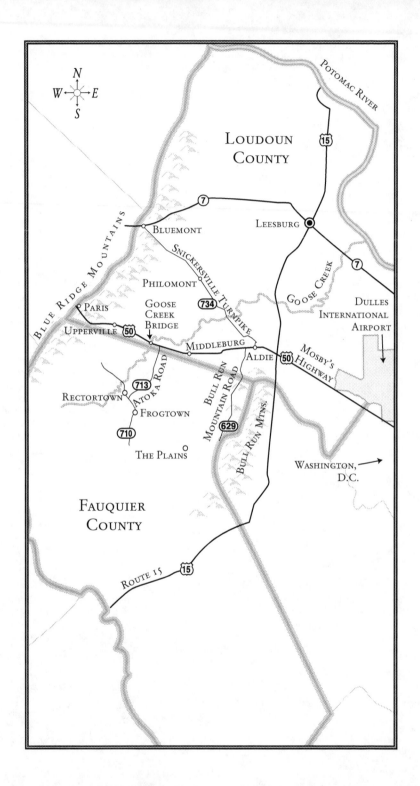

MONTGOMERY ESTATE VINEYARD

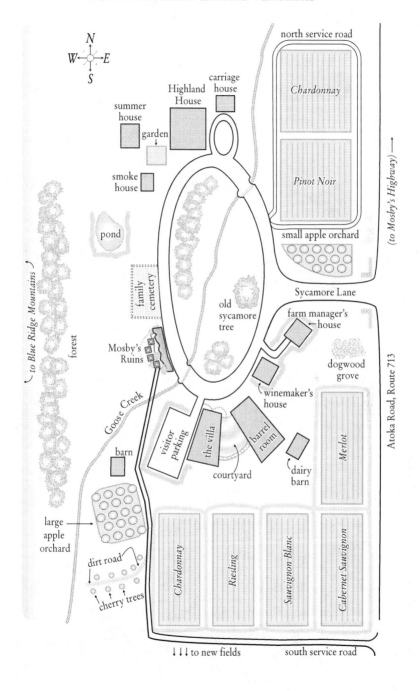

THE SAUVIGNON SECRET

We are all mortal until the first kiss
and the second glass of wine.

—Eduardo Galeano, Uruguayan journalist, novelist, writer

CHAPTER 1

———◦◦◦———

I didn't want to kill Paul Noble. Yes, I said I did. Worse, I said it in a public place. In my defense, half a dozen people at that same meeting chimed in. "Get in line" or "join the club" or "you and me both."

It was a figure of speech, and everyone in the room—twenty-five northern Virginia winemakers like me—knew it. At least that's what I thought at the time. So when I found Paul hanging from a beam a few weeks later in the old fieldstone barn he'd converted into an artist's studio, the first thing I thought was, "Oh, my God, someone really did it."

My second thought was that I could see my breath because the room felt like I'd stepped inside a refrigerator, which was odd on a sweltering July day. A blast of arctic air blew down my spine, bringing with it the faint but unmistakable sickening-sweet stench of death. How long had he been here? A few hours—maybe more—based on his mottled face, bugged-out, vacant eyes, and the slightly blackened tongue protruding from his mouth. I put a hand over my own mouth, swallowing what had come up in my throat. At least the glacial temperature had slowed down decomposition.

A paint-spattered stool was overturned in a wet spot on the carpet underneath Paul. He'd soiled himself—his khakis were stained—but the rug was damp from something else. An empty bottle of wine lay on the rug on its side next to a broken wineglass. I didn't need to lean in to see what he had been drinking. A bottle of my vineyard's wine, Montgomery Estate Vineyard Sauvignon Blanc. We'd won a couple of awards for it.

It was still possible to make out something in faded gold silk-screen on the wineglass. Nothing I recognized. No logo, no fancy calligraphy of a vineyard's name or a commemorative occasion, just a cartoonish figure of an empty-eyed man whose hands were clasped over stubs of ears, mouth open in the perfect round O of a scream.

My stomach churned again. I reached out to steady myself on the glass-topped table Paul used for his tubes of paint, palettes, and jars of brushes, pulling my hand back in the nick of time. The Loudoun County Sheriff's Department would be all over this place as soon as someone—meaning me—phoned in a suspicious death, and they'd check for fingerprints, fibers, and whatever they could find that would tell them who Paul's most recent visitors had been. No point contributing evidence I'd have to explain later.

I backed out of the barn into a wall of triple-digit heat. Though Paul had made many enemies with the way he did business, that kicked-over stool looked like suicide. Talk about an unlikely person to kill himself. Only two days ago I'd been on the phone with him and he'd been as ornery and mean-spirited as ever.

The only remaining brother of Noble Brothers Fine Wine Importers and Distributors, Paul Noble had the exclusive contract to distribute my wines to restaurants and stores, a monopoly he ran like a tin-pot dictator and the reason so many vineyard owners hated him. If you wanted your wine sold anywhere outside your tasting room, it worked like this: Paul told you what he'd pay for it, and you said okay. Tell him no or "if you think I'm giving it to you for that price, you're out of your mind," and no one else would, or could, buy it. Hence the word "exclusive" and the reason he got away with rock-bottom offers that forced more than one small family-owned vineyard to throw in the towel after their profit margin flatlined.

These were hardworking people—friends, not some faceless business ventures. Paul was nothing more than a wholesaler middle-man who pocketed a share of someone else's blood, sweat, and toil. For that we could thank the Twenty-First Amendment to the Constitution, which repealed Prohibition but kept a choke hold over the distribution of "demon alcohol," spawning the Paul Nobles of this world. It wasn't fair, but it was the law.

Paul had called me two days ago. A Tuesday. The minute I saw his name flash on my phone's caller ID display, I knew I was in for it. He didn't waste any time telling me he could no longer buy my Cabernet Sauvignon for the price we'd agreed in the spring, and if I wanted him to take it now, I had to throw in my Sauvignon Blanc, medals and all, for another fire sale price.

"We had a deal," I said. "You promised."

He'd caught me as I was walking through the courtyard that connected the barrel room where we made wine with the tasting room where we sold it. In the distance, the vineyard was summer-lush and green, framed by the soft-shouldered Blue Ridge Mountains. I loved this view, especially at sunset when the honey-colored light spread across the fields and gilded the vines like a scene out of a dream.

"Look, Lucie, it's not my fault the economy's in the toilet," he said. "I can't sell it if I buy it at that price now."

I deadheaded flowers in a wine barrel planter filled with rioting petunias and variegated ivy, snapping off wilted blossoms and thinking evil thoughts about Paul. He could keep our agreement and sell it at the old price, but it meant cutting his own profit.

"Paul," I said. *"Please."*

"Sorry, kiddo. No can do."

"I can't even cover my costs if I sell it to you for that price."

"It's just for now," he said. "Things'll improve and we'll do better next year. We all have to tighten our belts, you know."

Paul's belt went around a waistline that was forty-plus inches. He flew to Europe regularly to negotiate deals on the wines he imported, where he also bought his handmade shirts on Jermyn Street and his bespoke tailored suits on Savile Row in London, his favorite tasseled loafers at Gucci in Rome, and his silk bow ties from haute-couture designers in Paris.

"Maybe we can talk about this," I said.

"Sweetheart, come on. I'm trying to help you here." He sucked air through the straw of whatever he was drinking. A perfect metaphor for our conversation and the way I felt. "You know as well as I do that unless you meet my price, your wine will just sit in the warehouse. No one will touch it. They'll buy something else."

"That's not true." I rubbed a small spot between my eyes where my pulse had started to pound.

I knew this game. He muscled me to cut my profit and then he did the same thing to the retailer. Everybody bled but him.

"Look, I gotta go. Someone just walked in. Think it over. You've got two days." He hung up before I could make a stunned reply.

One of the threadbare jokes about owning a vineyard is that it's a surefire way to make a small fortune: all you have to do is start with a large one. I didn't have a large fortune when I took over the family business four years ago, thanks to Leland, my father, who never met an investment opportunity—or get-rich-quick scheme—that hadn't called out to him and his wallet until he died in a hunting accident. After his death, an inheritance from my mother's estate helped me get back on my feet, but that money was gone after fixing what Leland had let get run down and planting more vines. Throw in a rough spring earlier this year when my winemaker took a break to wrap up personal business in California, and an unexpected hard frost in May that killed half our crop, and I was teetering on the precipice again. Paul's phone call couldn't have come at a worse time.

For the next forty-eight hours I'd stewed about that ultimatum and the unfairness of what he was trying to do to me. Finally I decided to drive over to his home outside the pretty Quaker village of Waterford, rather than meet him in his Georgetown office, and tell him to go to hell. That was before I discovered him hanging from a rafter in his barn above a pool of my Sauvignon Blanc.

I shaded my eyes against the hard slant of the noontime sunshine and looked across Paul's golf-course-perfect lawn to the fields and woods beyond. The main road was a half mile away at the end of his long driveway—more like a private road. A car could have come and gone easily without being noticed, certainly not by any neighbor since the nearest one was down the road apiece. The only vehicle I'd seen after driving through the tree-lined streets of Waterford had been a John Deere tractor on the outskirts of town. The farmer pulled over and waved so I could pass him near the cemetery entrance on Loyalty Road.

Had someone else come by earlier, before I got here? What if he—or she, or they—killed Paul and then staged the hanging so a murder looked like suicide? And what if they were still here, waiting? Was I alone now?

I shuddered and took a long, slow look around the house and grounds. Except for the twittering of birds hidden in the trees and the faint buzz of the cicadas, the place was as hushed and silent as a cathedral.

I pulled my phone out of my purse. Once I called the sheriff's department, I'd be halfway down the slippery slope, letting myself in for a heap of trouble. First, I was the one who found Paul. Then there was that argument we had the last time we spoke and the fact that I recently said in public that I'd like to kill him—even if it was in jest. Throw in my wine bottle at the scene and the reason I'd come over here unannounced: to have a showdown with the deceased.

On the plus side, I didn't murder Paul Noble.

I punched in 911 on my phone and made the call.

CHAPTER 2

Loudoun County, Virginia, stretches across more than five hundred square miles of winding country lanes, villages plucked from a sweet, nostalgic memory, and rolling hills dotted with farms, weathered barns, and pastures where Angus cattle and expensive Thoroughbreds graze. It is also the fastest-growing county in the United States, thanks to a burgeoning high-tech industry that brought with it pockets of high-density subdivisions, strip malls, and multilane highways. Still, it would be awhile before I heard the sound of sirens in this rural corner of the county.

As I sat on the steps of Paul's barn to wait for the first cruisers to show up, the tip of my cane caught in the chink of a broken stone. I pulled it out and laid it next to me.

Six years ago a car driven by a former boyfriend missed the turn at the rain-slicked entrance to my vineyard late one night, plowing into one of the pillars that had guarded our front gate since before the Civil War. The boyfriend walked away. I did not.

After a couple of months in the hospital and two surgeries, the accident left me with a deformed left foot and a limp. A cane helped my balance. One day I planned to ditch the stick despite what my doctors said about it being permanent, which was why I still used the adjustable metal one the hospital gave me. If I ever moved on to a wooden cane it would feel like I'd given up hope.

From somewhere in the magnolia came the chipping sound of a

cardinal. My disability had been the consequence of poor judgment, excessive speed, and one too many beers on that memorable night, but it still had been an accident.

This felt different. Had Paul deliberately taken his life? And if so, what pushed him over the edge? The empty bottle—my wine—and the broken glass looked like he might have taken his time with one final drink, or a couple, before putting a knot in that rope and climbing up on that stool, so it seemed as if he planned this. Not that I wanted to go back into that barn, but if he had been murdered, surely the room would feel different? The presence of the other person, or persons, who killed him would linger or somehow be felt, like a vibrating hum that disturbed the air. Instead Paul's death seemed quiet—a sad, whispered goodbye, not an end that screamed violence.

I heard the first wail of sirens in the distance. A few minutes later, a tan-and-gold sheriff's department cruiser pulled up in front of the barn. A large, well-built African-American deputy unfolded himself from the driver's seat and looked me over, none too happily, as he got out of the car.

"Well, well, Ms. Montgomery," he said. "What are you doing on this side of the county? You the one who phoned in a suspicious death?"

Deputy Mathis, known as Biggie to his fellow officers, had also been the first on the scene at my vineyard a couple of years ago when a tornado unearthed a human skull. Mathis had a shrewd stare and a laserlike way of zeroing in on a person, as though he saw right through your head to where your brain was rapidly trying out and discarding explanations and excuses and alibis. I had done nothing except stumble on Paul's dead body and I wasn't guilty of anything, but already he made me squirm just as he had that day at the vineyard.

"Yes," I said. "In the barn. He hanged himself . . . he's been dead awhile. There's a horrible smell."

Mathis lifted his eyes to the sky like he was offering a silent prayer and shook his head as if lamenting another senseless death.

"Friend of yours?"

I hesitated. "Business acquaintance."

"Name?"

"Paul Noble."

"Anything else you want to tell me?"

The question was conversational, but I felt the prickle of electricity running through his voice.

I looked him in the eye. "Nothing, other than I found him like this when I walked into the barn."

Mathis tilted his head and considered that. "I see."

He called for backup, the crime scene team, and the EMTs as he pulled on a pair of latex gloves retrieved from the cruiser, knowing full well he'd left me like a kid waiting outside the principal's office trying to figure out if outright suspension or just detention hell was next for me. Just wait until he started asking the serious questions, like what I was doing here, and the details concerning my dispute with the deceased.

He pushed the barn door open. "You touch the door handle?"

"Yes."

"Anything else?"

"I don't think so. No, nothing else."

I followed him inside because he didn't tell me not to and heard him swear quietly when he saw Paul.

"Don't come any farther and don't touch a thing."

"Yes, sir."

I wrapped my arms around my waist against the bracing cold and watched him walk over to the body. He started to bend down to get a closer look at the bottle and the wineglass.

"Before you do that, there's something you ought to know."

He straightened up and his knee joints cracked. "And what would that be?"

"That bottle of wine is from my vineyard. Right now that's the only place you can buy it. Paul's a wine wholesaler. We have an exclusive contract and he sells my wine to restaurants and stores."

"Did you give him this bottle?"

"No."

Mathis's mind worked fast. I knew he was way ahead of the game, but he asked me anyway. "Care to characterize the nature of your business relationship?"

Here it was. "This is going to sound awful."

"Try me. You'd be surprised how much 'awful' I hear."

"He gave me two days to make up my mind whether I'd sell that wine—Sauvignon Blanc—and my Cabernet Sauvignon at a price where I was practically giving it to him."

"So you drove all the way over here to have it out with him?"

"He was dead when I got here."

"You didn't answer the question. And unless you've been sitting here since, say, midnight, I know he was dead when you got here. It's cold enough to hang meat in this place."

"We didn't actually have an argument. He gave me an ultimatum and I wanted to see if I could change his mind if we met in person," I said.

"You come by here often since you two do business?"

In spite of the temperature, I felt the heat rise in my face. "No. This is the first time."

"Great," he said. "Just great."

Outside the barn more vehicles pulled up and car doors slammed rapid-fire like gunshots. The barn door swung open, letting two uniformed men and a woman into the studio.

A minute later the door opened again, and before I could turn around someone said, "Hey, Biggie, what's shaking? Who's the vic?"

The memory-laced familiarity of that voice was a shot of relief, as if the cavalry had arrived. Bobby Noland was my childhood friend since the time he and my brother, Eli, let me hold the shoe box they used to keep the frogs they caught in our pond. The innocence of our relationship grew strained when I tutored him for honor society service hours in high school because he was flunking almost every subject. He bolted after graduation to join the army, and by the time he came back from two wars he was different, changed, scarred by locked-away stories. Every so often I'd see a haunted look in his eyes and wonder what still tormented him—an enemy soldier he'd killed or a buddy dying in his arms? But he'd returned to the old hometown, and the first thing he did was surprise us all by joining the sheriff's department. Everyone always figured Bobby would be dealing with the law when he grew up—just from the other side of the jail cell.

Mathis cleared his throat. "Hey, Detective, it's not shakin' too good for this guy. Name of Paul Noble. His home, his art studio, apparently. I believe you know Ms. Montgomery here. She's the, uh, RP."

Bobby's eyes shifted to me. "Lucie," he said. "I know I'm not going to like the answer to this, but how come you're the reporting party here?"

I told him about my relationship with Paul, and he nodded, none too pleased, as he ran a hand across his military buzz cut. He hadn't let his hair grow after his latest National Guard tour in Afghanistan. Kit Eastman, his fiancée and my best friend, told me he'd kept it stubble short so it was harder to tell his hair had gone prematurely gray—almost white.

Now he walked over to Paul and looked down at the items on the carpet underneath him. I caught the double take when he recognized the wine bottle.

"So you had a meeting with this guy today, and when you turned up, he was swinging from that rafter?" Bobby asked.

I caught Mathis's eye. "No meeting. I just came by."

"To shoot the breeze?"

I answered that question, too, and Bobby looked as thrilled as Mathis had been. One of the uniformed officers appeared in the doorway, the woman.

"House is locked up and the car is in the garage, Detective. The place is deserted."

"Get a warrant," Bobby said. "Where's Jacko?"

A short, dark-haired officer I hadn't seen before stood in the doorway. Mid- to late thirties, maybe. A few years older than I was. "Here. Who's the wind chime?"

Bobby's and Mathis's faces cracked into small smiles, but my stomach turned over once again. As much time as I'd spent around Bobby, I couldn't get used to the gallows cop humor that came with his job, but then I didn't spend my days walking into scenes like this or dealing with the depraved and inhuman things people did to one another.

"Paul Noble. In the wine business," Bobby said. "How long you reckon he's been here?"

Jacko walked over to Paul. "Ten, maybe twelve hours. Of course the fact that it's so cold you could freeze your nu . . ." He stopped and glanced at me. "I mean, it's pretty freaking cold in here. My apologies, miss. No disrespect intended. Detective Jackman, CSI. You are—?"

"Lucie Montgomery. RP."

The corners of his eyes crinkled but he kept a straight face. "Family member or friend of the deceased?"

"We had a business relationship."

"I see." He looked relieved not to have offended a grieving relative.

"You were saying, Tom?" Bobby asked him. "About the time of death?"

Jackman set a black case on the floor and pulled on gloves as one of the male officers moved around the room taking photographs. "Well, the room temp's screwing things up, but the guy's stiff as a board so lividity's set, tongue is black, and there are beginning signs of purging."

"What is purging?" I asked.

"The fluid leaking from his nose and mouth," he said. "I'd say time of death was anywhere from midnight to two A.M. last night. Maybe earlier, but not longer than eighteen hours."

Bobby did the math on his fingers. "So maybe as early as yesterday evening around six or eight, but more likely midnight to two."

"That's the best I can do. We'll know for sure after Dolan weighs in." I'd heard Bobby talk about Dolan. He was the new medical examiner. Jackman added, "Could be a case of coming and going."

Bobby nodded. "I was wondering."

"Pardon?" I asked.

"Autoerotic asphyxiation." Jackman pointed to the vicinity of Paul's waist. "Sometimes the rope slips as they ejaculate and they can't do anything to stop it. His, uh, trousers show stains in the right place, though they're not down around his knees. Maybe a fantasy or something."

He let that sink in and watched my face turn scarlet as I lowered my eyes and worked out what he had just said.

"A sexual . . . accident?"

"Yup. Some people are into kinky. You know anything about this guy's sex life?"

I blushed again. "No. I don't even know if he had one. He was very private. So you think he did this to himself? How can you be sure he wasn't strangled?"

"Like I said, the medical examiner will determine cause and time of death," Jackman said. "But in a hanging you always look at the jawline. If the rope follows it, then it's self-inflicted. Strangulation would produce a different mark on the neck. The rope would be pulled straight back. Look at his body, the way it's weighed down by gravity."

I looked, following the rope line on Paul's neck as Jackman traced it in the air with a finger. Then he pointed to a large canvas sitting on the floor propped against a beam. "If this painting was an indication of what was going on inside this guy's head . . . pretty creepy stuff. Self-mutilation. Cannibalism. Wonder what he did for fun if this was his hobby?"

The canvas—an oil painting—was filled with writhing, tormented nudes in so much misery and agony that I needed to look away. Jackman was right. Paul Noble's art was the work of a tortured soul.

"Get pictures of those paintings, will you, Smitty?" Bobby said to the photographer.

Jackman turned back to Paul and squatted by the wine bottle and glass.

"The bottle's from Ms. Montgomery's vineyard. She says that she didn't give it to him." I didn't know if Mathis was genuinely trying to be helpful or just speed the process of putting more nails in my coffin.

Jackman gave me a sharp look. "And the wineglass?"

"No idea," I said. "Vineyards give them out all the time as souvenirs. We silk-screen logos to commemorate a special event or the release of a new wine, but I don't recognize that one."

"That design reminds me of a painting I saw somewhere," Jackman said. "You know the one?"

"E.T.," Mathis said. "That little guy. The alien."

Jackman gave him a withering look. "*E.T.* is a movie."

"I've seen paintings of E.T." Mathis sounded defensive. "Looks just like him, if you ask me. What do you think, Detective?"

Bobby scratched the back of his head. "Yeah, I suppose it could be."

I stared at the glass and a memory clicked into place.

"The Scream," I said. "It looks like Edvard Munch's painting *The Scream.*"

"At least somebody here's got culture," Jackman said. "That's the one I meant."

"Yeah, you probably saw it on the back of your cereal box, Jacko," Mathis said.

"Okay, guys, let's get busy," Bobby said. "Lucie, why don't we talk outside and let them get on with it?"

He held the barn door for me. The heat was even more oppressive, or maybe I was starting to get dehydrated. Bobby grabbed my arm.

"You okay? You look like you're gonna pass out. Have a seat. I know it was rough seeing him like that."

"I'll be fine," I said, but I let him help me sit down on the step. "Are you just going to leave him there?"

He sat next to me. "It's a crime scene, Lucie. He's gone. We can't cut him down until we process everything around him. It might destroy evidence if we do."

"Right."

He didn't flinch at the reproach in my voice.

"I'm sorry. That's just the way it is. It's an inhuman business sometimes. I don't make the rules and you know that."

"It's such a ghastly way to die. It must have been slow and painful."

"If it's any consolation," he said, "the victim loses consciousness in about twelve to fifteen seconds, so it's pretty fast. Of course, you get some jerking around when the body spasms, so it seems like it's going on longer than it is. Then it's over for good."

"I don't understand why he did it."

Bobby gave me a long, hard look. "Suicides are pretty tough to fake," he said, "but not impossible. And they usually leave a note. This guy didn't, as far as we know. Biggie said you came over here today because you were mad as hell at the vic."

"Not mad enough to kill him."

He shrugged. "I understand. I don't need to read you your rights, Lucie, and you're not under arrest. But I need you to account for your whereabouts between now and midnight last night."

"Oh, come on. You're kidding, right? Even if I wanted to, I'm hardly strong enough to kill Paul Noble, then hang him from that beam. He probably weighed at least two hundred pounds when he was alive. I weigh a little more than half that. It's just not possible."

"Lucie," Bobby said, "I'm not kidding. I've seen plenty of people do things that they swear aren't possible, believe me. Where've you been since midnight last night and can anybody verify it?"

"Home alone," I said, "and no, nobody can verify it."

CHAPTER 3

———

Bobby didn't give me a lot of grief about my whereabouts and nobody being able to vouch for me, probably in part because he knew about my nonexistent social life, but mostly because we both knew I didn't kill Paul. After that he said I was free to go, though he might have more questions for me down the road.

"How much longer will you be here?" I asked.

He looked at his watch. "It's two now. Probably another three to five hours. As long as it takes to process the crime scene."

He got up from the step and held out a hand to me. "Come on, I'll walk you to your car. I've got one more thing to say to you."

I let him pull me to my feet. "What is it?"

He handed me my cane. "When you get home, pour yourself a good stiff drink, and before you go to bed watch something on television that'll make you laugh. Works for me."

He put an arm around my shoulder and gave it a friendly squeeze. It was so out of character, that little unexpected tenderness, that I couldn't find the words to answer him. All this time I'd figured Bobby was so tough he deflected the horrors of his job the way bullets bounced off Superman's chest. Now I found out he needed to numb himself with Scotch and reruns of *Seinfeld* or *Everybody Loves Raymond* to chase away nightmares.

"You okay?" he asked after a moment.

"Yeah, fine." My voice sounded almost normal. "Thanks for

the advice. I'll probably have that drink later on, but right now my grandfather's arriving on the afternoon flight from Paris. I'm just barely going to make it to Dulles in time."

"You'll get there," he said. "No speeding, hotshot. I'm not fixing any ticket, okay?"

"I never speed."

"Sure you don't. How come I didn't know Luc was coming for a visit? Last time he was here he promised on his next trip he'd bring a couple of Cuban cigars and we'd smoke 'em together. Kit should have told me he was going to be in town. Didn't the two of you spend five hours a couple of nights ago yakking on the phone about what shade of white her dress should be?"

I started to laugh, glad to change the subject to something silly, and he grinned. My wedding gift to the two of them was hosting their ceremony and reception at the vineyard. Kit and I had been planning nonstop for the past few months.

"There's a big difference between bone and blush, even if it's lost on you, buddy," I said, and his smile broadened. "And it was only three hours. I didn't know Pépé was coming until the day before yesterday. You know how he is."

"I hope he's going to be at your July fourteenth shindig. Be nice to see him again and have man talk instead of listening to you and my fiancée discuss whether your nail polish needs to match your shoes," he said.

"Oh, go ahead and elope. See if I care." I opened the door of my red-and-white-striped Mini Cooper convertible and gave him a mock-glare of annoyance. "He's coming to the party on Saturday, but then he's leaving first thing Sunday morning. Flying on to San Francisco to give a talk to some business group on a retreat outside Sonoma."

"California, huh? No wonder you can't keep up with him flying all over the place. At least I'll catch him on Saturday night." He shut the car door.

"Me, too. And thanks, Bobby."

"For what?"

The moment of good-natured teasing vanished as swiftly as a wispy cloud in the sharp blue sky above. The haunted look that aged him so much more than his thirty-three years flashed across his face. "You know what," I said.

"Don't mention it. You better get going."

He squared his shoulders and headed back to the barn. I drove away in the white-hot sunshine of a beautiful afternoon while he returned to the cold, dark studio with its tormented paintings. Later today he would cut Paul Noble's body from the noose where it hovered over the room like the angel of death.

My grandfather, Luc Delaunay, had called at sunset the Tuesday of my phone conversation with Paul. I'd been out on the back veranda sitting in the glider and finishing a bottle of white as I watched the fireball sun slip behind the low-slung Blue Ridge Mountains to the west. That evening the sky had been the creamy orange and robin's egg blue of a faded watercolor, and the ragged silhouette of the tree line at the edge of my land looked like dark lace against the light sky.

When the telephone rang inside the house I reached for my cane, but the machine kicked in before I could make it across the foyer. I knew it was Pépé the moment he cleared his throat like a rumbly bullfrog, as though preparing to deliver a speech to a filled auditorium.

"*Eh, bien, ma chère Lucie, c'est moi. Désolé que tu ne sois pas là.*"

I threw myself in my mother's favorite Queen Anne chair next to the demilune phone table, picked up the receiver, and cut off the answering machine. My grandfather's voice, which would almost certainly be filtered through the acrid smoke of a Gauloise and a snifter of Armagnac, sounded subdued as it echoed through the two-story foyer of the old house.

"I'm here, Pépé," I said in French. "I was outside watching the sunset."

Across the hall in the parlor, the mantel clock chimed eight. Two in the morning in Paris. It would be at least another hour before Pépé, a notorious night owl, would be ready to go to bed.

"Is everything all right?" I asked. "How was your trip to Vietnam?"

"*Formidable.* A couple of *vieux potes* decided to rent a junk and

sail the Halong Bay in the north. Did you know the name means
'where the dragon descends to the sea'?" As usual, he didn't wait for
my reply. "It was spectacular, *ma chère,* the sea the color of emeralds
and hundreds of stone grottoes rising from the water like cathedral spires or the scales on a dragon's back. Someday we'll go back
together. You must see it."

I smiled. Pépé kept in touch with a far-flung network known as
"the old chums" who were friends from his years in the French diplomatic service and, before that, in the Resistance during World War II.
No ten-countries-in-ten-days senior citizen package tour for him. My
eighty-four-year-old grandfather chased dragons in exotic lagoons.

"I'd like that," I said, "but I'm glad you're back in Paris, even if it's
only for a little while. When are you going to Morocco? Sometime
in the fall, isn't it?"

Like the song went, you couldn't keep him down on the farm
after he'd seen "Paree." In fact, it was hard enough keeping him in
"Paree." Ever since he lost my grandmother almost forty years ago,
he'd been a restless soul bereft without the love of his life. The wan-
derlust and the trips were how he coped with loneliness.

"Yes, yes," he said. "Morocco in September. A camel safari along
the southern border, plus the usual cities . . . Fez, Rabat, Tangiers.
But first I am coming to *les États-Unis.* I'm sorry to surprise you at
the last minute, *ma belle,* but it just came up."

I straightened up in my chair. "You're coming *here*?"

I'd long ago stopped being astonished by my grandfather's spur-
of-the-moment trips, especially when he announced he was about to
show up on my doorstep, but something in his voice said this time
was different.

"Let me guess," I said. "You're already at the airport, aren't you?
On the plane?"

He chuckled and I heard him sip his drink.

"Not quite, but I am packing my *valise.* I arrive in Washington on
Thursday afternoon. No need to put me up. I know how busy you
are. I'll stay in a hotel," he said. "Though I would like you to come
with me to a dinner party Friday night. Juliette and Charles Thiessman are having a few friends in to celebrate *le quatorze juillet.* Bastille
Day. You know the Thiessmans, *bien sûr*?"

Old family friends, they were Pépé's generation. I'd always found them hard to warm up to and the feeling seemed to be mutual. A dinner party at their home would be a very dull evening.

"Of course I do," I said. "Though Charles has become quite a recluse in the past few years so I haven't seen him for ages. Juliette pops into the shops in Middleburg every now and then. And you're staying here, by the way, not in some hotel. We have this discussion every time you spring it on me that you're arriving in the next few hours."

"If you're sure—"

"Pépé, you know I am. How long are you staying? Awhile, I hope?"

He sighed. "Not this time, *chérie*. I'm flying to San Francisco on Sunday to give a talk in a place called Monte Rio. It's in Sonoma County, near the Russian River."

I barely heard his description of the place. Another hit-and-run visit. Next time I'd tie him to a chair.

"Only three days? That's all?"

"It looks that way."

"Will you at least come to our Bastille Day party at the vineyard on Saturday night?"

"Of course. And I promise, the next visit I'll stay longer."

"You always say that."

"You do know that airplanes also fly from Washington to Paris, *n'est-ce pas*? You remember flying? It's very convenient, very quick," he said. "Do you want to call Charles and tell him we'll both be there on Friday?"

"Ouch. Okay, sorry for nagging. I know I'm overdue to come to France," I said. "It's just always so busy here. And would you mind calling Charles, since you seem to be in touch with him? I think their number is unlisted now."

"And you don't have it?" He sounded surprised. "A shame, since your mother used to be so close to Juliette. She practically adopted Chantal when she moved to America after marrying your father."

"That was a long time ago," I said. "Mom used to take me over to her house to visit. I remember Juliette talking about you all the time, the old days after the war when she first met you."

Pépé cleared his throat. "She was very kind to me when your grandmother died. Back then she wasn't married to Charles. I didn't meet him until they returned to Paris after Nixon named him your ambassador to France. She always made sure I was invited to their parties and dinners at the embassy." He paused to exhale a long breath of smoke and I knew he, too, was recalling old memories. "Frankly, I was surprised that Charles called me about this dinner on Friday, rather than Juliette . . . he especially asked for you."

"Me? Why?"

"I believe he has planted a small vineyard now. Perhaps he wants to ask you for advice."

"Pépé, he does have a vineyard and it's strictly off-limits to everyone," I said. "He makes his wine by himself, but he doesn't sell it anywhere. No tasting room, nothing. The other winemakers call him the Lone Ranger because he doesn't mix with any of us or show up at any of the wine festivals or competitions. It's really odd."

"Well, perhaps he wants to give you a private tour," Pépé said.

"If he did, I'd be the envy of every winemaker in two counties," I said. "I wonder what he really wants."

"I would imagine we'll find out on Friday."

"I guess. I'm dying to know what he does in that 'sanctum sanctorum' all by himself. You never know, it could be alchemy."

I heard Pépé's quiet laughter before he said goodbye and hung up.

By the time I got to the international arrivals waiting area at Dulles Airport after leaving Paul Noble's barn, the Air France passengers were already exiting customs, passing through double metal doors into the terminal. I scanned the crowd for my grandfather, hoping I hadn't missed him and he'd decided to take a cab to the vineyard. The fare—probably in the neighborhood of two hundred dollars—wouldn't faze him in the least. Finally the doors opened with a hiss, and a solitary figure emerged, gingerly pushing a luggage cart with a small brown-and-tan plaid suitcase and beat-up leather briefcase laying on it. The surprise was the cane, which he'd hooked over the cart handle.

At his age, and after that long transatlantic flight, it shouldn't have upset me, but it did. I had a quick moment to study him before he spotted me outside the metal guardrail. For the first time, his skin seemed nearly transparent, taut against the bones of his face in a way that sharpened his features so they looked sunken and almost hawklike. He must have sensed me staring because he glanced up and waved his arm like an infielder waiting for a pop fly, a smile lighting his frail face. I smiled back and went to the exit to wait for his kiss and our usual wrangling over who would push his luggage cart. Pépé was old-school chivalrous, and no amount of women's liberation or talk of equality between the sexes would ever persuade him that the small gallant courtesies a man performed for a woman—holding a door, helping her on with her coat—were passé.

Neither of us said a word about his new cane, but this time I put up only a faint protest over the luggage cart since I was going to lose the battle anyway. He patted my hand as he always did, and we walked down the ramp to glass doors leading to the shuttle buses and the hourly parking lot, which automatically slid open.

"I'm sorry," I said, hearing his small *ouf* as we stepped outside and he absorbed the brutal temperature change. "I should have warned you. It's over a hundred today. With the humidity it feels like one hundred and eight. Probably more. We're setting new records with this heat wave."

Across the street, rows of cars shimmered like a mirage. The asphalt felt squishy beneath my feet. Pépé pulled a handkerchief out of the pocket of his trousers and mopped his forehead.

"You forget how many summers I spent in Washington at the embassy after the war. In those days there was no air-conditioning." He glanced sideways at me. "Is something wrong? You seem upset."

"Are you sure you're all right? I know it was a long trip for you—"

I shouldn't have said it. He stopped the cart, looking exasperated.

"Now don't you go treating me like an old man. Just because I'm a little tired and maybe a bit unsteady on my feet is no reason to act like I've got one foot in the grave," he said. "That's your cousin's department. I can take one of you nagging me to take a nap or hovering over me like I'm in my dotage, but not both. Don't you start, too."

The reprimand had been delivered lightly, but he meant it and

I'd hit a nerve. He pushed the cart over to the car without speaking and put his suitcase and satchel in the trunk when I opened it. "Don't be upset with me," I said. "I just worry, that's all. I don't want anything to happen to you." His face softened. "One does not like to admit that one is getting older. I'm sorry, *chérie*. I shouldn't have snapped at you."

We climbed into the stifling car and I blasted overheated air-conditioning through the vents.

"We'll be seeing Dominique tomorrow, by the way," I said. The refrigeration kicked in and I switched the blower to low so it didn't sound like a jet engine before takeoff. "Juliette is using the Inn to cater her dinner. Dominique will be working, but she promised to take a break from supervising in the kitchen to see you. And she's coming to the vineyard on Saturday for our party."

Dominique's mother and my mother had been sisters, two years apart in age but so alike they could have been twins. Ten years ago, after my mother died when her horse threw her jumping a fence, Dominique moved from France to help Leland take care of my wild-child kid sister, Mia. My capable cousin, who'd been studying to be a chef, managed to get Mia under her thumb while also landing a job at the Goose Creek Inn, a local restaurant with an award-winning reputation for its romantic setting and superb cuisine. Dominique took over the fledgling catering business, and before long it, too, was racking up accolades just like the Inn. When the owner, who had been my godfather, passed away a few years ago, he'd left her both businesses in his will.

"Ah, then Dominique will have plenty of opportunities to monitor my napping," Pépé said to me.

We both grinned.

"She loves you. We all do."

"And I love you all, too. Now please tell me why you're so agitated, *ma belle*? That's twice you've missed the turn for the exit out of the parking lot."

I gave him a lopsided smile and pulled up to the tollbooth. After I paid the parking fee I told him about Paul Noble.

"The police believe he died while playing a sexual game?" Pépé asked.

"That's one possibility. The other is that he deliberately hanged himself," I said. "Except people commit suicide because they're depressed or they feel hopeless. A couple of days ago Paul called me and bullied me to sell him my wine practically at cost. I wouldn't have pegged him as either depressed or hopeless after he was done working me over. He was pretty ruthless. Talked about business plans for next year, too. Who does that if he's thinking about ending it?"

"Nevertheless you don't seem to believe that it was an accident?"

"If Paul was into erotic fantasies or extreme sexual games, then you'd think there would be rumors. There wasn't so much as a peep about him."

"You knew him well?"

"No, though I tried. I thought it would make dealing with him easier, but he was so . . . cold, I guess. All business, no social chitchat. After a while I gave up. Besides, he didn't seem to care about working with the local vineyard owners like his older brother did. A lot of people were mad at him because he was heartless. Folks blamed him when two really good wineries went out of business last year. They couldn't make a go of it anymore. Nice people. Lost everything."

"Could one of the owners have been angry enough to kill him?"

I signaled to turn onto Route 28 and merged with the usual early evening rush-hour logjam.

"Oh, gosh no. At least I don't think so. I mean, they weren't like that."

He gave me a don't-be-naïve look.

"No, Pépé. Neither of them did it. I'm sure," I said. "Believe it or not, for a while the deputy from the Loudoun County Sheriff's Department who turned up on the scene thought I might have done it. There was an empty bottle of my Sauvignon Blanc and a wineglass next to Paul's body. Plus it was no secret I disliked him. The reason I drove over there was because I was mad at him."

"The police suspect *you*?"

"Not really. Bobby Noland showed up later. He knows I didn't do it."

"Ah, Bobby. I have a couple of cigars for him," he said. "Do you think someone wanted to cast suspicion on you by leaving your wine bottle there?"

I moved from one slow-moving lane of traffic to another that crawled along only slightly faster. "No, that's too far-fetched. Besides, no one knew I was planning to drop by today."

"You'd be surprised how angry people become when they believe they are being cheated, or their livelihood is being stolen," he said. "It doesn't take much to push them to the kind of violence we've had in France. You've heard of the CRAV, haven't you? The Regional Committee of Viticulture Action, in English. A clandestine group of winemakers who, a couple of years ago, sent the president a video promising blood would flow if he didn't stop importing cheap wine from Algeria and Spain, and didn't do something about the over-production driving down the price of French wine on the world market."

"I read about those people. They sounded scary."

"They were scary. They bombed government buildings, tanker trucks, supermarkets," Pépé said. "They drained thousands of euros' worth of wine from tanks at agricultural cooperatives and let it seep into the ground. Once someone tried to plant a bomb along the route of the Tour de France. Thank God he was caught in time. The press called it 'wine terrorism.' "

"It isn't like that here, Pépé. It's nowhere near that bad," I said. "Plenty of people were mad at Paul, but not enough to consider blowing up his warehouse. And I honestly don't believe it was murder, after what the crime scene detective said about how hard it is to fake a suicide. I think Paul killed himself and we'll probably find out why sooner or later."

"It wouldn't take much to tip the scale for that kind of anger and violence to take hold in America." Pépé shook a warning finger at me. "It's what I've been asked to talk about in California next week—the lessons your government can learn from what happened to us."

"We had September eleventh," I said. "That changed everything. We have the Department of Homeland Security now. They reclassified wine as a food so we have to report every part of the production process to the Food and Drug Administration under some bioterrorism law. It's mind-boggling, all the paperwork we have to file. Records of everything we transport, everything we receive, what we add to the juice, batch lots, packaging materials . . . even each batch of grapes and the blend of each wine. It drives Antonio and me crazy. Sometimes I wonder why we even bother or if they ever do anything with all that information."

"The first time something happens, you won't wonder anymore." My grandfather sounded ominous.

"Who'd do something to wine?"

He shrugged. "How hard would it be? A group of tourists drive by a picturesque view of vines planted alongside a country road, say your vineyard on Atoka Road, and get out of the car to take a photograph. At the same time one of them scatters something that the wind will take and blow through your fields. They drive off and disappear forever. Gradually all your vines wither and die. Or a disgruntled employee adds something to one of your five-thousand-gallon tanks of wine just before bottling. How many people could he sicken or maybe even kill?"

We'd finally reached the turnoff for Route 50, Mosby's Highway. The homestretch. I put on my turn signal and we left Route 28 as I thought about what he'd just said.

Maybe we weren't so insulated from the kind of violence he was talking about. In France it was homegrown—a group of angry winemakers being driven out of business—not the threats of faceless foreigners. What would it take to push some of my fellow vineyard owners who had lost everything over the brink?

Maybe Pépé was right.

"I guess it wouldn't be that hard to do after all," I said. "Would it?"

CHAPTER 4

Friday the thirteenth dawned bright and hot, promising to be another scorcher for the record books. I showered and dressed, tiptoeing past Pépé's bedroom and avoiding the creaking treads on the grand spiral staircase. Halfway down the stairs I could still hear my grandfather snoring like a lumberjack from behind his door.

I fixed breakfast—coffee, croissants, and fresh goat cheese from a nearby farm—and carried it out to the veranda, along with the *Washington Tribune.* The heat and humidity had already leached the color from the sky, leaving it a dingy white. A film of haze had settled over the Blue Ridge.

Paul Noble's death was billboarded at the bottom of page one of the *Trib,* though the story had been moved inside to Metro. I didn't recognize the black-and-white thumbnail photo in the teaser; it looked like an old one taken years ago when Paul had more hair. Fortunately, the headline writers hadn't come up with anything cute or sensational, so it simply read: "Loudoun Businessman Found Hanged." The article was in the middle of the front page of Metro with a larger, more recent photo of Paul standing on the rooftop terrace of his luxurious Georgetown office building posing like a minor potentate. The Potomac and two backlit sculls whose rowers were perfectly in sync was the backdrop, probably a crew team from one of the D.C. universities. Thankfully the reporter wrote only that a "local woman" had discovered his body. No mention of anything kinky involving his death, so perhaps autoerotic asphyxiation had been discounted or maybe Bobby decided to keep that lurid possibility out of the press for now. Alcohol had been found at the scene, leaving the reader to draw his or her own conclusions about factors contributing to the tragedy.

A car door slammed in my driveway. I set down the paper and went inside. At this early hour it was probably Antonio. We'd been talking about whether we needed to do more spraying to deal with possible powdery mildew. But it was my brother, Eli, who let himself in the front door as I walked into the foyer. His red polo shirt had a stain like a Rorschach inkblot and his trousers looked like he'd slept in them. His dark brown hair, which he usually wore moussed or gelled in some gravity-defying style, fell naturally across his forehead as though he'd just stepped out of the shower. I liked it that way, glad he seemed to be shedding the manicured, pampered Ken doll persona his ex-wife had inflicted on him, even if he did trade it in for the rumpled, frazzled single-father-of-a-three-year-old look, which he was.

"Hey, babe," he said. "What's up?"

Calling me "babe" was still part of the Brandi hangover, though it was a lot better than some of the names he had for me when we were kids.

"Coffee's hot," I said. "And I have croissants. Did you eat breakfast?"

"I finished the milk and the soggy stuff at the bottom of Hope's cereal bowl." He glanced down at his shirt. "I dropped the bowl when I was cleaning up. I think it left a stain."

"You can't really see it," I said. "Is Hope at day care?"

He nodded. "I feel like I'm abandoning her every time I drop her off. She won't let go of my neck. It's like I'm being strangled with love."

Brandi's rich new boyfriend had made it clear he wanted someone who could travel with him on a whim and wouldn't be tied down with a child, so Eli ended up with full custody of his daughter. It had taken my breath away how fast my ex-sister-in-law had shed herself of Eli and Hope, but truth be told, I was glad she was out of the picture.

He rubbed a spot by his ear and my heart ached for him. "You two are coming here this weekend, of course?" I asked.

"You bet. We might not make it through fireworks, though. One of us gets nightmares."

"Maybe when she's older."

"I meant me."

I grinned. "The family pyromaniac? Ha. You're lucky I never told Leland who stole all those Roman candles he thought he'd stockpiled the first time he and Mom decided to have fireworks for July fourteenth."

"He guessed." He looked rueful. "Hence the nightmares."

He followed me down the back staircase to the kitchen and sat in his old childhood place at the scarred-up table while I fixed his coffee and got out a jar of my homemade strawberry jam—his favorite—for his croissant.

"Pépé upstairs sleeping?" He traced a finger over marks we'd made as kids pressing too hard with our pencils when we did our homework at the soft pine table. I nodded. "Hope still calls him Beppy. She can't wait to see him."

"He's flying to California on Sunday," I said. "Quick trip. But at least you'll get to spend Saturday evening with him."

"Uh-huh." He was still tracing curlicues and squiggles.

"We thought we'd make the party a clothing-optional event."

"That's good."

"Eli, are you listening to me?"

He looked up. "Huh? Sure, I am."

"What'd I just say?" I set a plate and coffee mug in front of him. "Not that I'm not glad to see you, but aren't you supposed to be in Leesburg? Say, maybe, at work?"

"Maybe yes, maybe no." He opened the jar of jam and carefully set the lid on the table. When he looked up, I saw just how beat down he really was. "Maybe I got laid off."

"Oh, God, you're kidding," I said.

"Would I kid about that? I missed a couple of deadlines while Hope had chicken pox. Clients got pissed off and went to another architectural firm. I'm job hunting, babe, but with the housing market the way it is right now, there's not much new construction out there, which means no work for builders and even less for architects like me." He touched his thumb and forefinger together showing no daylight. "And I'm that far away from getting evicted from our apartment because I can't make rent. It was either that or pay the day care bill."

"Move in here." I said it without thinking.

He looked up and our eyes locked.

"Is that a serious offer?"

"Of course it is. It'd be great to have someone in the house besides me. Mia's not coming back from New York and I just rattle around here by myself. It gets . . . lonely sometimes."

What I didn't want to say, much less think about, was that I never expected to be living on my own with my thirty-first birthday looming on the horizon in a few weeks. I always thought that by now there would be someone to share it with, maybe even a family.

He was silent for a moment. "I'll pay you rent, we're not freeloading. Cover our share of the groceries . . ."

"We can talk about that later. You know what I really need? Someone to fix the gazillion things that need repairing around the place. We could trade that in return for room and board."

"Luce, I don't want your charity."

"Eli, you haven't seen my list."

"Are you sure about this?"

"I think it would be great. I'll get to spend more time with Hope." He eyed me. "And you, of course."

He grinned and punched me lightly on the arm. "You know, I just thought of something. How about if I fix up the old carriage house and turn it into a studio? Maybe I could pick up enough work on my own to make a go of it, especially if I could keep Hope at home with me. What do you say?"

He busied himself spreading a perfect layer of jam all the way to the edge of his croissant while I stood there and watched him.

"I say your nose just grew an inch, Pinocchio. 'I just thought of something.' Jeez, Eli, I must be losing my edge. You didn't used to be able to play me that easily. You had this whole scheme all cooked up before you showed up, didn't you? Please don't tell me you spilled milk on your shirt on purpose and fished an old pair of pants out of the laundry basket just to make me feel sorry for you," I said.

He looked sheepish. "Ixnay to the clothes stunt. To be honest, I didn't think of it."

"Eli!"

He pretended to duck. "I didn't mean to set you up, but you're a good sister, Luce. Family means everything to you, so I kind of figured you might offer to take us in. Well . . . hoped."

"But you *did* set me up."

He flashed a cheeky grin and I threw a dish towel at him.

"In the nicest possible way. All kidding aside, I owe you. Raising a kid on my own . . . man, who knew? Now Hope will have you around because, let me tell you, I just don't get this girl stuff." He shook his head and set the towel on the counter. "Did your barrettes have to match the lace thingies on your socks when you were little?"

I didn't know whether to laugh or cry. "You bet they did."

"I don't suppose you have a to-go mug I could borrow? I could take this on the road. And, uh, I could get a van lined up from a buddy, but I can't have it until Sunday. We don't have much stuff. That work for you?"

He'd started rummaging through the cabinets for the mug, but I knew it was so I wouldn't see the giveaway expression of "mission accomplished" on his face.

"Jesus, Lord, Eli! Yeah, of course it's fine. I'll have the housekeeper air out your old room in the attic. Hope can have Mia's room since Dominique's bedroom has turned into the guest room. Pépé's got it now . . . that is, unless you've got other plans you haven't let me in on yet?"

He turned around grinning as he tossed the to-go mug in the air and caught it one-handed. "Nope, that's kind of what I figured you'd do."

"Glad I at least called that one right."

He planted a kiss on my cheek—a first for him—and said, "You're a good egg, you know that? I'd better take off. I met a guy who might be interested in a kitchen renovation. We're getting together in half an hour at his place in Aldie. I'll call you, Luce. Tell Pépé I'm sorry I missed him, but we'll catch him at the party tomorrow night."

"Right. See you later," I said, but he'd already vanished up the staircase.

A moment later, I heard the roar of his car engine and he was gone.

I cleaned up the kitchen, propped a note for Pépé against the coffeemaker asking him to call me when he woke up, and left for the winery. The Mini stirred up plumes of reddish-brown dust as I drove down Sycamore Lane, the private road we'd named for the two-hundred-year-old tree, now mostly a lightning-shattered trunk, which stood at a fork that branched off in one direction to the vineyard and the other to my house.

The talk on the radio station call-in show was nonstop anxiety about the drought and the possibility of water rationing. For anyone who grew crops or raised livestock in this still-very-agricultural county, the parched weather had been devastating. But a vineyard suffered less because vines actually thrived when the stressed roots had to dig deeper into the soil for nutrients and moisture. The good news for all of us was the cool front coming through later in the day. Though it wouldn't bring rain, at least the soupy humidity would vanish and the temperature would drop pleasantly into the eighties.

I pulled into the winery parking lot and parked next to Francesca Merchant's BMW. For Frankie, running the tasting room and planning all of our events was her empty-nester hobby after retiring from a high-powered government job in Washington that I'd never actually understood, and being the perfect eighties television show PTA-soccer-music–bake sale mom. Fortunately for me, she'd taken on her position at the winery with the same zeal and energy. In fact, she'd mostly taken over running the sales end of the business and I was spoiled rotten for it.

I climbed the flagstone steps to the ivy-covered villa designed by my mother where the tasting room and business offices were located. The whitewashed walls, large stone fireplace, and furniture covered with cheery Provençal fabric in the enormous rectangular room were her homage to her childhood summer home in the south of France; for me, everything was still marked with her indelible stamp and eye for beauty—a place she loved. Morning sunlight streamed through the glass panes of the four sets of French doors, striping the quarry tile floors and Persian carpets, glancing off the exuberant oil paintings of the vineyard, and reflecting off the mosaic tiles on the bar so they glowed like jewels. Frankie had classical music on the satellite radio—it sounded like Vivaldi—turned up loud.

I smelled coffee coming from the kitchen and heard her singing "dum-dum-dum-da-da-dum" with the loud off-key abandon of someone who believes no one is listening. A moment later she came through the swinging door carrying an enormous cobalt Biot vase filled with red gerbera daisies, red and white roses, and white star-gazer lilies. She'd switched to "la-la-la."

She stopped openmouthed when she saw me, setting the vase on an oak trestle table we used for overflow wine tastings and rearranging the already-perfect arrangement. I watched her hands flying, busily tucking and turning the flowers and the vase.

Frankie always looked smart and pulled together, even if she'd just spent the morning digging up weeds in our flower gardens. Today she wore a ruffled white silk top, black capris, and hot pink sandals. She'd pushed a pair of hot pink reading glasses up on her head to keep her shoulder-length strawberry blonde hair off her face.

"Morning," I said. "Those are gorgeous. Red, white, and blue for the weekend?"

She looked up and pushed a loose strand of hair behind her ear with her forearm. "I hope I'm not getting too carried away with this French tricolor theme. Antonio told me no Mexican in his right mind would wear a beret, so that's out. How long have you been out here listening, by the way? You should have yelled 'yoo-hoo.' "

"Listening to what?"

She grinned. "I always wanted to be an opera singer, did you know that? Too bad I can't carry a tune in a paper bag. There's coffee in the kitchen."

"Singing has to be the only gift you don't have," I said, "and I thought you sounded pretty good."

"Just for that I'll fix your coffee. Paper's on the bar. I hate to be the one to tell you, but Paul Noble committed suicide. Can you believe it?"

"Yeah, what a surprise."

Frankie took one look at my face and said, "What?"

"You know the local woman who found him?"

"Oh, God. Please don't say it was you."

My phone rang in the pocket of my jeans and I pulled it out. The display read "private number" but I knew the caller.

"It's a long story," I said and answered the phone.

"Lucie, love, glad I caught you."

"Mick Dunne." I sat down on a bar stool. "It's been awhile."

Frankie picked up the newspaper next to me and began reading, throwing me looks like daggers. I mimed "coffee?" and she rolled her eyes indicating I was hopeless and left for the kitchen.

In a perfect world, Michael Dunne is the archetype "great catch" every mother wants her daughter to marry. Tall, dark, handsome, well educated, youngest son of a prominent British political family, and, oh, yes, a self-made businessman worth millions. He went foxhunting with the old-money crowd, played polo with the lads, and bred some of the finest Thoroughbreds in the region, including a stallion who'd raced in the Derby and two jumpers whose riders earned ribbons in the last summer Olympics.

I'd fallen hard for Mick. But it wasn't long before I discovered the other women who also had him in their sights and Mick's problem with fidelity and commitment. We tried for a while, but I never stopped wondering if anything, or anyone, would be able to satisfy his restlessness. So I left before he did, before he told me that I wasn't the one, and now our relationship had evolved into that edgy ex-lovers' place where temptation, lust, and I-can't-do-this-again intersected. I coped by staying away from him as much as possible.

What complicated matters, or made them more complicated, was that Mick had moved here a few years ago after growing bored with the successful pharmaceutical business he owned in Florida and selling it, with the surprisingly romantic idea of living the indolent life of a Virginia gentleman-farmer who raised horses and owned a vineyard. The horses were his passion, but he had long since tired of the tedium involved in growing grapes and impatient with the three-year wait before he could bring in his first harvest. He'd leaned on me for advice, and I helped him as much as I could—before, during, and even after our affair. Call me noble.

Earlier this spring he tried to strike a deal with me after he lost nearly everything in a massive financial scam: I would buy his grapes outright, and Quinn Santori, my winemaker, and I would make his wine, bottled under a new label that included both vineyards. Then, two weeks ago, I found out he had earned back most of the money, as suddenly and spectacularly as he lost it, on a wildly successful IPO investment and a moribund real estate deal that finally paid off big. Now he was back in the game again: horses and wine. He was on the verge of hiring a smart young South African winemaker, but at least through this harvest he wanted to retain Quinn and me as advisers.

Mick always phoned in the morning, usually after he got back from his daily hack, so the timing of his call wasn't a surprise. But I knew, the way any woman knows after she's slept with a man, that the undercurrent in his voice meant he wanted something from me, and whatever it was, I probably wouldn't like it.

"You're right. It's been entirely too long," he said to me now. "I miss you, darling."

I'd guessed correctly. How big was this favor?

I took a deep breath. "Like a toothache when it's gone, sweetheart. What is it, Mick?"

His laugh was too hearty. "You're a cruel woman, Lucie Montgomery, stabbing a poor bloke through the heart."

"First I'd have to find it and don't try to butter me up."

He laughed again. "God, I really do miss you. And you know what I mean. We were good together."

I shivered, grateful for the distraction of Frankie setting down a coffee mug in front of me.

"Mick, I've got a million things on my plate—"

"All right," he said, "I'll get to it. I'd like to bottle some wine right now."

I almost sloshed my coffee on the bar. "You mean buy someone else's grapes? What brought that up?"

I could hear his shrug through the phone. "Everyone does it."

It was true. Vineyards often bought grapes grown elsewhere and made wine they could then sell in their tasting rooms before they were able to harvest their own crop. It was a way of building a brand, and it helped financially during the lean years with no income to offset the massive start-up costs of salaries, equipment, and root-stock.

But his timing was odd.

"Why now?" I asked. "We should have talked about this months ago. Harvest is only six, maybe eight weeks away."

"I can get a good deal on a couple thousand gallons from a terrific vineyard that's cash-strapped," he said. "A friend told me about it."

A fire sale. A lot of that going around lately. Maybe one of Paul's other clients.

"Who's selling it?" I asked.

"Rose Hill Vineyard."

"Are they new? What part of Virginia are they from?"

"It's not a Virginia vineyard," he said. "They're out in California, in Napa. Calistoga, to be precise."

"*California?* You want to buy California wine and bottle it to sell in Virginia? Why?"

"Because it happens to be top-drawer stuff and she's selling it for a song, that's why."

"Mick," I said, "you won't even be able to call it Virginia wine. You'll have to label it 'American wine.'"

I could hear his exasperated sigh on the other end of the line. "So? And don't give me all that *terroir* stuff. Who cares where it comes from as long as it's good?"

That *terroir* stuff. *Terroir* was the indefinable "something" that made wine taste of the place, the soil, the land where it had come from. It made each wine unique—why the great Bordeaux wines came only from that region in France, just as the most famous Rieslings were from Alsace, and why a wine from Virginia, with its hot, humid summers and freezing cold winters, would never be mistaken for anything produced in the temperate climate and endless sunshine of California.

"I care," I said. "I'm a Virginia winemaker. What you're talking about is *Mondovino,* that documentary on the globalization of wine-making. You're saying *terroir* counts less and less so soon we'll all be making the same generic wine, regardless of where we live. Chardonnay will be Chardonnay will be Chardonnay whether it's from France, Virginia, Australia, or California."

"Lucie." He was blunt. "I know what a purist you are, but I'm a businessman. I can buy this wine for a steal. And I'd like some help from you."

I could be just as curt. "Hire the bottling guys and you're all set."

"Not if I need to blend it."

"You want me to make your blend?"

"Yes, I do. I'll make it worth your while, I promise."

Money. He hit me right in my Achilles' heel. I knew he'd pay a bundle, but I didn't understand why he had to go to California for his grapes.

"How do you know it's not plonk and that's why you're getting it so cheap? There's plenty of wine you could buy right here in Virginia."

"Because Charles Thiessman told me."

"Pardon? Who told you?"

"Charles Thiessman. I was over at his place last night. He's the one who put me on to this deal. He promised it's a Cabernet Sauvignon to die for."

"Is that so?"

"Yes. Listen to me, darling. The man knows what he's talking about. He opened a bottle of his private reserve Cab. My God, Lucie, I'd stack it up against the best Bordeaux in France," Mick said. "Charles told me your grandfather is here for a couple of days before flying out to California to give a talk. I was thinking maybe you could go out there with him and handle the negotiations for me in Napa while Luc is in Sonoma. Try the wine, agree on the blend."

"I don't know, Mick."

"What if we talk about it tonight over dinner?"

"I can't. I've got a previous commitment with my grandfather."

That also involved Charles Thiessman.

"All right, then how about tomorrow? Come for breakfast in the rose garden or at least have tea? Someone else is going to buy this wine if I don't grab it up."

"I . . ."

"Lucie, love, I wouldn't ask if I didn't really need you. And the timing is perfect."

Perfect for whom? What was he talking about?

"All right, I'll come," I said. "Tomorrow morning for tea."

I hung up.

"Everything okay?" Frankie asked me.

"Yeah, fine. Mick wants me to check out some wine he wants to buy and, if I like it, make his blend."

"You said yes?"

"I did."

That made three times I'd walked into a setup with my eyes wide open in the past couple of days. Eli this morning, and just now Mick.

And setup number three—I was pretty sure of this, though I didn't understand why—was Charles Thiessman. He wanted something from me, too.

CHAPTER 5

Pépé and I drove up the winding private road to Mon Abri, Charles and Juliette Thiessman's handsome stone-and-stucco Greek Revival home, shortly after seven thirty that evening. I had been here once a few years ago, for memory's sake, the only year their house was on the annual spring garden tour, and many times as a child when my mother was alive.

In those days, Juliette and my mother would spend endless mornings strolling through the weed-choked remnants of gardens and scrubby lawn left to seed of the Thiessmans' new home. I remember them holding bowl-sized cups of café au lait between their hands as though they were praying, while I became invisible as children do when adults are totally absorbed in some project. Even now I can still hear their voices and the musical trill of their laughter, passionately considering, discarding, then reconsidering plans for sweeping, many-hued perennial gardens that would bloom year-round, climbing roses twining around a graceful bower, a vista of flowering cherry trees, a pergola, a wisteria-covered bridge over a yet-to-be-built lily pond surrounded by rustic garden benches. Juliette's vision was to re-create Monet's Giverny gardens in Middleburg, calling it "Mon Abri," or "my refuge." My mother, who revered Thomas Jefferson's *Garden Book* as the set-in-stone bible of what to plant in Virginia, warned her that unless she planned to throw a net over the entire yard, the deer would call it "my dinner."

Over the years some of my mother's advice obviously had prevailed, as we drove past dozens of white blooming crape myrtle at the entrance to the circular drive where the house sat on a knoll surrounded by now-mature dogwoods, as well as masses of azaleas, rhododendrons, hydrangeas, and rioting flower-filled gardens. A valet took the keys to the Mini and drove it off to a nearby field to park it among the Mercedeses, Jaguars, Lexuses, BMWs, and Porsches of the other guests. What had surprised me was that nearly all the license plates seemed to be from D.C. Not a gathering of neighbors, then.

"I thought this was going to be an intimate get-together with a few friends," I whispered to Pépé as we climbed the steps to a columned veranda and a butler opened the door.

"*Moi aussi,*" he said. "At least, that's what Charles said."

Inside it looked like the house had been redecorated since my childhood days—the garden tour had been outdoor only. In the foyer, Juliette had duplicated the exuberance and lush abundance of Giverny with sun-drenched glazed yellow and ocher paint on the walls and brilliant floral fabrics splashed on two settees and the cushions of a couple of rush-seat chairs. Bright red geraniums potted in brass urns sat on either side of doorways leading to a library to the right and a formal living room to the left. Colorful botanic prints lined the walls of the staircase to the second floor. An enormous vase of tuberoses with greens tucked among them sat on a pedestal table in the middle of the marble floor, their fragrance lightly scenting the room.

Juliette, white hair swept up into a chignon and wearing a gold and white gown that looked vaguely Greek, found us before Charles did, catching her breath as the fingers of one hand fluttered over her heart when she saw my grandfather. I thought her cheeks became pink under her perfect makeup as her eyes lighted on Pépé, a warmth and affection in them that struck me as more than casual friendship. Then she saw me and froze. Her lips moved, and I knew she was murmuring "Chantal," since I am the portrait of my mother at this age, or so I've been told.

With the courtliness that I love so much about him, Pépé reached for Juliette's hand and kissed it, bowing lightly and breaking the awkwardness that had fallen like a spell over the three of us. "Juliette, *ma chère. C'est tellement bien de vous revoir.*"

My grandfather had known her for decades, but he still used the formal *vous* with Juliette. *Tu* implied an intimacy to someone of his generation that I was somehow glad he didn't feel was appropriate between the two of them.

Juliette withdrew her hand and touched Pépé's shoulder like a caress. "It's good to see you, too, Luc," she said in French. "And Lucie. For a moment, my dear, I thought I was looking at a ghost of Chantal . . . I don't know why. I'm so sorry."

"It's all right," I said. "I take it as a great compliment."

Her smile seemed strained. "Please, both of you make yourselves at home. Get a drink. The waiters have champagne, but there is a bar outdoors by the swimming pool where there is anything you wish. It's just through the library and out the door to the back terrace."

The doorbell rang again. Her eyes strayed past us as the front door opened and closed and more guests arrived.

"We'll find Charles," Pépé said, "and leave you to your duties as hostess."

"Thank you. We must catch up later . . . so many things to talk about," she said. "I'm so glad you've come. Charles is terribly anxious to talk to you, Luc. Both of you, in fact."

As she walked by us to greet the new arrivals, I'm sure I heard her say in a voice meant for my grandfather's ears only, "*Tu me manques énormément.*"

I miss you terribly. She didn't use *vous*. She had used the intimate *tu* with Pépé.

Pépé accepted two champagne flutes from a waiter as we walked into the library. He handed one to me without bothering to ask what I wanted to drink as he usually did, and I knew what Juliette had said had disturbed him.

In contrast to the vibrant foyer, the library was dark and masculine. Though it appeared to have none of her lighthearted decorating joie de vivre, Juliette's presence still overwhelmed the heavy furniture, floor-to-ceiling shelves of gilt-edged leather-bound books, and antique maps because of a frankly sensual oil portrait that hung over the fireplace. I recognized her instantly, in spite of the fact that it must have been painted when she was a young woman about my age, some forty or more years ago. She had posed in a shaded garden or a wooded setting of mottled pale and fierce greens, head thrown back just a little as she sat languidly in an oversized rattan chair. Barefoot, her long dark hair carelessly pinned up as though she were hot and wanted it off her shoulders, she wore a strapless silk gown the color of a sultan's rubies. The dress was so low cut that the French word for it is *osée,* something between daring and risqué. I found it impossible not to stare at Juliette's décolleté, her ethereal beauty, the contrast of milk white skin against bloodred fabric, and the laughter dancing in her dark eyes as she watched someone or something out of view that amused or entertained her.

"Did you know Juliette in those days?" I asked my grandfather.

His eyes flickered briefly at the portrait. "Yes."

"Do you know where it was painted?"

"In France." With uncharacteristic abruptness he said, "We should find Charles."

I saw Charles on the other side of the swimming pool seated at a long stone table lit by flickering votive candles and talking to a group of men and women, all of them holding drinks. The withering heat had vanished as predicted, clearing out the humidity. A cool breeze rustled an arrangement of ferns and ornamental grasses growing in a planter set above a waterfall that spilled into the pool. Stone urns filled with more scarlet geraniums sat on pedestals at each corner of the octagonal pool and on either side of the waterfall. Someone had already turned on the lights so the water glowed celadon and turquoise like a tropical lagoon and the underlit plants threw swaying shadows on the white stucco wall behind them.

Charles, like Juliette, fixed his stare immediately on Pépé and me, getting up and excusing himself to his other guests. He was dressed like an aging matinee idol or Hef at the Playboy mansion—bottle-green velvet smoking jacket with silk lapels and cuffs, collarless open-neck white dress shirt, navy ascot and pocket handkerchief, charcoal trousers, black patent leather shoes.

Though my mother had been fond of Juliette, she had never warmed up to Charles, whom she considered a cold fish. Even now,

I saw something steely in his dark eyes as he joined us, shaking hands first with Pépé and clapping him on the back, greeting him in flawless unaccented French. He extended a hand to me, clasping mine warmly in his.

"It's been a long time, Lucie," he said in English. "So glad you both could make it."

I smiled and said nothing. Charles had invited us tonight for a reason. How long would it take him to get down to business and tell us what he wanted? I hadn't seen him for years, yet he seemed well steeped in the details of my life and my business. How else could he have pulled puppeteer strings to get Mick to persuade me to site-sample some fabulous California wine, with the bonus and perfect timing of accompanying my elderly grandfather on his trip to the West Coast?

"I spoke to a couple of friends who flew out to the Grove today for the opening ceremony tomorrow, Luc," Charles said. "You'll be well looked after, meet a lot of good people. Those lakeside talks are always one of the highlights of the campout. Of course the alcohol's first-rate, flows like water. You'll drink some fabulous vintages, I promise you."

"The 'grove'?" I said. "What campout?"

Charles looked from me to Pépé. "Didn't you tell her?"

"Eh . . . no." My grandfather shook his head. "I wasn't certain how much of what you told me was confidential."

Until now I'd assumed Pépé had been invited to give a talk at some organization's annual meeting, probably the featured speaker after a dinner of chicken with mystery sauce or dry roast beef with vegetable medley at a generic convention hotel.

Instead he was going camping. And Charles had arranged that, too.

"What's going on?" I said. "Why all the secrecy?"

Charles's smile was tolerant. "The Bohemian Grove is no secret, but it is private. The club, which is based in San Francisco, is probably the most prestigious gentlemen's club in the United States. Been around since 1872. They've been camping each summer practically since that first year. After a while they managed to buy a couple thousand acres in a redwood forest on the Russian River so they'd have a permanent place to camp. They named it the Bohemian Grove."

"The Bohemian Club is legendary, *chérie*," Pépé said. "Some of the most powerful men in the United States belong, or have belonged—including several of your presidents."

"All these important men camp together in the woods, out in the middle of nowhere?" I asked. "What exactly do you do that you need so much privacy?"

"Please." Charles waved a hand. "There's been enough rubbish written about conspiracies and subterfuge or that the members are an elite 'guild of illuminati' getting together to plan their strategy on how they'll rule the world—picking political leaders and manipulating financial markets. None of it's true, I assure you. It's strictly a social gathering."

"Don't tell me you spend your time roasting marshmallows and telling ghost stories," I said. "Or do you?"

Charles pursed his lips. "Actually, I'm not a member. The waiting list is years, even decades, long. But I've been a guest there enough times to know what does go on. Obviously you meet . . . well, the right people. But it's a couple of weeks to kick back and unwind with friends—get away from all the daily pressures."

"And you camp in tents like the Boy Scouts?"

The idea of Pépé spending several nights on the ground in a sleeping bag at his age worried me.

"Some do," Charles said. "Some of the camps are more rustic than others. There are about a hundred or so, scattered throughout the woods. Others would remind you of a European hunting lodge with artwork on the walls and beautiful furniture. Even a piano for the sing-alongs. Don't worry, Lucie. Your grandfather's staying in Knockabout, one of the more elegant, well-appointed campsites."

He signaled for someone to refill our glasses. A striking dark-haired woman who looked about my age came over holding a bottle of champagne.

"Is everything all right, Ambassador?" she asked. "Can I bring you another martini?"

He nodded. "Jasmine, isn't it?"

"Yes, sir." She refilled Pépé's and my glasses with an expert flick of her wrist. "I'll be right back with your drink."

"Are you leaving for California on Sunday as well?" I asked Charles.

"I'm not going on the campout this year." His words were clipped, though he tried to soften them with a small smile. "But I've made all your arrangements, Luc. Ah, here's my drink. Thank you, my dear."

Jasmine glanced at Pépé and me as she handed Charles his martini. Her eyes met mine briefly and something flickered behind them. After she left, the three of us stood together in uncomfortable silence. We'd exhausted the topic of the Bohemian Grove and Charles had yet to explain why he'd really invited us tonight. By now, though, I suspected he'd figured out that we knew something was up.

He smiled and sipped his martini. "I'd like it very much if the two of you would join me for a drink after the other guests have left at the end of the evening. I have a small retreat, I guess you'd call it, on the property. There's a bottle of Château Margaux waiting for us."

A top-drawer bottle of wine.

Pépé glanced at me. "Thank you for the invitation, but it's really up to Lucie. She's the driver."

"No worries about that," Charles said at once. "One of the staff will drive you home in my car afterward. I promise your own car will be back at Highland House first thing in the morning."

"Would this private drink have anything to do with Mick Dunne?" I asked.

I'd caught Charles by surprise and an annoyed look crossed his face. Then he recovered. "Ah, I see you two have spoken. As a matter of fact, indirectly it does have something to do with Mick. The California wine, yes?"

I nodded.

"There's more to it than that. It's rather complicated and I prefer to discuss it when we're alone." He lifted his glass to his lips again. His hand shook and the drink sloshed over the rim and dripped on the sleeve of his velvet jacket.

"Damn."

A waitress materialized and blotted the spot, taking his glass for a refill. Charles looked up.

"Promise me you'll say nothing to Juliette about this."

"We don't really know what 'this' is," I said.

"Please be patient. You will soon enough." He dropped his guard and I saw fear in his eyes. "You see, my life's in danger and I need your help, Lucie. Please don't turn me down."

CHAPTER 6

Charles clammed up after that remark, ending the cryptic conversation about needing my help and slipping into his jovial host persona as another couple joined our group. Pépé met my eyes, his message unmistakable: Let it go; we'll find out later.

It wasn't as though I had a choice. Whatever Charles was up to, it was clear that he'd gone to a lot of trouble to engineer this get-together. What was not clear, but becoming a looming possibility, was whether it might turn out to be an overblown melodrama that was much ado about nothing. Or, to give him a modicum of credit, about very little except an old man's wish to see if he could still move players around on a chessboard.

Pépé had reminded me on the drive over to the Thiessmans' that Charles had held high-ranking positions in administrations dating as far back as Dwight Eisenhower, dipping into consulting work when he wasn't the political flavor of the moment. And of course, there was his ambassadorship to France during the Nixon administration. What Charles did fell into the need-to-know category, hush-hush stuff that utilized his background in science—chemistry, Pépé said—with an expertise that had been in demand by the Pentagon and elsewhere in the military establishment. I had asked if Charles was a spy or in intelligence, and Pépé had smiled enigmatically, saying he'd occasionally wondered about that himself.

Charles had retired a decade or so ago, but it must have been tough to relinquish the glamour and trappings that came with the rank of ambassador, or even ex-ambassador, the fizzy excitement of the social and diplomatic world he and Juliette inhabited. The seductiveness of Washington's power surely must have called to him like a Siren, tempting him to take what he wanted—everyone else did it—as his due after so many decades of service. Was he having trouble moving off center stage, becoming a spectator rather than a player? Did he need proof that he still had what it took, that he hadn't been sidelined by younger, more virile men—and, God forbid, women—who replaced him? Charles, I guessed, was something of a chauvinist.

I said no, thank you to more champagne from an attentive waitress who wanted to top off my glass, since it was already making me light-headed. Or else it was the slowly blooming feeling that I had stepped onto the set of an old black-and-white movie where the last scene of a story that began long before I was born was about to be filmed. I have no idea what triggered it: Charles's fifties-era attire, Juliette's giddy coquettish airs befitting a much younger woman—and that portrait in the library—or the realization that all the other guests except me had probably come of age in the aftermath of World War II or earlier.

I caught a flash of white and gold across the pool, and then Juliette stood beside her husband, linking her arm through Charles's and informing him in a low voice that the Hanovers were inside and dying to talk to him. I heard her quiet remark about an oxygen tank and not getting Mr. Hanover overly excited. He was in the library if Charles wouldn't mind joining him there. Charles excused himself, and the other couple departed, leaving Juliette with Pépé and me. Something crackled in the air between her and my grandfather. For a split second, I felt like the child who accidentally stumbled into an intimate conversation between adults, overhearing a stray remark on a subject about which they felt vaguely ashamed.

"We've just had a greenhouse built behind the swimming pool." Juliette seemed to be reaching for something innocuous to talk about. She waved a hand at a wrought-iron gate in the stucco wall and rambled on. "I'm so sorry Chantal isn't here to see it. I miss her the most when I'm working in the gardens, especially among the roses. Would you like to have a tour?"

Of all the subjects she could have chosen, I wished she had brought up anything but my mother. I often thought Pépé grieved even more deeply than I did over her death, perhaps because he still hadn't gotten over the devastation of losing his wife when he had to deal with the death of an adored daughter.

Juliette glanced at me as a courtesy, but I knew she'd been speaking to my grandfather.

"I'd love to see your greenhouse," I said, "but if you'll excuse me, I ought to find your powder room. You two go along. I'll catch up later."

Pépé shot me a martyred look as though he wouldn't be responsible for his actions without a chaperone, but I gave him a bland see-no-evil look and smiled. He was a big boy; he could handle this.

The powder room off the foyer was occupied. As I waited, the noisy sounds of the kitchen staff preparing dinner floated down the hallway. My cousin would be there, cool and collected, calmly making sure everything was in order with her staff, the meal, her host and hostess.

I walked down the hall and pushed open the swinging door. Juliette's enormous French country kitchen was warm and inviting, dominated by a collection of brass and copper pots suspended from a wrought-iron rack over a granite island and walls filled with colorful plates and oil paintings. Above all, the fragrant aroma of baking and the odors of garlic, onions, herbs, and spices mingled with meat and, I thought, fish, smelled wonderful.

Jasmine, the waitress who had filled my champagne glass and gotten Charles his martini, stood at the large Viking stove, whisking something in a copper saucepan.

"Can I help you?" she asked, mopping her forehead with the sleeve of a chef's jacket she now wore. Her voice was low and pleasant, and in the brighter lighting of the kitchen, I noticed the tiny beauty mark by her upper lip, the quizzical tilt of her dark eyebrows, and intelligent eyes.

"Smells wonderful in here," I said. "What's for dinner?"

"Roast chicken with garlic and herbs, pan-seared trout with summer vegetables, new potato gratin . . . the menu's à la française, of course, for Bastille Day. Crepes for dessert, fresh berry compote, and *mousse au chocolat*. All the herbs, vegetables, and fruit are from Mrs. Thiessman's garden or her greenhouse. Even the olives. She cured them herself. The chicken is from the organic butcher in Middleburg and the fish from someone I found who catches it fresh."

Her French accent sounded native and she obviously worked at the Goose Creek Inn as more than a waitress. I knew almost everyone on the staff, but I hadn't met her.

"We haven't been introduced," I said. "Dominique told me she hired a new chef last month, so I guess that would be you. I'm Lucie Montgomery."

"I figured you might be." She looked up from her sauce again, a game expression on her face, eyes avoiding my cane. "You own the vineyard. I'm Jasmine Nouri. Your cousin did hire me as an assistant chef, but it looks like I'm probably going to be helping out more with the catering business. Tonight, though, she thought I was too new to solo and she needed to supervise."

I wondered when Jasmine Nouri would find out that if Dominique had been around when God made heaven and earth, she'd feel the need to supervise Him before he went solo on this brand-new creation thing He was trying out.

She must have read my mind because she said, "Don't worry. Everyone from the bookkeeper to the guy who takes care of valet parking has made sure to tell me she likes to keep her finger in every pot. Literally."

"That's because so far no one in the family has found her Off switch," I said. "And now we're all pretty sure she doesn't have one."

Jasmine smiled.

"Where did you work before you came here?" I asked.

She shrugged. "Everywhere. Most recently a restaurant in Portland, Oregon."

"Virginia's a long way from Oregon."

"Umm." She turned off the gas and set the saucepan on another burner. "I'd better get busy. Dominique will have my head if this evening isn't perfect."

"Sorry, I didn't mean to distract you. I'll just say hi, then disappear," I said and slipped out the side door.

My cousin glanced up from grinding her cigarette butt under the heel of a black sandal. She looked like she did the time I caught her in the kitchen adding a can of broth to her made-from-scratch chicken stock.

"*Merde,* you scared me," she said. "I thought it was Juliette. She believes cigarettes are the devil's creation. They're totally banned from the house."

"Serves you right if it had been Juliette. When are you going to quit? You'll get cancer."

"Pépé smokes like a chimney. He's eighty-four and he doesn't have cancer. We've got good genes," she said. "Where is he, by the way?"

"Visiting the greenhouse. Juliette is giving him a tour."

"Just the two of them?"

I nodded and Dominique shot me an unreadable look that I didn't like.

"Where's Charles?" she asked.

"She sent him to the library to talk to a guest who's on oxygen. You know, I think I'm the only person here tonight except for your staff who is under sixty. Maybe even under seventy."

My cousin didn't smile. *"Merde,"* she said again. "I knew it."

"What?" I asked.

"She's still in love with him. After all these years."

"What are you talking about? Pépé and Juliette?"

Dominique automatically slipped her pack of cigarettes out of the pocket of her slim-cut black trousers and I glared at her.

"Oh, all right," she said and shoved them back. "But it calms my nerves when I smoke."

"Forget the cigarettes and tell me about Pépé and Juliette."

"I forgot that you wouldn't have known. It started after Grand-mama died. My mother told me the story one night when we stayed up really late and drank too much champagne. He was so lost on his own. Juliette . . . well, she lived in the same building on Boulevard Saint-Denis, so they all knew each other." She bent and picked up her cigarette butt, holding it between her thumb and forefinger like it was some rare specimen that needed to be preserved. "She got in the habit of coming by to bring him dinner. She'd say she just cooked a little more than they needed and that he would waste away to nothing if he didn't eat. Sometimes my mother and I would drop by his apartment and there'd be a pretty bouquet of flowers, or pastries from the *boulangerie* across the street. My mother said she always knew they were from her. Juliette was married at the time to a troll who beat her. She finally left him."

"And?"

"Well, I think she was hoping . . . you know. "

"That Pépé would ask her to marry him?"

She nodded.

"Were they, I mean did they . . . I mean . . ."

"Did they have sex? Is that what you mean?" Dominique rolled her eyes. "And who do you think was going to ask him that? You know Pépé. *Mon Dieu,* he's so private. They could have done. The troll traveled a lot so it wouldn't have been difficult to arrange, living in the same building. To be honest, I don't think they did. He's too much of a gentleman and she was married."

"But after the divorce?"

"He was sent to Brussels for a year since he was still doing some consulting for the foreign ministry. It was a blessing, kept him really busy, but of course he was living in Belgium. Then my mother heard Juliette was moving to Washington to take a job as a secretary at the embassy. She thought Pépé pulled strings to get her the position. Juliette left France and apparently decided to turn over a whole new broom." Dominique spoke English fluently but despite years of living in America, idioms continued to baffle her.

"You mean forget about Pépé?"

"My mother always thought that's why she left," she said. "Juliette met Charles in Washington right around the time he was named ambassador to France. She married him and moved home, into the residence on the Rue du Faubourg Saint-Honoré with her new husband, and all of a sudden she's living down the street from the Élysée Palace. Parties, balls, receptions, lots of fancy entertaining, and a huge staff to help. My mother said she was absolutely *aux anges.* She was such a beauty, too—her picture showing up all the time in *Paris-Match* and *Vogue.*"

I nodded and thought about the portrait in the library. Maybe that teasing smile had been for my grandfather and he'd been there when she posed for the artist. It would explain why he'd been so abrupt when I asked him if he knew where it had been painted.

"Charles and Pépé never got to be close friends, did they?"

"You know Pépé," she said. "He's such a gentleman and always polite, but I don't think he ever warmed up to Charles. And Charles didn't strike me as so dumb he didn't realize his wife still carried a torch for another man. It wouldn't surprise me if Juliette married Charles just to get back at Pépé—then she had to live with her decision. The irony of it is that Charles has a reputation as a womanizer, though he's discreet and they pretend to be a happy couple."

"My God, how complicated."

Was this what Charles wanted to talk to us about after dinner? Something personal? His marriage? The kitchen door opened and Jasmine's head popped into view.

"The lady of the house is asking for you. I told her you were in the bathroom." She waved something at my cousin. "Breath mints. I figured you could use them."

Dominique and I exchanged glances. "Well," she said, "here we go."

On our way inside I said, "I like your new chef."

"She's amazing," Dominique said. "I was lucky to get her."

"How'd you find her?"

"She contacted me. She was born in France, spent a lot of time there, but grew up here. Her father was Iranian, a university professor. American mother, died last fall. Apparently she brought up Jasmine in a home that only ate organic produce, anything locally grown. They owned chickens, a goat, that sort of thing. Jasmine worked with Juliette on tonight's menu, so all the fruit and vegetables could come from her garden."

"I'm impressed," I said. "At least the food is going to be fabulous."

"It is. Which reminds me. We've been planning a dinner at the Inn where everything on the menu was grown or raised within a hundred miles of here. We've had so much interest that I was wondering if we could move it to the vineyard."

"Sure, no problem. Talk to Frankie and we'll get it on the calendar."

"There won't be time. It's next Friday." She saw my alarmed

look. "Don't worry. Jasmine's got it all organized. There's nothing to worry about."

"You're letting Jasmine run this?"

"It was her idea," Dominique said. "She's very capable, Lucie. Besides, you know what they say—never let a gift horse in the house. How could I say no?"

"When you put it like that," I said, "I suppose you couldn't."

Juliette seated Pépé at her table and exiled me to a remote corner of the living room with an elderly crowd who talked about the old days at their various foreign posts and the new days with their aches and pains, and the hassles of dealing with Social Security and Medicare. Mercifully everyone began leaving at eleven. By eleven thirty Pépé and I were the only guests remaining. Charles took me aside after Juliette excused herself to settle up with Dominique and her staff.

"I explained to Luc where the lodge is located," he said. "It's only half a mile down our private road, easy enough to find. Make yourself at home and I'll be along shortly."

"Charles." Juliette returned from the kitchen, lightly touching his sleeve. "Do you have the check to pay the caterers? I thought I had it, but I don't."

"It's in the library," he said. "I'll take care of it."

He disappeared, leaving the three of us alone. I waited, hoping the floor would open up so I could drop through, rather than witness the anguished looks that passed between Pépé and Juliette.

"When will I see you again?" Juliette held out her hands to my grandfather, who clasped them without taking his eyes off her face.

"I don't know," he said. "I leave for California on Sunday. After the trip, I'll be returning to France."

"Can't you stay a day or two longer?"

"I don't know."

"Please try. We could see each other again."

Even now I don't like to remember the look of loss and longing that passed between them. I cleared my throat and turned away, pretending to have a coughing fit. When I finished, Pépé was kissing both of Juliette's hands.

She blinked rapidly. "Good night, Luc."

"Good night, *ma chère* Juliette."

"Thank you for dinner," I said.

Juliette gazed at me like she had no idea who I was. "Yes, yes, of course."

I followed my grandfather outside, where one of the valets had the Mini waiting in front of the entrance. We got in the car without speaking. I believe Juliette came to the door and watched us drive off, but I couldn't be sure because I kept my eyes glued to the road so I didn't have to see the utterly bereft look on Pépé's face.

The lights from the Thiessmans' house glittered in my rearview mirror until I turned down the side road where Charles's lodge was located and we were swallowed up in darkness.

What Charles wanted to talk about and why we had to retreat to his private eyrie to talk about it was anybody's guess. Now it wouldn't be long before we found out. Hopefully by then my grandfather would have composed himself. Charles's wife was in love with him. And after tonight, it seemed Pépé was at least a little bit in love with her, too.

CHAPTER 7

My grandfather's silence filled the car until I felt so claustrophobic I had to roll down my window. The night air rushed in, sharp and stinging, as though summer had evaporated in the past few hours. The unexpected smoky tang of autumn scented the breeze and whipped my hair in my eyes. I shivered and rolled up the window again, but at least now my alcohol-buzzed brain felt like it had been jolted out of its stupor.

As soon as I drove beyond Juliette's gardens and her greenhouse, the gravel road plunged into a thicket of woods that closed around the car. I put on the brakes because I had been speeding, and in the murky swirl of fog my headlights turned trees, underbrush, and impenetrable black holes an unnatural yellow-green. Overhead the canopy of trees wove together and blocked out the night sky so it felt like we were winding through a tunnel or a cave.

"Are you sure this is the right way?" Pépé asked after a few minutes. "Maybe you should have turned left at that fork in the road beyond the house."

"I thought you told me Charles said right."

We rounded a corner and he said, "I think I see a light up ahead."

"I wonder what he wants to talk about. He said it was life or death."

"Juliette knows he's upset about something," my grandfather said.

"She has no idea about what?"

Pépé tilted his head, as though he were weighing his answer. I wondered if he was thinking about Juliette or me. "She says she does not."

"You don't believe her?"

"I think she has her suspicions," he said. "She asked if I would do what I could for him."

"And you said yes."

"I said I would try. But Charles specifically asked for you to come this evening, *ma belle,* and you're the one he asked for help." He gave me a sideways glance. "I don't know what, if any, role he has in mind for me."

"Mick Dunne got me to agree to fly out to California to sample some wine Charles talked him into buying," I said. "Mick knew you had business out there, too, so he figured I could accompany you and, um, we'd . . . be together. And Charles was the one who set you up to talk to this Bohemian Grove group."

"How interesting. Obviously it's no coincidence. I wonder what Charles has got up his sleeve."

I rounded another bend in the road and the light grew larger, winking like a wicked eye between the tree branches.

"I guess we're about to find out," I said. "I hope that's the lodge, or else we're really lost."

I parked in front of a rustic cabin that sat in a clearing surrounded by Charles's smallish vineyard. The cloudless blue-black sky was star filled and serene. A scuffed-silver half-moon hung high above the trees and brushed the tops of the vines so they looked frost rimed. The luminescent clock on my car dashboard showed ten minutes to midnight.

"Should we wait for him?" I asked.

"He said to make ourselves at home." Pépé was already starting toward the front door. "And he left the place unlocked."

The hinges creaked as he pushed open the door, and for an instant I expected the Big Bad Wolf or a wicked witch disguised as a kindly grandmother to appear and bid us to come inside. The room could have been the reading room in a gentlemen's club, with a pair of black leather wing chairs and a matching sofa pulled up around a polished granite coffee table, all grouped in front of a large stone fireplace. The walls looked like old barn wood that had been beautifully refinished. The sconces and matching chandelier in the middle of the room were made of antlers. Tiny red shades over the candlesticks muted the light so it seemed almost viscous, except for the warm pool of spreading color that came from a Tiffany lamp hanging over the bar. A rug in the center of the room was a dead animal skin—a zebra. Something dark and furry I couldn't identify lay in front of the fireplace.

"I didn't know Charles was a hunter," I said. "It's cold in here."

"He's hunted for as long as I've known him. When he lived in France he used to go off to Scotland with a group of friends every year," Pépé said. "Juliette loathes blood sports so I suspect that is why he has this place in the woods, so far from the house. Here, *chérie,* take my jacket."

"I can't. You'll freeze."

He draped his navy suit coat around my shoulders. "I'll be fine."

I walked around the room, examining the signed photographs that lined the walls. Pépé did the same from the other direction. Each one showed Charles, with practically every American president since Harry Truman or with sober-suited men I didn't recognize, with the exception of Winston Churchill. All the pictures looked official; there were no candid snaps of him and Juliette on a vacation cruise, at Christmas, a special dinner somewhere. I wondered why there had been no children.

I scarcely recognized Charles in the early black-and-white pictures: smooth-faced and dashing, reed slim, clear-eyed, with a pompadour of wavy dark hair and a slight grave smile befitting the seriousness of the moment. What hadn't changed was that cocky self-confidence in his eyes, the lack of self-doubt. No wonder Juliette had fallen for him after living with a troll who beat her.

One picture that had particular prominence showed Charles shaking hands with the then president of France, Georges Pompidou, on what looked like the day he presented his diplomatic credentials as ambassador to France. Juliette, ethereal and as lovely as she'd been in the portrait in their library, stood behind him looking radiant. It was the only picture in the room in which she appeared.

Behind me a door opened and closed with a quiet click and I spun around.

It appeared as though Charles materialized out of nowhere, until I noticed the door set into a wall that had been camouflaged to look like a bookcase. He was holding something partially obscured in his hand. For a wild moment I thought it might be a gun. Maybe I'd been right after all: He had come to have a man-to-man talk with Pépé about his wife's infatuation with my grandfather. But when he raised his arm I saw that it was a wine bottle, dark like the color of old blood.

"I didn't mean to startle you both. I went in through the cave to get the wine and came through the back door." He opened and closed it again so we could see the neat trick of how it disappeared into the wall. "Clever, isn't it?"

He crossed the room and flicked a switch next to an oil painting of a pair of foxhounds. Instantly a fire blazed to life in the stone fireplace.

My grandfather looked surprised and Charles grinned. "Gas," he said. "I know it's a lazy man's way of getting out of building a real fire, but I enjoy it. No need to wait for it to burn down at the end of an evening."

So this was the refuge he retreated to when he wanted to get away from . . . what? Or whom? I wondered if Juliette had even seen the inside of this place.

"Do you spend much time here?" I asked.

He gave me an indecipherable look and said, "Depends on your definition of 'much.'"

I decided not to ask the obvious follow-up.

"Please, come and sit by the fire," he said, "while I pour the wine. I had it opened about an hour ago. I'd like to see how it's developing. It might need a little more time."

He handed me a glass and I nearly dropped it. Silk-screened on the wineglass was the logo of the openmouthed alienlike figure that had been on the broken glass in Paul Noble's studio. He handed Pépé a similar glass and took a third for himself.

"Is anything wrong?" he asked.

I looked into his eyes and saw a shadow pass behind them. What-

ever his reason for bringing us here, now it seemed it had something
to do with the death of Paul Noble. Somehow Charles had learned
that I'd found Paul hanging in his studio and he knew about the
wineglass, too. I wondered who had told him and when this game
was going to end. I was tired of being played.

"I saw a wineglass with the same design on it the other day, but
you know that already, don't you?" I said in a curt voice. "Where did
you get these? They look like old glasses, not the inexpensive ones
we give out as souvenirs at the winery."

"Lucie—" Pépé cautioned me.

"They are," Charles said. "I haven't used these glasses in more
than forty years."

"Why tonight? A celebration? Or is it in memoriam? And
shouldn't we be drinking Sauvignon Blanc?"

Charles's mouth tightened. "You're right," he said. "The Margaux will have to do. It's from the correct year."

I looked at the bottle. "What happened in 1970?"

"I'll get to that. Now, please, have a seat."

He waited until Pépé took one of the leather chairs and I sat on
the sofa before he sat down in the other wing chair. The fire flickered merrily.

"Do you mind if I smoke?" My grandfather indicated a large
glass ashtray on the coffee table.

I'd noticed it earlier. The White House logo was etched into
the glass, probably a souvenir from another era, in the days when
nobody minded if the president lit up and dinners ended with
brandy and cigars in one of the formal state rooms.

Charles pushed the ashtray over to Pépé. "Be my guest. Juliette
doesn't come here. She's absolutely against tobacco, and don't get her
started on hunting."

He smiled without amusement and raised his glass. "Thank you
both for indulging me."

Pépé and I raised our glasses in silence. The wine was out of this
world.

"I'm going to tell you a story," he said, "and I'd appreciate it if you
would let me tell it my way. I promise I'll answer all your questions
when I'm finished."

Pépé snapped his lighter shut and it made a little metal clink. He slipped it in his pocket and took a drag on his cigarette, closing his eyes. I kicked off my sandals, tucking my feet under my long dress and laying my pashmina across my lap like a blanket. Pépé's jacket was still around my shoulders and I pulled it close. Charles settled back into his chair and receded into the shadows.

"In 1970, Nixon was still in the White House," he said, "but it wouldn't be long before he got mired in Watergate and it brought him down. We were still in Vietnam, the '68 riots had ended but they still left vivid scars on the national conscience, and the war, which had ended Johnson's presidency, was more unpopular than ever. Nixon wanted to get us out of there and he did, calling it 'peace with honor.' Our worst enemies were the Sovs and it was the height of the Cold War."

Pépé crossed one leg over the other and exhaled a stream of smoke. Like Charles, he'd lived through these years. The history lesson was clearly for my education.

"I was a history major in college," I said. "So I did read about all this, you know."

Charles made a small noise and Pépé chuckled.

"Ah." Charles's voice was dry. "Ancient history?"

"Prehistoric."

"I see," he said after a moment. " 'I know of no way of judging the future but by the past.' Do you know who said that, history major?"

"You?"

"Patrick Henry."

" 'Give me liberty or give me death'?"

"The same. A Virginian. A Founding Father. The lesson applies now, too."

"You'll explain that?" I said.

"I won't need to." He sipped his wine. "In 1970, I was the Deputy Director for OSPR."

"English, please," I said. "For the uninitiated?"

"The Office of Strategic Programming and Research. Later it went under the Pentagon's umbrella, so it became DOSPR. *D* for 'Defense.' Dosper was one of the most nimble and competent agencies in the federal government. The jewel in the Defense Department's crown. You wanted something done, that was the place to go. No bureaucratic red tape to snarl you, no congressional hearing to ask permission first. We had carte blanche to make it rain."

"How convenient," I said. "What exactly did this organization do?"

"Oh, remnants of it still exist. But the original program was started in the late fifties, when the Sovs caught us off guard with Sputnik. They beat us in the space race and we had no clue what was up their little Commie sleeves. You can't imagine how devastating that was."

Pépé nodded and I stared at both of them, wondering what it must have been like during the years when our former World War II ally had become the "Evil Empire" and people like Charles called the Russians "Commies" and "Sovs" like something out of an old spy movie.

Charles drank his wine. "So in order for us never to fall behind, and for that never to happen again, we set up a sort of freewheeling think tank of creative people who spent their days playing military what-if and then figuring out how to invent the technology. You've benefited from some of the results . . . advancements like global positioning systems, voice-recognition software, things like that. It wasn't just building things that went boom or the next James Bond–type toy to put in the arsenal. The sign on the door to my office was a quote from Einstein: 'If we knew what we were doing, it wouldn't be called research.'"

He shifted in his chair. No one laughed.

"The wine is really opening nicely, isn't it?" He stared into his glass. "Still got some life in it after all these years."

I nodded, wishing he'd get on with it. Charles was leading up to something important, but at this rate we'd still be here tomorrow morning.

"You were saying about your position with OSPR?" I asked. "Or DOSPR?"

Charles fixed his gaze on the fire. "I'm getting to that, what I did. R & D is the heart of playing what-if. You have conventional warfare—soldiers fighting each other on a battlefield—and then you have unconventional warfare," he said. "Both are as old as time.

People have been using some variant of biological and chemical weapons in wartime as far back as the ancient Greeks."

Pépé sat up straighter in his chair. I'd been about to take a sip of my wine, but I stopped and uneasily waited for him to go on. Charles had changed the direction of this conversation with as much subtlety as shifting tectonic plates.

"Unconventional warfare took a different direction in the twentieth century, gassing troops in the trenches during the First World War to name one of the most graphic examples," he said. "Then during World War II the use of airplanes to drop bombs that would cause widespread destruction took what-if to the next level. What if you could fill a bomb with some pathogen or crop agent and drop it over a city or farmland? You wouldn't destroy buildings, but the damage would be incalculable. Think of how many people you could sicken or kill, wiping out food supplies for decades because you'd poisoned the soil, how paralyzing it would be to a country."

He saw my eyes widen. "I'm not talking about the good guys, Lucie. Imagine the Nazis with that technology and you live in Paris or London in the 1940s knowing there's a goddamn bull's-eye painted on your back on a war room map in Berchtesgaden."

"Go on, Charles," Pépé said. "Lucie and I are listening."

Charles sipped his wine. "Where was I? Oh, yes, the U.S. had its own programs—biological and chemical warfare—all conducted in the utmost secrecy. Then the war ended and things started to wind down. I'm going to fast-forward through some of this, but in the aftermath of the war there was a massive ethical and moral debate about whether to continue or abandon something so heinous, so reprehensible to the American psyche. That was what the politicians and civilian leaders wrestled with. So the military decided to move the program under its own tent, though by then we had field-tested the A-bomb and discovered that it worked."

I was glad to hear the small note of irony in his voice.

"Weren't plans for the atomic bomb drawn up at the Bohemian Grove?" Pépé asked.

"The Grove is rented out all the time to people who want to use it when the members aren't there." Charles sounded irritated and a little peevish. "It's true there was a planning meeting held there for the Manhattan Project, which led, of course, to the A-bomb—but it wasn't a plot concocted by the Bohemian Club, I can assure you."

Pépé set his glass down on the table and reached for his cigarette pack. "I see."

Charles shot him an inscrutable look. "Fortunately or unfortunately, depending on where you stood, the Cold War ramped up and that breathed new life into BW and CW research, saved the programs. We couldn't afford to fall behind again."

"You mean biological weapons and chemical weapons?" I said.

He nodded. "Some of it was run out of a small installation—Fort Wilton—just down the road in Maryland. We built on what was accomplished during the war: germ warfare, chemical warfare, plant and animal toxins, it's a long list. But with any kind of research comes field testing. To be blunt, testing on animals only goes so far."

He paused and now I was starting to guess where this was going.

"The Japanese did the most experimenting on human subjects during the war, and in return for us not prosecuting them for war crimes, we got a peek at their results. It was a Faustian pact, but it happened." He shrugged. "Hell, we did our own testing here at home—open-air tests using simulants and then monitoring the results. No one knew at the time, of course. It wasn't the sort of thing where you sent out permission slips door-to-door."

I choked on my wine. "You're talking about our government testing biological and chemical weapons on its own citizens?"

"Lucie, there were hearings on this in the late seventies. It *is* ancient history," he said with the weariness of someone who had been over this ad nauseam and was tired of defending it. "We only did what was absolutely essential, took no unnecessary risks. You may have studied all this in your history books, my dear, but you're forgetting these were the Cold War years when kids hid under their school desks during drills to prepare for a nuclear attack. It's a cheap shot to look back and condemn; it was different living through those times."

He got up and poured the last of the Margaux into our glasses.

"Charles, you took none for yourself," Pépé said.

"I'm switching to brandy. Care to join me, anyone?"

"*Non, merci,*" my grandfather said, and I shook my head.

He walked behind the bar, setting a bottle of Rémy-Martin on the counter. "In 1969, Nixon bowed to ethical and moral pressure to stop the program. He signed orders that all chemical and biological weapons development and testing was to cease. They dismantled the lab at Wilton, let people go, moved equipment, animals, everything elsewhere."

He splashed cognac into a snifter. "You can probably guess what I'm going to say next. A small group of biochemists, brilliant young scientists who'd been hired as contractors, thought it was insane to shut down our program when other countries were forging ahead."

He came back to his chair, swirling the burnished liquid in his glass with the practiced ease of habit. I wondered why he wasn't drunk yet. My own head was spinning. Writhing figures, like the sinewy one on my glass, danced in the flames of the fire and waved their arms.

Charles resumed his talk as he sat down. "It was easy enough to keep them off the grid. Wilton was the perfect place to do it. Plenty of other stuff went on that no one talked about. They were a tight-knit group, all good friends. They hadn't wanted to split up anyway."

"What did they do?" I asked.

"Mostly the same thing they'd been doing before."

"Including experimenting on humans?"

"I'm getting to that," he said. "Don't rush me."

Pépé caught my eye and made the universal gesture with one hand that meant *Calm down.*

"Sorry."

"First you need to know about these young people," Charles said. "Who they were. It's important."

Pépé nodded and exhaled a stream of smoke. I settled deeper into the cushions of the sofa.

"They used to get together on weekends after work. One of the girls' families had a beach house on Pontiac Island in Maryland. Beautiful place, that island. Only a few hundred inhabitants. A two-lane bridge from the mainland and then you're transported to another time where life moved more slowly. In the beginning it was idyllic." A ghost of a smile flickered across his face.

"You, also, went to the beach house?" I asked.

"Once, for a birthday party, and one other time, but I didn't socialize with them. There was a lot of drinking, weekends got a bit wild." He paused, a distasteful expression on his face. "It led to some rather casual and open sexual activities, not my thing at all. Besides, I was married to my first wife."

I waited for him to elaborate, but he didn't.

"One of the girls, Maggie Hilliard, decided their little group needed a name—you know how girls are." He gave me a tolerant smile and I bit my tongue, resisting the urge to ask him for his own interpretation of how girls were. "Some folderol invented one night when everyone was in their cups at the cottage. But it stuck. They called themselves the Mandrake Society."

"Why?" I asked.

"Mandrake was a plant that had been used as long ago as the ancient Greeks," he said. "It's a deliriant causing hallucinations. Used to induce sleep. It's part of the nightshade family. The Greeks used mandrakes in war, scraping the bark and putting it in wine that they left for the enemy to discover. The foreign troops drank it and, once drugged, their captors easily overcame them. It was one of the earliest biological weapons. The name was sort of an inside joke among the five of them."

"I've heard stories about mandrakes," I said. "If you pull one out of the ground it starts screaming. Anyone who hears the sound will die."

"I see you know your mythology," Charles said.

"More like my Harry Potter."

"How amusing," he said in a dry voice. "There is another legend, a bit of folklore, that a mandrake will only grow where the semen of a hanged man has dripped to the ground."

He steepled his fingers, and I shuddered.

"Do you mean Paul Noble?"

"I heard one of the stories about the possible cause of Paul's death," he said. "It is a bizarre coincidence, you must admit."

Pépé pointed to the figure on his glass. "So this creature was the symbol of the Mandrake Society?"

Charles nodded. "Maggie had the wineglasses made for everyone. I used to have a set of six. These three are the only ones left."

I set my glass on the coffee table with a sharp little clink. Charles stared at me.

"Do continue about this group," Pépé said.

Charles leaned his head against the back of his chair like he was contemplating what to say. "They needed to continue field testing," he said finally. "On humans. So they advertised for volunteers. Offering money."

"You mean discreet ads in newspapers?" I asked. "Like they used to do before the Internet?"

"Of course not." He sounded annoyed. "It was easy enough to find people who needed spare cash if you knew where to look . . . people sleeping in the rough. Homeless individuals."

"Oh, my God," I said. "They got people who were desperate for money to volunteer to be experimented on?"

"*It happens all the time.* How else do you think they test new drugs? Don't judge, Lucie." Charles sat forward and shook his finger in my face. "They were protecting *you.* The people who volunteered were patriots. They wanted to help."

I kept my mouth shut. Drug testing was one thing. This was about creative ways to kill people.

Charles sat back again. "There was, well, an unfortunate incident. One of the volunteers, a homeless man who said his name was Stephen Falcon, was also mildly disabled. Autistic, I guess, is how you'd describe him today. Unfortunately, he died during one of the experiments. It happened in the lab, very traumatic, upset the hell out of everyone." He held out his hands palms up as though entreating us to understand the small setback. "There was nothing anyone could do to save him. A tragedy, obviously."

I couldn't tell if he meant for the Mandrake Society or for Stephen Falcon. Neither Pépé nor I spoke. Pépé's lips were pressed together and his face was the color of ashes.

"Of course, we took care of his burial. Actually, he was cremated. We didn't find a next of kin." He looked rueful. "That was our undoing, where we went wrong. His real name was Stephen Falcone. He wasn't homeless; he'd run away. At the time he was living with his sister in D.C., Elinor Falcone. She found out that he'd volunteered for our program from someone who knew Stephen and tracked us down. I went to see her."

He gave an elaborate shrug. "I told her that her brother had died serving his country and she should be proud of him. After all, he was autistic—what kind of future could he have? She was well compensated for her loss, spared his future medical expenses, what have you. In return, of course, she couldn't talk about what happened to him."

Blood money. I blinked hard listening to Charles's description of the "favor" he had done Elinor Falcone.

"Did she keep her word?" Pépé asked.

He waved a hand. "Oh, yes, she did, indeed. But it didn't end there. Stephen's death . . . I don't know . . . it changed everything. The Mandrake Society got together one night at the cottage and, from what I heard, everyone got stinking drunk, really crazy out of their minds. Theo Graf, the head biochemist, said he was done with the group, the experiments, everything. He planned to quit, leave Fort Wilton and go somewhere else. Maggie was so upset that she said they ought to come clean about what really happened to Stephen. Aside from the fact that they were operating a program that shouldn't even exist, there was the issue of what charges they might face—manslaughter, or worse. Everyone's careers would be ruined. A tragedy when they all had such brilliant, promising futures."

"How many 'others' were there?" Pépé asked.

Charles ticked them off on his fingers. "Besides Maggie and Theo there were three others," he said. "Two men and a woman. Mel Racine, Vivian Kalman, and . . . Paul Noble."

"Paul Noble was a biochemist who worked for a secret weapons program at Fort Wilton forty years ago?" I should have seen it coming, but it still floored me. "That's a long way from owning a multimillion-dollar business distributing wine."

Charles shook his head. "Not as far off as you think. When you consider it, there's a lot of chemistry in wine."

"What happened at the cottage that night?" Pépé asked. "You didn't finish the story."

Charles took a deep breath as if the memories still pained him. "I told you Theo left the place in a rage. Got in a car though he never should have been behind the wheel. Maggie went after him, although she was drunk, too. They were, ah, a couple, sleeping together on the quiet since fraternizing with colleagues was frowned on. Theo was crazy about her, so she figured she could talk some sense into him." He paused and cleared his throat. "Maggie never made it off Pontiac Island and Theo didn't know she had followed him. The car she was driving was found the next morning where she drove it off the bridge. Her body washed up on the beach."

The writhing figures kept dancing as the fire blazed with the same intensity as when Charles had flipped the switch . . . how long ago? It seemed like we'd been here all night.

"Maggie's death and the incident involving Stephen Falcone sent Theo off the deep end," he said. "He was . . . I don't know . . . wild, out of control. The day he came to my office for the last time—"

Charles stopped speaking and pressed his lips together.

"What happened?" Pépé asked finally.

"He made some crazy accusations. Claimed her death wasn't an accident, and that the others had done something to tamper with the car to keep her from talking about Stephen. It was preposterous, of course. He even accused me of being part of the conspiracy." Charles's voice rose and his face grew flushed. At first I thought it was shame, or maybe the cumulative result of enough alcohol to float an ocean liner, but as he went on, I realized he was outraged.

"Theo swore that if he ever found a way to prove that Maggie had been murdered, he'd make sure everyone paid for it. I can still hear his voice that day," he said. "Shouting over and over that he'd see to it each of us lost someone we loved as much as he loved Maggie. I told him he was absolutely cracked, out of his mind."

Charles took an unsteady breath. "At the time, I dismissed it as, well, you know, an idle threat, nothing he would really act on. Besides, what was he going to uncover about Maggie's death except the truth? She was blind drunk and she drove off a bridge in the middle of the night and drowned."

He swirled his brandy and finished it with his eyes closed. When he opened them he said, "I disbanded the group after that. What choice did I have? They all left, went elsewhere, and it fell to me to clean up. Erase Stephen Falcone's death. Erase the Mandrake Society altogether. So I did." He reached over and picked up his empty wineglass. "But I did keep these as a reminder to myself. Not a day passes that it hasn't haunted me."

THE SAUVIGNON SECRET   69

"Did it haunt Paul Noble, too?" I set down my own glass and wished I hadn't drunk from it. "You must have gotten together from time to time and it came up?"

"Actually," he said, "we avoided each other. It wasn't hard to do." He got up for more brandy, swaying slightly. Pépé and I exchanged glances.

"I kept track of them all over the years," he said. "Though we were never in direct contact again, you understand."

"What happened to everyone?" I asked.

"Theo disappeared . . . just vanished. I heard that he was killed in a car accident while he was in Europe about twenty years ago. Even saw a copy of a grainy photo in an Austrian newspaper that looked like him." He shook his head, remembering. "I can't tell you how relieved I was. Then Vivian died. Heart attack last winter. She'd retired to France. That just left Mel and Paul."

He ticked off two fingers. "Mel was out in California, the Bay Area. Owned a couple of car dealerships . . . talk about a lifestyle change. He set up a wine club and rented out temperature-controlled storage to people who needed a place to keep their high-end collections. He bought an old bank building and converted the vault into a cellar. Paul, well, you know what happened to him. But a few years ago when I was out in Monte Rio at one of the Bohemian Grove's summer campouts, someone brought a couple of cases of wine made by a new winemaker in Calistoga. Named Teddy Fargo. Turned out the guy also grew roses so he named the place Rose Hill Vineyard. Graf spelled backward is F-A-R-G. Theo's middle initial was O for Octavius. I began to wonder if it could be Theo."

"That's the vineyard you recommended to Mick Dunne," I said. "Told him that he should buy wine from them. But I'm sure Mick said 'she' and not 'he.' "

"The new owner is a woman," Charles said. "About six months ago Theo, or Fargo, sold the vineyard and vanished. A couple months later Mel Racine was found dead. It looked like a heart attack, same as Vivian. He'd been drinking, too. Guess which wineglass the police found in his office, next to his body?"

He stared at both of us. No one said anything.

"Then two days ago, Paul committed suicide. Something drove

him to it—or someone," he said. "I think Fargo is Theo. I think he decided to hunt down the remaining members of the Mandrake Society after all this time. I think he's kind of flipped and he's carrying out the threat he made forty years ago."

"Did Paul Noble know about Mel Racine's death?" Pépé asked.

"Not from me." Charles's morose mood seemed to deepen. "At first I thought it was just what it was. We're all getting up there in years now . . . hell, Mel was probably in his mid- to late sixties. I just figured it was a heart attack. But when I heard about Paul and that wineglass, I called in some favors and learned that they found a Mandrake Society wineglass next to Mel, too."

"What about Vivian? Any wineglass there?"

"I don't know. I've checked with some old French contacts, but I'm still waiting to find out."

"You think Theo was responsible for their deaths?" I asked. "That he's this Teddy Fargo person?"

"I do. It would explain finding the wineglasses with Mel and Paul. Theo was a brilliant biochemist," he said. "He could get away with murder, especially if no one was suspicious about the causes of two seemingly unrelated deaths. The police wouldn't bother with a tox screen."

"Paul Noble's death appeared to be suicide," Pépé said.

"I still think Theo was involved, though I'm not sure how. And maybe it wasn't suicide."

"What does this have to do with Rose Hill Winery—and me?" I asked.

"I need to know if it's really Theo," Charles said. "And I'm betting the clue that would confirm it can be found at his old winery. Somewhere on the property, there will be black roses."

"There's no such thing as a black rose. They're just very dark red roses," I said. "It's fiction."

"All the same, they were Theo's passion. Obsession, really. They'll be growing there somewhere. No one will wonder if you ask for a private tour of the winery," Charles said. "Especially if you're there to buy wine. Trust me, those roses will be in a garden where no one would see them if they were just visiting the tasting room."

"Why don't you fly out to Calistoga and take a look? Why me?"

He smiled. "And tip my hand? Not a chance. It's equally possible I'm barking mad, still haunted by old ghosts. There are days when I wonder myself. Like I told you, I saw a photo of Theo in a newspaper. Supposedly he died two decades ago. To be honest, I feel a bit of a fool even telling you all this."

I glanced at my grandfather, but he remained mute. My choice. My decision.

"All I'm asking is that you find out whether there is a garden with black roses at that vineyard. That's it." Charles's tone was reasonable, but he was also pleading. "And the wine, I promise you, is first-rate. I'm not worried that you'll advise Mick Dunne not to buy it. I have that much faith in it. So you see, it's a win-win situation. You also get to accompany Luc to California, spend more time together."

Win-win for whom?

"And then what?" I asked. "What if I find these roses?"

Charles sucked in his breath. "Then, I guess, I'll be one step closer to believing I'm right and that Theo could be alive."

"Then you'll go to the police?" Pépé asked.

"I . . . maybe not the police, but someone. Dragging up Stephen Falcone in this day and age could be like throwing gasoline onto that fire right there," he said. "Can you imagine opening up the Pandora's box of an off-the-radar project involving human testing gone wrong, having it show up in some newspaper next to a story on waterboarding or Guantánamo?"

Charles shook his head, without waiting for an answer. "I told you Theo swore he'd hurt someone each of us loved as deeply as he loved Maggie."

The fiery figures rose up and became more menacing. The room grew hostile, unwelcoming. I resisted the urge to glance at the windows where a ghostly face from Charles's past might be staring through the glass at the three of us.

Pépé's voice was hoarse. "Juliette."

Charles nodded. "Juliette. Who else?"

Of all the mental and moral blackmail Charles could have brought to bear on me that night—and I wouldn't have thought there was anything—he'd found the path to my heart. He knew Pépé would suffer if something happened to his wife and I'd refused to do one small favor that might change the outcome of this situation, save her somehow.

I stole a look at my grandfather. His hands gripped the sides of his chair and he was staring into the fire, a bleak expression on his face. He wouldn't ask me outright; it was my decision.

"All right," I said. "I'll do it."

CHAPTER 8

———— ∞∞∞ ————

Even now when I think back on that night in Charles's lodge, the three of us sitting around an absurdly comforting fire in the middle of July during the hottest summer since they started keeping records, I have a hard time remembering what really happened and what I imagined had taken place. Charles's tale of Theo Graf—a scientist he'd believed was dead for more than twenty years who suddenly popped up in California and decided to exact revenge for the accidental death of the young girl who'd been his lover almost half a century ago—sounded like the frayed memories of an old man with a guilt-ridden conscience. Or a narcissist who believed that a series of coincidences involving other people somehow revolved around himself.

The tenuous thread that held Charles's logic together was a set of wineglasses with the Mandrake Society's "logo" on them found near the bodies of Mel Racine and Paul Noble, and a fearful belief that Graf might have faked his death, flipped his name around to Fargo, and, for no obvious reason, decided to make good on a decades-old threat.

I have even hazier recollections of discussing this with Pépé when Charles finally called on a gardener who lived on the premises to drive us home that unnaturally cold night. The man's placid, almost bovine, demeanor when he appeared at the door to the lodge, minutes after Charles phoned him, made me wonder if this were a regular occurrence, and whether it was a little secret to be kept from Juliette that one of her groundskeepers moonlighted as a chauffeur for her husband's boozy get-togethers. I suspected he was well paid for keeping this extracurricular activity to himself.

"Do you think it's possible that Teddy Fargo is hunting down anyone who was associated with the Mandrake Society? And that he's really Theo Graf?" I asked Pépé as the driver pulled out of the Thiessmans' gravel driveway onto the two-lane country road.

The moon had disappeared and, out here in the middle of farmland, no streetlights illuminated the hairpin turns and unspooling ribbon of hills that our driver navigated with the speed of someone who believed he was being chased. With the exception of two carriage lanterns at the entrance to a gated driveway that flashed by and the dimmed instruments on the dash, the night closed around us like a cocoon.

My head rested on Pépé's shoulder. I had finally gotten him to put his suit jacket back on. It felt comfortingly scratchy against my cheek, smelling of his cigarettes and old-fashioned aftershave with a mingled hint of my light floral perfume.

"It does sound far-fetched, doesn't it?" he said. "Who knows what tricks his mind is playing on him after so many years? He's obsessed with Juliette not knowing a thing about this—and he's had no one else to discuss it with until tonight."

"I wish he'd told us the truth about those wineglasses before we started drinking," I said. "It was sort of creepy once we knew their history."

"Charles always did have a flair for drama," Pépé said. "And embellishment."

"Maybe that's all this is," I said.

"You are going to check out this wine for Mick anyway, *n'est-ce pas?*"

"Yes, I suppose so."

"Then look for these so-called black roses and that will be the end of it with Charles. At least it will bring him some peace." He patted my hand. "And Juliette, as well."

His voice softened when he mentioned her name.

"Okay, I will."

"And you will be with me for the trip out west," he continued. "I'll change the reservation at the hotel in San Francisco and you can stay with my friend Robert Sanábria when you go up to Napa. I'll join you after my talk. He lives in Calistoga so you'll be right where you need to be." Another pat on the hand and he said, sounding happy, "It's an ill wind that doesn't blow someone some good, eh, *ma belle?*"

I showed up at Mick Dunne's for tea on Saturday morning, Bastille Day, looking and feeling like something the cat dragged in. His housekeeper, a pretty, petite Hispanic girl with long, dark hair pulled into a loose bun, told me Mick was out by the pool and asked me to wait while she went to get him.

"It's okay," I said. "He's expecting me and I know where to go. I'll find him myself."

She was new. He'd had another housekeeper when we were seeing each other and I slept here from time to time.

"Of course." She bobbed her head, courteous and respectful, but something about the heavy-lidded flicker of her eyes told me she'd heard that line before, and each time it had been a woman who'd said it.

With a little twinge of jealousy, I wondered whom Mick was sleeping with now. Surely there was someone.

I had to walk through his gardens to get to the pool. When Mick bought his home a few years ago, he discovered that the previous owner, who had studied botany as an avocation, had worked with a horticulturist to identify and label the many exotic species of trees, shrubs, and flowers that bloomed on the park-like grounds of his estate. Mick tracked down the horticulturist and persuaded him to take the job of full-time groundskeeper, giving him carte blanche to purchase whatever new or unusual specimen he wanted. The current passion was succulents, or so I'd heard. Desert plants and cacti that looked like modern sculpture and could wound like weapons weren't my thing; my favorite was the lush, luxurious sunken rose garden with its pretty two-tiered fountain. Mick told me that coming upon the rioting tumble of roses—espaliered climbers, bushes, shrubs, floribunda, tea roses, hybrids—the first time he saw the house had brought back a flood of memories of his childhood in London and the days when his route walking to and from school had been through Regent's Park and Queen Mary's Rose Gardens. He'd bought the house on the spot.

After that, each time I came here I couldn't help but hear school-boy voices and see shadows flicking in and out of the sunlight, imagining blazers heaped in a pile on the ground, dress shirts untucked, ties askew, the thud of a soccer ball being passed back and forth imitating the agile footwork of the current football idol who played for Arsenal or Man United.

Mick was on the phone by the side of the pool, still dressed in riding attire after being out with the horses for their morning exercise. He sat at a glass-topped table under an umbrella, legs splayed out in front of him, running a hand through his long, dark hair, intent on the conversation and the caller. I could tell by the way he sat, and his demeanor, that it was business.

He looked up and saw me, raising a finger to indicate that he would be only a moment as the housekeeper came outside carrying a silver tray with a Portmeirion teapot, matching dishes, a cloth-covered basket, and a pretty cut-glass bowl of summer berries.

Mick's house, like mine, had been built on a hill where it commanded a spectacular view of the Blue Ridge. The former owner had taken advantage of the way the hill dropped off to a long vista of the Piedmont anchored by distant mountains and had put in an infinity pool—a swimming pool with no edge or rim on one side that gave the effect of water disappearing at the horizon, almost as if it were joining the sky. In reality it cascaded like a waterfall into a smaller pool below where it was pumped through filters back into the main pool. The effect always took my breath away.

Mick clicked off his phone and tossed it on the table, getting up and pulling me to him. He kissed me swiftly on the lips and held me so close I smelled horses and sweat, and a faint whiff of what-ever his housekeeper used to wash his clothes. His arms tightened around me.

I placed my hands on his chest. He sensed the restraint and pulled back.

"What does it take for a girl to get fed around this place?" I asked. "You did promise tea."

I hated that his easy sexuality could still knock me off balance—and that he knew it—the implied intimacy of lovers who had just gotten out of bed or the shower together. Mick was a man of angles and planes, nothing soft or yielding about him, both in his business dealings and his physical features. His face was fair and smooth shaven, but it had been burned brown by years in the Florida sun and wind whipped from riding fast horses while foxhunting and playing polo at dizzying breakneck speed. He looked lean and hard muscled, more like a rugged American cowboy than an English gentleman.

"I'll feed you myself," he said and grinned. "It's good to see you, love. Thanks for coming by. Please . . ." He gestured to the table and two chairs.

We sat across from each other and, as if she had been waiting behind the boxwood hedge, the housekeeper appeared with another tray, this one with little bowls filled with jam and thick cream, a plate of lemon slices for the tea, a sugar bowl, and a small pitcher of milk.

"Do you fancy coffee?" he asked. "Or is tea okay?"

"Tea's fine," I said as he picked up the pot, nodding dismissal at the girl. "This looks lovely."

"You look absolutely shattered," he said as the gate to the pool closed and we were alone again. "Something wrong?"

"My grandfather and I had drinks with Charles Thiessman at his lodge last night. Or more like very early this morning."

Mick smiled. "That gardener bloke drive you home, too?"

I nodded and our eyes met like a couple of guilty underage kids who'd conspired to get drunk as lords behind their parents' backs. "I told him you and I had spoken about this California wine he talked you into buying. He seemed surprised we'd discussed it."

What Charles hadn't said was how much he had told Mick about Teddy Fargo, or Theo Graf, and about his obsession with learning whether black roses grew somewhere on the property. My guess was that Mick knew only what Charles believed he needed to know and nothing more.

"Truth be told, I was surprised he came to me with the information in the first place. Apparently he's got loads of contacts in the wine world out in California." Mick indicated the rose garden. "I think it was the connection with roses. This place in Calistoga is supposed to have quite the fabulous rose garden attached to it." He gave me a lopsided grin. "Which probably explains why they call it Rose Hill."

"He did mention the roses." I stabbed a slice of lemon with a tiny fork. "Did he say anything specific about them to you?"

Mick didn't answer right away. "About the roses? What do you mean?"

I stirred my tea. Mick was shrewd. I shouldn't have brought up the subject if I didn't want him to connect the dots.

"Nothing. I just thought he went to a lot of trouble getting my grandfather invited to this Bohemian Grove meeting and then indirectly arranged through you for me to accompany Pépé to California."

Mick burst out laughing. "You've got this the wrong way around. Being invited to give one of the lakeside talks at the Bohemian Grove is huge, Lucie. The most important men on the planet belong to that club. Crikey, it's easier to marry a royal and get yourself a title than it is to join that lot. I have friends whose fathers were still on the waiting list when they died—and I'm talking decades."

"So you know about this Bohemian Club, too?"

He nodded. "Who doesn't? I think it was Herbert Hoover who called their July campout 'the greatest men's party on earth.' I'd cut off a limb to be a member, even with some of the boys' own silliness that goes with it."

He untucked the cloth that swaddled the breadbasket, releasing the warm, fragrant aroma of fresh scones.

"Did your housekeeper make these? They smell heavenly."

He smirked. "Taught her everything she knows about English cuisine. Quick study, that Victoria."

"Oh, so she had five minutes to learn, did she? 'English' and 'cuisine' don't belong in the same sentence, you know."

"You bloody frogs are all alike." He made a face as he broke open a scone and heaped berries on it. "Think you invented cooking."

"No, we just perfected it." I drank some tea. "What about the silliness at the Bohemian Grove? Is Pépé going to have to put on a goofy hat or wear his underwear outside his trousers, like some fraternity hazing right of passage?"

"Nothing that unimaginative. There's clotted cream for the berries, English clotted cream." He passed me the bowl. "They've got this opening ceremony each year that could sound a little dodgy, if you didn't realize it was just a bunch of lads letting off steam and bonding. The caveat is they're the richest, most powerful men in the world. The club has a motto: 'Weaving spiders come not here.' Shakespeare. *A Midsummer Night's Dream*. It means no business is to be transacted while you're at the Grove, but let me tell you, a hell of a lot happens during that campout."

"What do they do for their opening ceremony?"

"Oh, they dress in robes like monks and light some funeral pyre in the middle of a lake to represent worldly cares and cremate the bloody thing. So for a couple of weeks, you shrug off the burdens and worries you haul around the rest of the time and you're free to do things like pee openly against trees and drink like a fish. They also put on concerts, plays . . . the entertainment is supposed to be incredible."

"How very bohemian sounding," I said. "Especially the tree peeing."

He waved a hand and said through a mouthful of berries, "Not that kind of bohemian—long hair, unwashed tie-dyed shirts, and angst-filled poetry. Don't forget they were founded in the 1870s. It meant London, beau monde, a club that was a place for eminent men who used their wealth to do good."

I picked up the teapot and refilled our cups. "It sounds like a combination Boy Scout jamboree and fraternity party, if you ask me. No girls allowed."

Mick winked at me. "That's half the fun. Luc will have a grand old time."

"In the meantime, I'll be at Rose Hill Vineyard talking to the winemaker about your Cab," I said. "And discussing the blend."

"I spoke to her yesterday. She's expecting you." He pulled a paper out of his shirt pocket. "Here's her contact information. Said to ring her when you want to show up. She's fairly tethered to the place so she'll be there."

He handed me the paper. I stared at the name and phone number in his bold scrawl.

"Brooke Hennessey?" I rubbed my thumb over his writing. "That name sounds familiar."

"You know her? Not too many female winemakers out there. I should have figured you did."

"No, not that. Hennessey . . . I wonder if she's related to Tavis Hennessey?"

"Who's that?" he said.

"He owned a vineyard in Napa awhile back. Quinn worked there," I said and stopped.

Atoka was a small enough town that everyone knew the gossip about everyone else, but Mick and I had never discussed Quinn's past in California and the shadowy circumstances under which he left his former employer. Even I didn't know exactly what had happened. Quinn avoided any questions or even an attempt to bring up the subject.

"Oh, so that's the guy?" Mick said. "I heard about it. It's common knowledge; you must know that. The winemaker at Quinn's old winery got caught selling adulterated wine on the black market in Eastern Europe and went to jail. Canfield, wasn't it?"

"Cantor. Allen Cantor."

"Cantor. Yeah, that's right."

He sipped his tea like he was waiting for me to rush to Quinn's defense, a jury member who needed extra convincing the defendant didn't do it. So Mick believed the rumors that where there was smoke there had been fire.

I set my teacup down and pushed the saucer away. "Quinn didn't know anything about what was going on, Mick. He was completely in the dark."

"I heard that."

"It's true."

"Quinn's a smart guy—"

"He didn't know."

The vineyard had been called Le Coq Rouge. It went under after Cantor went to jail, and the owner, Tavis Hennessey, couldn't recover his financial losses, coupled with the damaging impact of what had been written in the press. Quinn left and moved to Virginia. A few weeks before my father died he hired Quinn, deciding it wasn't necessary to do a background check after Quinn told him his salary requirements were minimal. Back then Montgomery Estate Vineyard was nearly broke and our previous winemaker had returned home to France, so Leland was desperate. He saw Quinn as the answer to his prayers. Soon afterward Leland was gone and I took over the winery. Neither Quinn nor I bargained on the other, but we'd made it work somehow.

Mick reached over and took my hand. "I heard that Quinn might not be coming back here, that he might stay in California for good. You going to hire a new winemaker to take his place?"

So that was the current rumor going around. Quinn left poor Lucie in the lurch.

"He'll be back for harvest." I withdrew my hand, hoping I didn't sound defensive. "I guess I'll have to stop by the General Store and straighten out Thelma and the Romeos."

In every small town in America there is someone who keeps tabs on everyone else, minds their business for them, and then genially shares it with everyone else on the planet. Our someone was Thelma Johnson, who owned the General Store, where she presided like a chatty, benevolent queen over her subjects, the good citizens of Atoka. Telling Thelma something was like the kids' old-fashioned game of telephone: little whispers passed around a circle, only to find out that what was said originally had been burnished and revamped into a tabloid-worthy headline with the over-the-top drama and throaty angst of one of her beloved soap operas.

The Romeos, her henchmen, were just as guilty. Their name stood for Retired Old Men Eating Out, but it could as easily have been Retired Old Men Eavesdropping Obsessively. I knew all of them practically like uncles because Leland had been a Romeo. Their whereabouts on any given day were as predictable as animal migration patterns: mornings gathered around the coffeepot at Thelma's, laying siege to her fresh-made doughnuts and muffins, then whiling away long, lazy afternoons that stretched into "It's five o'clock somewhere," and the dinner hour with drinks and a meal at some restaurant or bar in Middleburg or Leesburg. Social networking on the Internet had nothing on the pack of them as a faster-than-a-speeding-bullet means of disseminating information.

"When's the last time you talked to Quinn?" Mick asked. He kept his voice casual, but he was fishing.

"I can't remember. Not that long ago."

His eyes narrowed. "You can't remember, huh? Why don't you see him when you're in California, Lucie? Straighten things out. You do know where he's staying, don't you?"

"There's nothing to straighten out." I folded my napkin and pushed back my chair. "Except the gossip about him not returning. Thanks for tea, Mick. I'll call you after I get back from Napa."

He caught my hand and pulled me up. "Come on, I'll walk you to your car. You do know you're a lousy liar, don't you?"

"I don't know what you're talking about."

He slipped an arm around my waist, suddenly serious. "Sure you do. Look, love, I've been doing some thinking. About us."

"Mick—"

"Hear me out before you say anything." He put two fingers over my lips. "How'd you feel about giving us another chance? We know each other so much better now. We'd be good together, the pair of us—wouldn't make the same mistakes."

I shook my head and removed his hand. "I don't think so."

"I'm not taking an answer from you right now. Please at least promise me you'll think about it." We reached my car and he turned me so I faced him. "But first, darling, you've got to sort out your feelings about Quinn. I'm not talking about business, either, and you know it. See him in California, get it sorted once and for all. When you come back, let me know if you want to try us again."

He bent and kissed me like a brother. I think I mumbled something about him being completely and totally wrong before I got in my car and drove home.

But I knew, just as Mick did, that I couldn't go on flying solo. If there was going to be any future for Quinn and me—that meant the winery's future as well as our own—then Mick was right. I needed to seek out Quinn when I was in California and get some answers. Whether I liked them or not.

CHAPTER 9

Since childhood, I've always had a secret hideaway—a refuge where I can lick wounds, grieve a broken heart . . . cry. Growing up, it was the Ruins, the crumbling-but-elegant shell of a tenant house that had been torched by Union soldiers searching for the Confederacy's most famous renegade: Colonel John Singleton Mosby, the Gray Ghost, and his Partisan Rangers. After we converted what was left of the old building to a stage for concerts, plays, and lectures, I retreated farther, to the family cemetery. Generations of Montgomerys were buried there, beginning with Hamish Montgomery, who chose the site in the late 1700s after receiving the land for service during the French and Indian War, and ending, at least so far, with my parents.

Hamish had picked the flattened crest of a hill for its view of his beloved Blue Ridge Mountains, which now watched over him forever. Over the years, more of my ancestors were laid to rest on that open-air place, until the mid-1800s when Thomas Montgomery—who later died as one of Mosby's Rangers—built a low redbrick wall to surround and perhaps fortify the little cemetery, with a wrought-iron gate at its entrance.

I drove straight there from Mick's, parking at the bottom of the hill next to a grove of oaks and tulip poplars. Years ago, my mother had discovered a pair of mulberry trees struggling to live in the dense underbrush on one of the many occasions she'd brought Eli and me along to pull weeds and tidy up the grave sites. She called it our duty to our ancestors. Eli called it a waste of time; the weeds always grew back and it wasn't like the ancestors noticed anyway. For some reason I didn't mind the work, and that annoyed the hell out of Eli.

Finding the mulberry trees changed everything. It became a ritual during the summer months to stop and look for berries, picking handfuls and cramming them into our mouths until our lips and fingers were stained with sticky dark red juice. Eli thought it was hysterically funny to pretend he was dripping in blood and began popping up from behind a headstone where I was weeding, saying in a fake Transylvanian accent, "Bwah-hah-hah, I've come to bite you and suck your blood." The first few times he scared me until I dumped a vase of dirty rainwater on him and that was the end of the vampire act.

Out of habit, I checked the trees for fruit. Not quite ripe, but I ate some berries anyway and thought about Eli waving his red fingers like wriggling worms on a hot bright July day like this one, the three of us trudging up the hill with our trowels and rakes and a thermos of my mother's fresh-made lemonade or sweet tea. Now she was always here, and I was the one who cared for the graves, fulfilling the family duty to our ancestors.

I picked some wildflowers blooming nearby—joe-pye weed, black-eyed Susans, wild chicory, and Queen Anne's lace—and made a small bouquet. The gate creaked as I pushed it open, another chore for Eli's to-do list. I'd been here ten days ago on the Fourth of July to leave small flags at the headstones of all those who fought in wars as far back as the Revolution, so the cemetery still looked neat and tidy.

I dumped the wilted roses from the vase at my mother's grave and replaced them with the wildflowers. Then I sat, my back against her sun-warmed headstone, and called Quinn.

He answered on the third ring, breathing hard like I'd caught him in the middle of doing something involving intense physical labor.

"Lucie? Hey, what's going on? Haven't heard from you in a while. Everything okay?"

I leaned farther into the stone until I could feel the chiseled grooves of the words of my mother's epitaph: *I will go before you and light the way so that you may follow.*

Quinn's familiar baritone was so matter-of-fact, so normal, that for a moment it seemed like he'd never left, and I was just calling to find out where he was. At that moment, I missed him—and all the times we'd spent together in our up-and-down relationship— unbearably.

"Everything's fine," I said. "How's it going with you?"

"Good."

I should have known it would take a crowbar to pry anything out of him. Or some form of torture banned by the Geneva Conventions.

"What are you doing?" I asked. His breathing had slowed but it still sounded as though he'd been running or lifting heavy objects.

"Talking to you."

"Okay, wise guy, maybe I'll just hang up—"

"Hey, please don't!" He didn't seem to realize that I was kidding. "I'm sorry. It's good to hear you. I'm glad you called . . . I've been thinking about you."

Something caught in my throat. "I've been thinking about you, too. When are you coming home?"

He took a long time to answer, too long. Maybe I shouldn't have said "home." He was, after all, from California, born and raised. Maybe he was home.

"Soon . . . I promise. I've still got a few things to wrap up."

"Thelma and the Romeos are spreading the word that you're staying out there for good," I said.

His laugh sounded self-conscious. "Good old Thelma. I even miss her, too. Tell her that Ouija board of hers isn't always dead-bang right. And say hi to the Romeos for me."

I wanted to say I wished he'd deliver those messages himself in person, but I couldn't do it. "Sure, next time I see them. I guess if it's soon, you must have finally sold your mother's house?"

"Maybe. Cross your fingers."

"Quinn, even my eyes are crossed. Will you be here for harvest like you promised?"

"I won't let you down. You have my word."

He had said the right thing, but something was still missing. My heart, which had been pounding in my chest, slowed to a dull thud.

"Well," I said, "I've got some news. I'm coming to California with my grandfather. We're flying in to San Francisco."

A swallow flitted past me, landing on a nearby headstone. The cicadas seemed to amp up their volume, drowning out the silence on the other end of the phone.

Finally I asked, "Are you still there?"

"Yeah. I'm here."

"I can tell that news went over big. Look, it's just a quick trip and I'll probably be pretty busy. I'm sure you are, too—"

"Hold on," he said. "You caught me off guard, that's all. I've been working flat out all week. I owed an old friend a favor. We wrapped up bottling last night and I just finished racking over some Chardonnay. My head's someplace else."

"Oh." The racking over at least explained the huffing and puffing.

"So what's the deal? Pleasure trip? Sightseeing? When do you get here?"

"Tomorrow. It's business, not pleasure. Pépé will be in some town called Monte Rio in Sonoma to give a talk at the Bohemian Grove."

He whistled. "The Bohemian Grove? Are you serious? Luc must be going to that big summer shindig in the woods they have every July. Every mover and shaker in the country flies in for that. It's huge."

"So I've heard."

"What are you going to do? That place is men-only."

"Going to Napa—Calistoga—to check out some wine Mick Dunne is considering buying. He wants something to sell this fall before his own wine is ready . . . and he wants me to make the blend for him."

"Good for you."

"I can't do it without you. Please say you'll help me?"

He sidestepped that. "Where are you staying in Napa?"

"With a friend of Pépé's. Robert Sanábria."

"Sanábria? Jesus, Lucie, you're full of surprises. You know who Sanábria is, don't you? California Winemaker of the Year a couple of years ago. One of the heavyweights in Napa. I didn't know your grandfather knew him."

"You're avoiding the question."

"What question?"

"Will you or won't you help me blend this wine? You're so much better at this than I am."

"You must really want my help if you're buttering me up."

"You make it sound like I'm asking you to hang the moon someplace new," I said. "Mick pays well, you know that."

"Whose wine?"

"Cab from a vineyard called Rose Hill. It's in Calistoga on the Silverado Trail."

"I've heard of it," he said. "Winemaker is some guy named Fargo, I think."

"There's a new owner. It's probably a coincidence, but her name is Brooke Hennessey. I don't suppose she's related—"

He cut me off. "Jesus, Lucie! You left that until the end on purpose, didn't you? She's his daughter. Man, of all the gin joints in the world, Ilsa. Why'd you have to pick that one?"

"Please don't be angry. I didn't pick it." He'd blown up like a volcano as soon as I mentioned Brooke. "There's a lot more to the story that you don't know. I can't go into it now; it's too complicated."

"When is anything you do not complicated?"

I let that one pass. At least he hadn't turned me down. But he still sounded mad. I plunged ahead.

"So you're not in touch with Brooke Hennessey?"

"Last time I saw her she was sixteen. I heard she went off to Davis to study enology and viticulture like her old man. I never thought she'd stick it out, but she did."

"Will you please come with me to this meeting? Please?"

His laughter was harsh. "You make it sound like it's no big deal."

I waited and bit my tongue.

When he answered, it was grudging. "I suppose I knew sooner or later I'd run into her. Just didn't figure on it being now."

"Thank you," I said. "I'm really grateful. You have no idea."

"Oh, you'll pay for this, don't you worry."

"Send the bill to Mick," I said. "Why don't I call you when I get to town? Are you staying in San Jose at your mother's place?"

"I'm kind of moving around. Right now I'm in Sausalito. Keeping an eye on a friend's houseboat."

When he was being evasive like that there was always more to the story. Until now, I'd thought of Quinn as someone who belonged to the land, with his innate understanding of the rhythm and pace of the growing season, his intuitive knack for knowing exactly when to harvest the grapes and when it was wiser to wait. It never occurred to me that he might be equally comfortable on the water, that maybe he was an adept sailor who knew firsthand about navigating the pretty bays around San Francisco or had grown up surfing California's golden beaches like the sun-kissed boys and girls in the endless summers of old Beach Boys songs.

I knew almost nothing about his past, what his life had been like growing up. But that's how he'd kept it in Virginia and it seemed he hadn't changed now that he was back in California.

"A houseboat. How romantic."

"You would say something like that." At least his voice had lost its edge. "Look, it's really easy to get from Sausalito to the city. Where are you staying?"

"Oh, gosh, I have no idea. It was four A.M. when we were having the discussion about the trip and I forgot to ask. Probably somewhere downtown, knowing Pépé."

"The Embarcadero? Union Square?"

"I'm embarrassed to tell you this, but I really don't know San Francisco. The last time I was there was probably twenty years ago. All I remember was that it was big and hilly."

"It still is. When do you have to go up to Napa?"

"Sometime between tomorrow and Wednesday, when we fly home."

"So you'll have time to do some sightseeing," he said. "I could show you around, if you want."

"Would you? I'd like that."

"Yeah, I'll show you the real city. The good, the bad, and the ugly. We'll skip the tourist traps."

"How poetic. I thought you'd say you want me to leave my heart in San Francisco."

"There are worse places to leave it," he said. "Call me when you get in."

He hung up.

He was right. There were worse places to leave my heart. Like where it was right now. Missing him.

Our Bastille Day party passed in a blur of voices and laughter and music. At the end of the evening we set off our best fireworks ever from a barge in the middle of the small pond by the Ruins, watching them fizz red, white, and blue as they lit up the silhouette of the mountains and cascaded over the dense rows of vines. For the first time in the past few days I felt absurdly happy, even giddy, partly because of all the compliments we got from our guests and partly because I'd kicked back and drunk enough wine to make me tipsy.

Frankie had transformed the courtyard between the villa and the winery into the kind of Parisian brasserie Hemingway and Fitzgerald would have frequented—white linen tablecloths, flickering candlelight, bud vases with a single rose—a midsummery night tableau of heads bent together across bistro tables in earnest conversation or flirty romance. Swags of Japanese lanterns hung across the courtyard, and tiny white lights woven through the arcade beams and around the columns gave the scene a dreamy, fluid timelessness. Over the last few weeks Frankie had taken my mother's French records—the well-known *chanteurs* like Aznavour, Brel, Bécaud, Brassens, Piaf, and the classic rock and rollers like Patricia Kaas, Johnny Hallyday, Sylvie Vartan, Jean-Jacques Goldman, and dozens of others—and turned them into CD sound tracks. We played those during dinner until one of our favorite deejays showed up and started playing the kind of swingy dance music that emptied the tables and had people spilling into the arcades when the makeshift dance floor overflowed.

I caught sight of Pépé, genial and happy, sitting at a table the Romeos had staked out a few steps from the bar. Later I knew they'd disappear to smoke the Cuban cigars he'd brought from Paris. Eli came with Hope, who looked like a dark-haired angel in a white sundress with an enormous V-neck collar. I watched him catch her in his arms and swoop her up, whirling her around until they both were dizzy with laughter, her sweet face flushed and glowing, chubby arms clenched tight around my brother's neck.

Once or twice I noticed Eli staring at Jasmine Nouri, who had helped Dominique set up and serve the bistro menu for the evening. He seemed mesmerized by the way she threw back her head to laugh at something one of the waiters whispered in her ear, the candlelight strafing her dark, glossy hair and silhouetting her profile like a noble relief on a coin. A couple of waitresses joined her behind the serving table and the group of them linked arms, singing and dancing with Aretha, the Beatles, Smokey. Jasmine moved with the sensual grace of a natural dancer, and by now the waiter who had shared the joke had begun hovering around her like a moth around a flame. I saw something hungry in Eli's eyes as he stared at the pair of them, then Hope tugged his arm and they disappeared into the crowd.

Much later Kit Eastman showed up alone. She was still dressed in her work clothes, so I knew she'd probably spent another Saturday editing reporters' stories for the Sunday paper and buried under paperwork. In the swirling chiaroscuro of candlelight and shadow, she looked haggard and run-down.

She leaned in for our usual air kiss. "Hey, hon. Sorry I'm late."

"Where's Bobby?" I cupped my hand to her ear so she could hear above the bouncy doo-wop harmony of Frankie Valli and the Four Seasons.

"Blue Ridge," she yelled back. "Terrorism seminar. He says he's sorry he can't be here tonight, but duty calls."

We moved away from the music and the lights and stood in the shadow of the archway that led to the villa and the parking lot beyond.

"What kind of terrorism?" I asked.

Though Washington was fifty miles away, we were still considered to be the outer fringe of the D.C. Metro area, which was permanently on a state of high alert. The plane that crashed into the Pentagon on 9/11 had left from Dulles Airport on the eastern border of Loudoun County. Ever since that day, the sheriff's department seemed to be participating in a regular routine of training exercises and readiness drills.

"The bad kind," she said.

"Now I know why you're the *Trib*'s Loudoun bureau chief," I said. "What's your saying? 'If it's news, it's news to us'?"

She grinned. "It's called agroterrorism. People doing bad things to crops or the water supply or livestock. Really remote far-out stuff. Don't worry, they didn't get an alert or anything like that. They just need to know about it."

I didn't smile back. "*Agro*terrorism?"

"Well, you know. Loudoun's still an agricultural county, in spite of all the high-tech businesses out on Route 28. They're just preparing for whatever, unlikely as it is."

Whatever. The topic of Pépé's discussion at the Bohemian Grove in a few days. All of a sudden someone was talking about agroterrorism every time I turned around.

"Sure," I said as a small shudder ran down my spine.

"Looks like a good party." She scanned the crowd.

"It is. You missed dinner, but Dominique made so much food we'll have leftovers until Labor Day. You hungry? There's French onion soup."

"Oh, God. I've died and gone to heaven. I'm starved. I didn't leave the office all day. Ate the leftover stuff in the kitchenette. I think the sell-by date passed on a can of microwave chili." She patted her stomach and looked uneasy. "Can you get botulism from that?"

"I don't know. You feel all right?" I flagged down a waitress and asked her to bring Kit a bowl of soup and fix a dinner plate.

"I'm beat. More layoffs. The buyout days are over. Do more with less. You know the newspaper biz these days," she said. "What's left of it."

"Is your job in jeopardy?"

She shrugged and looked defeated. "Everyone's job is in jeopardy."

The waitress showed up with Kit's soup and two glasses of white wine.

"Mud in your eye," Kit said and we clinked glasses. "Bobby told me you found Paul Noble the other day. That must have been grim."

"It was. I don't suppose he shared any information about the autopsy results. If the medical examiner confirmed yet whether it was suicide or not."

"I sleep with the guy and it still doesn't cut any ice. You know Bobby. Sometimes I think I'm the last to find out anything. He makes me work my ass off for it, too."

"I guess that's a no."

"You guess right." She picked up her spoon. "What are you doing tomorrow?"

"Flying to California with my grandfather."

"You're going, too? Wow, when did that happen? You taking him sightseeing?"

"It just happened and it's business for both of us. Pépé's giving a talk and Mick asked me to check out some wine he might buy from a vineyard in Napa. We'll be back Wednesday."

"Bobby told me about Luc's talk. Why is Mick buying California wine?"

"Someone put him on to a good deal."

She nodded and I was glad, suddenly, that Bobby hadn't come along tonight because the reason I was traveling out West was indirectly linked to Paul Noble's death—at least in Charles Thiessman's mind. I didn't want to lie to Kit and I sure as hell couldn't lie to Bobby, especially if there turned out to be some truth to what Charles had said.

I sipped my wine and changed the subject to wedding talk, which Kit easily and willingly fell into. The deejay changed generations, switching from Stevie Wonder to Sinatra crooning "Fly Me to the Moon." I leaned back against the stone arch, letting the music and candlelight and animated voices and laughter wash over me.

Tomorrow I'd be in California, on the other side of the country, ostensibly to do an errand for Charles Thiessman and to accompany Pépé. But deep down I knew the real reason I was going was Quinn.

Eli and I once threw dice to see whether we'd keep the vineyard or sell it after Leland died, and I won. Seeing Quinn felt like another all-or-nothing gamble. Did he miss me the way I missed him, and would he come back to Virginia or stay in California for good?

I tilted my head and finished off my wine. By tomorrow at this time I'd probably know one way or the other.

I fought off the feeling of foreboding that our meeting wasn't going to go well and went back to discussing flowers and table linens with Kit as though I didn't have a care in the world.

CHAPTER 10

⎯⎯⎯⎯⎯ ⚬⚬⚬ ⎯⎯⎯⎯⎯

I bolted upright in bed when my alarm went off at three thirty A.M., disoriented until memory kicked in. Our flight left at seven; I'd booked a town car for just after four o'clock. Across the hall, I heard my grandfather stirring. Maybe he'd never even gone to sleep. Forty-five minutes later a sleek black car waited outside the house, dashboard lights and GPS glowing eerily as the driver got out to put our bags in the trunk. Pépé and I dozed as the car sped off in the inky darkness, waking as the swooped gull-like wings of the main terminal at Dulles came into view against a rosy sky.

The direct flight to San Francisco International arrived just before ten A.M. Pacific time. The Bay glittered like crushed dark diamonds as we began our final approach, and then the silvery blue city appeared from the thin haze of the marine layer, tip-tilted through the airplane window, a modern-day Atlantis emerging from the sea.

Pépé had booked us at the Mark Hopkins, where he had often stayed after the war when the embassy sent him to the West Coast on business. The half-hour taxi ride zipped along a highway that hugged the Bay, passing an enormous white-lettered sign embedded in the side of a mountain that read SOUTH SAN FRANCISCO, THE INDUSTRIAL CITY. Pépé narrated our route as we drove by the stadium and reached the beginning of the Embarcadero where the driver turned up Market Street and cut over to California.

American and California state flags snapped in the wind as we pulled into the hotel's circular redbrick drive. A valet opened the cab door, letting in an unexpected sharp, cool breeze. Perhaps I imagined it carried the mingled exotic scents of nearby Chinatown spices and the salt tang of the Pacific, but whatever it was, the air smelled different here, nothing I recognized from home in Virginia.

The hotel lobby was old-world opulent, alive and buzzing on a Sunday morning. I waited under a massive beaded crystal chandelier while Pépé sorted out our reservation for adjoining rooms with a Bay view, and then we took the elevator to the fourteenth floor. The first thing we did was open the curtains all the way and Pépé pointed out landmarks: the endless toy-sized bridge to Oakland, the TransAmerica pyramid, rows of piers jutting into the slate-colored water like an unfinished puzzle on the Embarcadero, and, peeking through holes in the marine layer, glimpses of Alcatraz, Treasure Island, and the round-shouldered mountains where Oakland and Berkeley lay on the other side of San Francisco Bay.

I touched my grandfather's arm. He looked pale and drawn in the cool morning light.

"Would you like to lie down? We didn't get much sleep last night."

For a moment I thought he was going to be annoyed with me for mothering him like Dominique did, but he nodded. "I might do that. What are your plans, *chérie*? Shall I order room service? You didn't eat much breakfast on the plane."

"Neither did you," I said. "I'm not really hungry, but you ought to eat something. Anyway, I promised Quinn I'd call him when we got here. I'm sure we'll grab a bite to eat together."

"Quinn," he said. "You have not spoken much about him. Is everything all right between the two of you?"

"Of course it is. Why would you even ask?"

"He has been gone awhile, hasn't he?"

"He's coming back, Pépé. Don't worry about it, okay? He's just taking a break to sort out the sale of his mother's house. I don't know why everyone is making such a big deal about him being gone for a few months."

I shouldn't have snapped at him, or sounded so defensive.

"I apologize," my grandfather said with stiff formality. "But it wasn't 'a big deal.' Merely a question."

I laid my head on his shoulder. "I know and I'm sorry for being an idiot. I shouldn't take my frustrations out on you."

"It's all right." He stroked my hair. "No apology necessary. But I guess you really ought to call him now, *non?*"

I nodded, still feeling guilty, and went to get my phone, accidentally dialing Kit. I punched End Call before it rang, took a deep breath, and called Quinn's number.

Before I saw him later today, I needed to get my head screwed on right.

Quinn's phone went to voice mail. I left a message that I was in town and tried not to let my disappointment show. Pépé, who hadn't gone to sleep after all and had ordered nothing more than a pot of coffee from room service, finally told me in the nicest possible way to quit wearing a path in the carpet and suggested maybe I ought to be the one to take a nap. Or pour myself a good strong drink from the minibar. I glanced at my watch. Eleven thirty here, two thirty in the afternoon at home. Was Quinn still helping out his friend at his vineyard? On a Sunday morning?

My phone rang fifteen minutes later and I pounced on it.

"Hey," Quinn said, "what'd you do, take the red-eye?"

"No." My heart was pinging like a small hammer against my rib cage and I felt light-headed. "Nonstop that left Dulles at dawn."

"Huh. That was fast. Where are you staying?"

"The Mark Hopkins."

He whistled. "Nice, veeerrrry nice."

"It is nice," I said. "The view is to die for."

"Great. So what are your plans?"

"Oh, nothing. Just . . . uh . . . getting settled."

"You up for a cup of coffee, maybe something to eat? Or you want to relax at your swanky hotel first?"

"I'd love to get something to eat. And some coffee."

"All right, how about the Buena Vista? Best coffee in town. It's dead easy for you to get there from the hotel."

"Sounds lovely. Is it a famous coffee shop?"

He chuckled. "Oh, boy. This is gonna be fun. You're not in Kansas anymore, sweetheart. You'll find out when you get here."

"Real funny, Toto. Just give me directions and I'll meet you, okay?"

"The full San Francisco experience. Cable car. It's the fastest way. Your stop is about a three-minute walk from the hotel. Walk down California to Powell and take the Powell and Hyde line to Beach Street. You get off at the last stop, Fisherman's Wharf. Any farther and you're in the water. The Buena Vista will be on your left, corner of Hyde and Beach. It'll take you about twenty minutes tops, unless you have a long wait for a cable car."

I scribbled down his directions on a hotel phone pad as fast as he gave them. "What time?"

"How about twelve thirty? Actually, better make it twelve forty-five. I'll wait for you outside. Or you wait for me."

He hung up as Pépé walked over and stood in the doorway between our rooms. "Everything okay?"

"I'm meeting Quinn at a coffee shop. A place called the Buena Vista."

Pépé's eyes lit up. "Ah, the Buena Vista. I haven't been there for years."

"You know it, too?"

"Of course. It's a San Francisco icon."

"What exactly is it?"

He grinned and said, in the same teasing voice as Quinn, "You'll find out when you get there."

I rolled my eyes. "I'm taking a shower."

Twenty minutes later I knocked on Pépé's door and told him I was leaving. He was sitting at a large desk in front of the picture window, coffee growing cold, papers spread out around him and fanned out on the floor. Apparently he'd gotten a second wind. The papers looked like his talk for the Bohemian Grove. I went over and dropped a kiss on the top of his head.

"I'll be back later this afternoon. I'm not sure when. See you for dinner?"

"If not dinner, at least for a martini at the Top of the Mark."

"I don't drink martinis."

"You do at the Top of the Mark, *ma chère*. Everyone does." He set down his pen. He still wrote all his speeches and correspondence with a Montblanc fountain pen that he'd used for years. My mother had given it to him. "I've phoned Robert Sanábria. He's in town, so he and I might meet somewhere for lunch or a drink. I promise not to be back too late."

I grinned. It would be just like my octogenarian grandfather to be out on the town hours after I got back to the hotel, outlasting his much younger granddaughter and breezing into the room, ready for martinis at the Top of the Mark whatever the hour.

"You're such a party animal," I said.

He chuckled, looking pleased with himself. "You're just saying that."

I got the last seat on an outdoor wooden bench facing the street when the dark-green-and-red cable car stopped on Powell Street ten minutes later. The conductor rang the bell, and I felt a giddy, manic thrill as we climbed Nob Hill then up and over Pacific Heights before plunging down the roller-coaster-steep street toward the water. There seemed to be no limit to the number of passengers the conductor was prepared to take on until, finally, the old-fashioned car was packed inside and out with people hanging on to the running board grab bars like barnacles on a ship. I glanced over my shoulder at the grip man inside the car, who flashed a practiced don't-worry grin and pulled hard on the long cable handle. More people hopped on than jumped off, until finally the conductor tugged the bell and we continued our downward dive toward Fisherman's Wharf.

I got off at the corner of Hyde and Beach, as Quinn had instructed, and watched the two men manually rotate the wooden car on a large turntable—like a lazy Susan built into the street—so it could grind its way back up the hill. Above an olive drab brick building across the street a red neon sign read THE BUENA VISTA.

Quinn wasn't among the people milling in front of the restaurant, but I caught sight of him, the familiar way he ducked his head and balled his hands as he sprinted across Beach Street with the easy grace of an athlete. His curly salt-and-pepper hair, so long it was over his ears last time I saw him, was nearly as short as Bobby's. He pulled off his sunglasses and scanned the crowd, grinning and waving when he caught sight of me. I waved back, smiled, and prayed he wouldn't notice how nervous I was.

Until this moment I hadn't wanted to imagine our reunion, whether it would be stilted or awkward or, worst of all, excruciatingly polite and formal after our painful goodbye in my bedroom that April morning. But he pulled me to him in a swift, fierce embrace, and my arms automatically went around his neck gripping him tight. We stayed locked like that for a long time without speaking, clinging to each other in the middle of the sidewalk, as the crowd brushed past us.

Finally he said in my ear, "I can't believe you're in San Francisco. It's great to see you. You look terrific, Lucie."

He stepped back and I let go of his neck. He was dressed in a Hawaiian shirt—he owned a closetful of them, even collected them—and jeans. I knew every one of his shirts; this one—sage green with blue and tobacco-colored palm fronds and coconut shell buttons—was new.

"Thanks. You look pretty terrific yourself. California agrees with you."

I regretted it the moment I said it, but it was true. He looked happy, content. The haunted, defeated look I remembered from back home last spring was gone. Here he'd made peace with himself, found a purpose, seemed fulfilled.

Something new and self-conscious flashed in his eyes. I pretended to fiddle with my cane and wondered if, or when, he was going to tell me he wasn't coming back to Atoka after all. This time it wasn't about the vineyard and whether he would return as the winemaker. This time it was about us and where we were going from here. I felt like I was back on that dizzying downward cable car—this time with no brakes.

He brushed my arm with the back of his hand, a familiar, remembered gesture. "How about a drink?"

I managed to smile. "I thought you'd never ask."

He grinned back and suddenly we were on our old footing—the safe territory where we kidded each other a little but kept our guard up and our emotions locked down.

"This isn't exactly a little coffee shop," I said. "Pépé knew about it, too. He said it's a San Francisco icon."

Quinn took my elbow with one hand and reached for the door with the other.

"Best Irish coffee outside of Dublin. And breakfast all day. You hungry, Virginia lady?"

"Starved," I said. "The last real meal I had was Dominique's French onion soup at our July fourteenth party last night."

He faltered as he followed me into the restaurant. Then he recovered and said, "I love her French onion soup. Fireworks good?"

"The best yet. Next year will be even better. You'll see."

"Yeah, pretty soon we'll be outrivaling the ones on the National Mall on the Fourth."

I was glad he said "we."

The Buena Vista was packed and noisy, an old-fashioned place of dark woodwork, mustard-colored walls, lazily spinning ceiling fans, and a long row of picture windows overlooking a leafy park with the Bay as a backdrop. People stood three deep at the bar, which ran the length of the restaurant, or sat jammed together around small tables lined up underneath the windows. The high tin ceiling amplified the laughter and chatter until it overflowed the room, absorbing Quinn and me into the easygoing crowd.

"Come on," he said in my ear. "You've got to see this."

A couple moved away from the bar and Quinn shouldered us into their places, ordering two Irish coffees from a white-jacketed bartender who nodded and lined up a row of glass mugs. I watched the blur of movement as he made our coffees and about a dozen others, assembly-line style, pouring and sloshing hot coffee and Tullamore Dew Irish whiskey from a few feet in the air with flair and the absolute abandon of one who didn't have to mop up the counter or floor at the end of the day. With maestrolike finesse he finished by pouring a thick head of cream into the mugs off the back of a silver spoon. I waited for the cream to turn the drink caramel-colored but instead it remained a perfect two-inch layer that sat on top of the coffee.

"How'd he do that?" I murmured to Quinn.

"Magic." He took our mugs and said, "The table behind you just opened up. Grab it while I pay for this, okay?"

We sat across from each other at a scarred table as the jostling crowd closed in around us. A waiter came by and opened a small ventilation window above our heads with a long wooden pole.

"Welcome to San Francisco," Quinn said.

The coffee was hot and strong, and the whiskey and cream went down like silk. He grinned, watching my face.

"Pretty good, huh?"

"Stop me after this one or you'll have to carry me out."

"I've done that before."

"You helped me. You didn't carry me."

He slurped his coffee. "That's not how I remember it."

We should not have traveled this road. It was one of the nights we'd gone to bed together. He looked like he realized belatedly, too. I stared into my mug while he studied the bartender making another round of drinks.

He picked up the two menus on the table and handed one to me. "How about something to eat? They make great eggs Benedict."

I set down my menu. "I can't do this, Quinn."

"Do what?"

"You know what. Act like we're on a blind date that isn't working out when the soup's arrived and it's a five-course meal."

He laughed, looking rueful.

"I know." He took one of my hands in his. "I left you with a lot on your plate when I took off and I'm sorry about that."

"It's okay—"

"Let me finish."

"Sorry."

"I still have some stuff I've got to work out here," he said. "In California."

"Does that mean you're not—?"

He put a finger to his lips. "Listen, okay? I promised I wouldn't let you down for harvest and I won't."

I pulled my hand away and gripped my coffee mug. Harvest. That was all we'd ever talked about. Nothing else, just this year's harvest.

"What about after that?"

"Lucie, don't."

"You don't know or you won't say?"

"Probably I don't know, so I can't say."

"I want you to come back." My voice cracked and for once I didn't mind that he knew I was pleading. "For good."

"I know," he said. "I care too much about you to screw this up. I've never been any good at relationships, you know that. A failed marriage . . . a bunch of women after that . . . no one who lasted."

"Then take your time." I locked my eyes on his. "Just don't shut me out, please?"

If I looked away, broke the spell, then maybe he'd say no. I'd clenched my teeth together so hard my jaw hurt. He nodded slowly and I relaxed.

"I won't," he said. "But let's take this one day at a time."

If I pushed, I'd lose him. "Okay. I can do that."

He touched his glass against mine. "I know you can."

We drank our Irish coffee without speaking, but at least the silence was no longer tense or even melancholy.

"So," I said, "are you going to show me San Francisco, California guy? How long before I start wearing flowers in my hair?"

He grinned and glanced at his watch. "Any minute now. They just show up. Usually right here." He reached over and tucked a strand of hair behind my ear. "And may I say that it is your uncommon good luck that I happen to be a fabulous tour guide? I know rings around those hop-on hop-off bus people."

"So humble," I said. "I've missed that about you."

"Wait until I take you to Napa, sweetheart. I'll show you places that'll make you think you're in the Garden of Eden."

I'd nearly forgotten the real reason I was here. Charles's little mission cloaked in a wine-buying trip for Mick. Now I'd involved Quinn as well—asking him to face the daughter of the man he once worked for without telling him what was at stake.

"I can't wait," I said. "I'm sure it will be wonderful."

He gave me a shrewd look. "What?" he said. "I'm not dissing Virginia, you know, so don't give me that cross-eyed stare you do so well about Virginia being first in wine because of Jamestown and Thomas Jefferson and California being late to the game."

"There's something I have to tell you," I said.

He sucked in his breath and watched me warily.

"No." I held up my hand. "It has nothing to do with us."

"Is this what was so 'complicated' yesterday?"

I nodded. "It wasn't Mick's idea to buy wine from Brooke Hennessey. Charles Thiessman set it up. You remember Charles, don't you?"

"Does he really exist? I thought he was like Mosby's ghost, only appearing on moonless nights to haunt other vineyard owners. He's too good to mingle with the rest of the Virginia winemaking riff-raff."

I smiled. "Oh, he's real all right. He and Pépé have known each other for decades. It's thanks to Charles that Pépé is giving that talk at the Bohemian Grove."

"What does this have to do with Brooke?"

"Well, nothing. No, actually, it does have to do with her. It's all sort of related."

"That's good, because I think I'm lost already."

"Sorry, but there's more."

"I can hardly wait."

"Charles is interested in Brooke's vineyard," I said. "It's not called Rose Hill for nothing. He says there are some exotic specimens of roses grown there, gardens in addition to the vineyard. He pitched the idea of Mick buying a couple thousand gallons of Brooke's Cab. Told Mick about the roses and all that, and made it sound like the wine was the next best thing to a first-growth Bordeaux. Mick went for it."

"Yeah, well, Mick doesn't give a damn about *terroir,* as long as the wine's good. And he's sort of a rose nut, isn't he?"

" 'A rose nut.' " I rolled my eyes. "You say 'tomato,' I say 'rosarian.' "

"Whatever."

"Charles wants to know if the previous owner cultivated black roses. Not real black roses, because they don't exist, but there are some roses that are such a deep, dark red that they're referred to as black roses."

"Why does he want to know this?"

"He thinks the guy who owned Rose Hill before Brooke is

someone he knew a long time ago." I finished the last of my coffee and set the mug on the table. "There's something else. Paul Noble hanged himself the other day."

"God, how awful." Quinn shook his head. "Sorry, but I'm having a hard time keeping up with the players in this story. Is he involved in this, too?"

I nodded.

"That's sad about Noble, but he was a bastard to vintners." He paused and said, "God rest his soul. How'd you hear about that?"

"Firsthand," I said. "I drove over to his house in Waterford to talk to him and found him in his studio. He'd been drinking. A bottle of our Sauvignon Blanc."

"Jesus, Lucie. What the hell's going on?" Quinn set his empty Irish coffee mug on the table and lined it up with mine. "This story gets weirder and weirder."

He stared at me as though he were considering something.

"Look, we can either have breakfast here or we can clear out and I'll take you to Scoma's," he said finally. "You're speaking so softly I can hardly hear what you're saying with everyone talking around us."

"That whiskey went right to my head. I could use a little air."

"Then let's go."

On our way out the door, he leaned over and said in my ear, "What are you involved in, Lucie? I still don't understand where you're going with this, but I can tell you right now that I don't have a good feeling about it."

I glanced over my shoulder as Quinn held the door for me. Three thousand miles away from home on the other side of the country and I felt Charles Thiessman's presence as though he were right here with us.

Suddenly I didn't have a good feeling about what I was dragging Quinn into, either.

CHAPTER 11

—⊶∞⊷—

We passed a park as we walked toward Fisherman's Wharf and the Embarcadero. The steady breeze carried the pungent, briny scent of the Bay and an unexpected fragrant smell of baking.

"It smells like bread," I said to Quinn.

"Sourdough. Boudin's is nearby. It's a pretty famous bakery out here."

The fog had burned off, leaving a tender blue sky that faded to white behind the dusky hills across the Bay. The water—lemon-lime with froths of white—looked tropical.

"You're thinking about Southern California," Quinn said, when I asked him if it was warm enough for swimming. "Northern California beaches are cold with great crashing waves and lots of cliffs and rocks."

He pulled out his phone and called Scoma's, asking if we could have a table for two in forty-five minutes.

"Are we walking to the restaurant?" I asked.

"Nope. There's a Scoma's here on the Wharf, but we're going to the one in Sausalito. Taking the ferry. It leaves in ten minutes."

The Embarcadero was a crowded, bustling tourist strip that seemed part kitschy outdoor carnival, part upscale yacht club. Quinn pointed out Alcatraz as we passed a busker with a sad Quixote face playing Dylan on an acoustic guitar. Sailboats tacked across the water, gulls screeched overhead, and the weather—sharp sunshine, crisp shadows, and that fresh riffing breeze off the water—was flat-out perfect. I could almost feel the physical tug this place had on Quinn—its freewheeling openness, the rugged scenic beauty, the live-and-let-live tolerance and lifestyle everyone sang about in those ballads about San Francisco.

He took my hand as we headed down a pier to a building with a BLUE & GOLD FLEET sign on it.

"What are you thinking?" he asked.

We passed a silver-faced mime performing next to a souvenir stand with T-shirts that read I ESCAPED FROM ALCATRAZ and cans of San Francisco fog. "Nothing, really. Pretty day."

"Yeah," he said. "Most of 'em are out here."

We stayed outside on the deck for the half-hour ferry trip to Sausalito. Quinn loaned me his jacket since the breeze was chilly on the water. I pulled it tight around my shoulders and breathed in his scent, remembering how it smelled on my own skin after we'd made love.

I'd seen the Golden Gate Bridge before, but never from the water and never the full majestic sweep of it—the towering orange-red spans backlit by the sun against an azure sky with tiny dark cars buzzing across like migrating ants. Beyond the bridge, the Pacific Ocean was a straight dark line on a limitless horizon.

"Get a good look at it," Quinn said. "You might not see it on the trip back. It disappears like a magic trick. Sometimes the fog rolls in late in the day; it's not just in the morning. The view doesn't get much better than this."

The ferry let us off on Sausalito's main street, Bridgeway, which curved along the waterfront. Scoma's was a charming wood-framed building located on a pier that jutted out over the water, not far from the ferry landing. A hostess led us through the restaurant to a light-filled room with a breathtaking view of the Bay. Quinn pointed out the landmarks: Belvedere, Angel Island, Treasure Island, and the Bay Bridge. To the right was San Francisco, watery-looking through a gauzy marine haze, like a distant kingdom.

Quinn told me I had to try the Dungeness crab, so I did; he ordered crab cakes. He chose a bottle of California Chardonnay, and we started by sharing a plate of oysters. Our waitress filled our water glasses and set down a basket of warm sourdough bread.

"You want to finish your story from the Buena Vista?" Quinn opened the breadbasket and held it out. "Tell me about Paul Noble and how his suicide ties in with Charles Thiessman and black roses."

I filled in the blanks while we ate. Somehow in this bright, cheery room, my tale seemed less disturbing, less menacing. It also seemed less plausible. As I talked, Quinn's lengthy silence and occasional are-you-kidding-me? arched eyebrow made me wonder if he didn't believe I'd lost a few marbles since April.

"So Charles believes the guy who owned the vineyard before Brooke has gone off the grid and is now finishing off whoever is left of this Mandrake Society after forty years?" he said when I was done. "Just supposing that's true, why now?"

"I don't know."

"Do you think Charles knows?" He asked the question in a calm enough manner, but I could tell he still wasn't buying any of this.

He picked up the bottle of wine and filled our glasses. I set down my fork. The meal had been fabulous.

"I'm sure he knows more than he told us," I said.

"Okay."

I folded my hands together and leaned across the table. "Look, I don't believe Thelma really communicates with my parents on her Ouija board, and I don't hear voices when no one's around. But if you'd been in that lodge with him that night, he made a pretty compelling case."

"After how much booze?"

"Oh, come on."

"Were you guys drunk?"

"Not really. I mean, yes, we were drinking." I pushed my wine-glass to the side. "We shared a bottle of Margaux."

"After cocktails and wine with dinner, no doubt," he said. "So was he drunk?"

"He kept pace with us, then he switched to brandy. He wasn't slurring his words until the end. But he wasn't that bad."

"Maybe that's all it was, then. He got sloshed and started babbling about something he's lived with like a noose around his neck for four decades."

"You could have chosen another metaphor," I said.

"Huh? Oh, sorry. Paul."

The waitress stopped by with dessert menus.

"I couldn't eat another thing," I said. "Just coffee, please."

"Look," he said after the waitress left. "If Charles is right, then something must have happened recently to this Theo guy, or Teddy Fargo, to open an old wound and get him thinking about revenge out of the blue."

"Presuming Teddy Fargo is Theo Graf," I said.

"Presuming."

"I think it's odd that both Paul and the other guy, Mel Racine, died with those Mandrake Society wineglasses next to them," I said. "That's got to be more than just a bizarre coincidence."

"I don't know why that name rings a bell," Quinn said. "Mel Racine. When I get back to the boat tonight, I'll look him up on the Internet."

"He moved out to the Bay Area," I said. "And he owned car dealerships. Those guys pester you with advertisements and deals worse than politicians at election time. If he's local, I'm surprised you wouldn't have heard of him."

"That's because you probably don't realize how much geography you're talking about in a big state like California," he said. "The Bay Area goes as far south as Santa Cruz and as far north as Napa."

I spun my coffee spoon around on the linen tablecloth like a needle on a compass. Quinn figured something must have happened to prompt Theo, or Fargo, to make good on a forty-year-old threat. What if he was almost right?

"Maybe it wasn't something that set Theo off," I said. "Maybe it was someone."

The waitress set down two coffees and the check.

"So who is the someone?" Quinn slid the leather billfold to his side of the table.

I poured cream in my coffee and automatically started to put some in his before I caught myself.

He smiled. "Go ahead. You know how I take it."

"A little cream and strong enough to strip paint." I finished pouring and opened a couple of sugar packets for mine. "To get back to your question, I haven't got the foggiest idea who it could be. All the players are dead, except Charles—and, I guess, Theo. And he's the only one who knows the answer. Too bad Theo's gone. Wonder if he's still in California."

"Whoa, there, sweetheart. Hold your horses. If this guy's running around bumping off his ex-colleagues, you really think it's a good idea to look him up and ask him what's going on?" Quinn said. "He might not like it too much."

"I didn't say I was going to do it." I gave him a cross-eyed stare. "But I wonder what he knows. And who or what made him go off after all those years."

Quinn set his coffee mug on the table. "There might be a way to find out what you want to know about Fargo without talking to him."

"Sure. Ask Brooke Hennessey. She bought the place from him," I said. "Though if I make her nervous once she realizes why I want to know, she might decide not to let me take a look around."

"I wasn't thinking of Brooke."

I waited, but he didn't elaborate. Finally I said, "Quinn?"

He worried his lower lip and stared out the window. "I know someone who would know anything that's out there about this Fargo guy. Good, bad, indifferent. Especially the bad stuff."

I wondered if whoever this was belonged to the old history Quinn never wanted to talk about.

"This guy sounds scarier than tracking down Fargo." I tried to make a joke. "Care to tell me who it is?"

"I need to make a call first," he said. "And if he's okay with it, I'll take you for a drive tomorrow. Show you more sights."

"Okay." He was talking in a deadpan voice that unsettled me. "Sure. But do you mind telling me what this is all about? I feel like I'm a couple of chapters behind, all of a sudden."

He lifted his head, a rueful expression in his eyes. "I should have guessed you'd be the one to make me face all my old ghosts, Lucie. Asking me to see Brooke again after all these years . . . that was such a kick in the teeth when you said her name the other day on the phone."

What was he talking about? "All what old ghosts? Who are we going to see tomorrow?"

He drummed his fingers on the edge of the table and resumed staring outside. When he spoke, I had to lean close to catch what he said.

"Allen Cantor."

The winemaker who had destroyed Brooke's father's business and brought Quinn down with him.

"I thought he was in jail," I said.

He worked the muscle in his jaw that always meant he was upset. "He was." His voice was grim. "He got out."

CHAPTER 12

———— ✦✦✦ ————

By the time we left Scoma's, the lunchtime crowd had thinned to a few remaining tables of diners, mostly couples lingering over coffee as we had done. It looked like the staff was beginning to set up for dinner.

Outside on the pier, the breeze had picked up and the sun had sunk lower in the sky. The light held an end-of-day tinge and our shadows were long and soft.

"What time is it?" I asked.

Quinn glanced at his watch. "Going on quarter to five."

"I should get back to the hotel, to Pépé."

"My car's in the lot down the road," he said. "I could drive you. Or you could catch the five o'clock ferry, if you want. It'd probably be faster, with all the weekend traffic heading into San Francisco."

"I wouldn't mind taking the ferry," I said. "Save you a trip into town through traffic, and then driving back here again."

"Yeah, you'll enjoy that, especially at this hour. There's some fog, but you might get a view of the Golden Gate again."

"Then that settles it," I said. "Walk me to the pier?"

"Sure."

He took my hand and we threaded our way single-file through the slow-moving crowds that clogged the sidewalk and lingered in front of the art galleries and pretty shops that lined

Bridgeway. When we got to the ferry landing, Quinn handed me a ticket.

"I bought two round-trip tickets this morning. Kind of figured you'd want to take the boat back to San Francisco."

My mouth dropped open. "How'd you know . . . you had this all planned out, didn't you?"

"Who, me?" He leaned over and kissed my cheek. "You don't want to miss your boat. It's leaving soon."

"There are so many ways I could respond to that."

He grinned and brushed his finger across my lips. "I'll call you about tomorrow after I talk to Allen."

"You sure about doing this, Quinn?"

"Yup." But his voice had tightened. "Off you go. Enjoy the view. Keep my jacket, you'll need it."

"Thanks."

I stayed on deck and watched him as the ferry pulled away from the pier. The wind gusted and nipped at his clothes, but he just stood there with his hands in his pockets and waited until the boat had left the harbor. I watched until he was so small I could barely tell when he turned and started up Bridgeway to his car.

The Golden Gate glowed vivid orange against the soft dark folds of the Marin Headlands and the sky looked like it was on fire. I found a sheltered spot on the deck where I watched the bridge drift in and out of view through wisps of mist—a tower or a section of the suspension cables or part of the deck—until finally the thickening fog swallowed all of it up for good. The breeze, now sharp as needles, was cold so I went into the cabin and watched the looming San Francisco skyline grow larger.

If Allen Cantor agreed to talk to us tomorrow, I might learn more about Teddy Fargo and who he really was or was not. The more I thought about it, the more I felt sure the answers I needed were here in California.

They just weren't to the questions Charles had asked.

When I got back to the hotel, Pépé was in his room, ready to take me to the Top of the Mark, with its 360-degree glass-walled view of the city, for a martini, or two, as he'd promised. A waiter led us to a window table overlooking the Bay with a view of the TransAmerica building. On the other side of the room, Pépé told me, you could see the Golden Gate and the Pacific.

The city lights made hard-edged boundaries between the land and water, burnishing the coastline so it gleamed like polished copper before fading into blackness farther up the Bay. Pépé handed me the one-hundred-martini menu and told me stories about how the Top of the Mark had been a popular hangout for soldiers and sailors shipping off to the Pacific Theater during World War II, pointing out the widows' corner overlooking the Golden Gate on the other side of the room, where wives and girlfriends had watched as ships sailed under the bridge until their loved ones disappeared from sight. We finally chose our drinks and decided to order hors d'oeuvres. Then we sat there, mostly without talking, drinking our martinis and listening to the pianist play songs that Pépé remembered from the war years.

When he swung into "In the Mood," Pépé asked how my day went with Quinn.

"Fine," I said. "We had lunch in Sausalito."

"And you also went to the Buena Vista?"

"Yes. For Irish coffee. In fact, I've had so much alcohol today, my liver is probably starting to pickle." I yawned.

"Your head is dropping into your glass, *ma belle*," he said. "We should go."

At the elevator he said to me, "I know you came to California to humor Charles's request about black roses, but I wonder if you would have done it if Quinn weren't here as well."

"You mean I'm using Charles's errand as an excuse for seeing Quinn?" I said.

"Aren't you?"

"I'm also supposed to be buying wine for Mick."

"Also engineered by Charles," he said. "But that's beside the point."

"Okay," I said. "I suppose I am."

"I thought so," he said, sounding satisfied as the elevator door slid open and we stepped inside.

He kissed me good night at the adjoining door to our rooms, and for a while I heard him moving about in his own room as I got ready for bed. Then the light went out on his side of the door and I lay down and closed my eyes.

Only once in my life have I lived in a city—Washington, D.C., years ago—so I'd forgotten that there is always light and motion and noise, no matter what the hour. After a while, I threw off the duvet and got out of bed, opening the curtains to the enormous picture window and letting in a flood of glittering, spangling light. In Atoka the view out my bedroom window is of moon-washed mountains, the dark lacy outline of the forest, my rose garden, and the stars; the only sounds come from nature—the serenade of the cicadas and tree frogs with an occasional hooting owl or the cry of a fox.

I pulled up the desk chair and sat next to the window for a long time, thinking about Quinn and my life back home and where things were going with us. After a while I remembered his promise to call after he talked to Allen Cantor. I found my phone in my purse, still turned to silent mode from the restaurant, and saw the missed call just before midnight.

"Sorry it's so late. I'm sure you're asleep by now. I got hold of Allen." His voice was terse and matter-of-fact. "He says he'll see us tomorrow. We've got to do some driving so I'll pick you up at seven thirty outside the hotel."

It was just after three in the morning. Quinn would be waiting for me in less than four and a half hours. I pulled the curtains shut and climbed back into bed. But my mind kept racing with edgy, just-out-of-reach thoughts.

I didn't fall asleep until nearly dawn.

I woke to what sounded like drums pounding. Pale streaks of daylight filtered through the cracks of the curtains and striped my bed. I threw back the duvet, grabbed my cane, and went over to the connecting door to Pépé's room. He stood there, immaculate in a double-breasted cream-colored linen suit, his gray hair slicked back with water, ready to take on the world. I'd caught a glimpse of myself in the mirror above the dresser before I opened the door. My hair was wild-looking and stuck out in weird clumps, and my eyes looked like two bruises, since I'd forgotten to take off my mascara before I went to bed.

"What time is it?" I felt breathless.

"Good morning, *chérie,*" he said. "It's seven o'clock. The limousine taking me to the Bohemian Grove is waiting downstairs. I wanted to say goodbye before I left. Sorry to wake you up."

I'd set my phone alarm for six thirty. When had I shut it off?

"Seven? Dammit to hell. I'm late."

"Order anything you like for breakfast." Pépé seemed to have decided to ignore my train-wrecked appearance and unvarnished language. "I'll see you tomorrow evening in Calistoga at Robert's. He's giving us his guesthouse, so we'll have a place of our own."

Meaning I wouldn't terrify Robert Sanábria if he saw me slipping into the bathroom first thing in the morning looking like I did just now.

"I'm sorry, Pépé, I didn't mean to bite your head off. I'll be there tomorrow. Quinn's coming in half an hour and I overslept. I'll get something to eat on the road."

"There is coffee in the pot in my room. Help yourself. You look like you could use a cup. Or perhaps the whole pot," he said. "Where are you and Quinn going?"

"I don't know. He promised to show me around."

It happened to be the truth and I was glad I didn't have to lie to my grandfather. For now I didn't want him knowing about meeting Allen Cantor to check up on Teddy Fargo, going behind Charles's back to see what else I could learn about this mission he'd sent me on.

"Will you and Quinn visit Rose Hill Vineyard today or tomorrow?" he asked.

"Probably tomorrow."

"Thank you for doing this," he said. "I spoke to Juliette last night. Charles isn't doing well. She's upset."

He sounded upset, too. I wondered who had called whom.

"Not well." I repeated his words. "Mentally? Or physically?"

"Both, I think."

Our eyes met. "Are you talking about him or her?"

"Why, Charles, of course."

"And Juliette?"

He sighed. "Yes, perhaps her, too."

"What's wrong, Pépé?"

He looked away. "I don't know. Something happened to Juliette and she's changed. I can't explain it. Lately she's so high-strung. It takes so little to set her off."

Just how often did they talk to each other?

"How long has that been going on?" I kept my voice noncommittal.

"A while." He fiddled with his perfectly knotted tie. "I never knew her to be melancholy, or moody like this before."

"You can't fix her problems. Or her marriage."

"I know that." His voice was sharp. "All I could do was tell her everything would be all right."

"Do you believe that?"

"No," he said, "I don't."

"Me, neither."

After he left, I realized I'd forgotten to wish him good luck on his talk in Monte Rio.

Quinn called my cell when I was in the shower. I grabbed it off the sink ledge while I was still dripping wet, just before it went to voice mail.

"I'm gonna be late," he said. "Traffic on the bridge."

"Don't rush." I swiped a towel and tried to dry the phone.

"Overslept, did you?"

"Absolutely not. I just don't want you to rush."

I heard him chuckle. "I'll call you when I'm about ten minutes away. What are you doing? Taking a shower?"

"How could I be taking a shower and talking to you?"

"Took you too long to answer. Splish-splash go back to taking your bath," he said and disconnected.

He picked me up just before eight in a black Porsche with the top down.

"Nice wheels," I said as he leaned over to open the door for me.

"They're Harmony's," he said. "I'm car-sitting, too."

I felt an unwelcome flash of jealousy. "Harmony?"

He glanced over at me and smiled. "Friend of my mother's. She's like an aunt to me. A child of the sixties. Flower power, hippies, Summer of Love, the whole enchilada. I think her real name is Penelope. She's an artist . . . hence the houseboat in Sausalito."

"And the Porsche?"

"She likes cool cars that go fast."

"I'd love to meet her."

"She's in Italy at the moment. Been gone since June. Went to Stonehenge for the summer solstice and did that Druid jumping-around stuff they do."

"Don't be such a cynic. It's not jumping around. They dance and celebrate summer and light bonfires," I said. "What's in Italy?"

"Good food, great wine . . . and Italian men."

"Then I'd *really* love to meet her."

He grinned. "Yeah, I bet you would."

We were zipping down vertigo-inducing streets—Quinn some-how timed it so he hit all the green lights—with the wind riffing my hair and cutting in behind my sunglasses. Since yesterday I'd been trying to put my finger on what felt so different about San Fran-cisco—aside from its obvious unique geography—why it was unlike anyplace on the East Coast or even all the European cities I knew.

As we drove past Union Square, with its startling tropical palm trees amid skyscrapers, and continued down Mason Street, Quinn rattled off names of the bubbling ethnic stew of neighborhoods, waving an arm to indicate roughly where they were—the Tender-loin, Japantown, Little Saigon—and I finally realized what it was: that despite the old-world roots and history of the city, it looked east to Asia, not west to Europe. Now I understood why Quinn loved it, why he belonged here. It was the perfect foil for his personality; San Francisco still thrummed with the gold rush brashness that grew it big, and the Russian roulette edginess of being built on earthquake fault lines where everyone knew it was a matter of when, not if. Even yesterday, I'd felt an odd little shifting when I'd been in the hotel, finally realizing that it wasn't traffic thundering along Nob Hill.

Quinn caught me staring at him and said, "What?"

"Nothing," I said. "Just that I like San Francisco."

He grinned and reached over to squeeze my hand. "You ain't seen nothing yet, honey. There's a map of California in the glove compartment. Get it out and I'll give you a geography lesson."

I found the map, opened it, and refolded it to show San Francisco and the Bay Area.

"The marine layer's pretty intense this morning," he said. "So we'll head up the Bay side of the Peninsula and go by Sunnyvale, Cupertino—that's Silicon Valley to you. Highway 1, the Pacific Coast Highway, is beautiful, but it takes longer and it's dangerous in the fog."

"Where are we going now?" I asked.

"Santa Cruz." He reached over and stabbed the map. "Sits at the top of Monterey Bay. Beautiful little town—fabulous beaches for surfing, very laid back, very mellow. You're gonna love it."

"What's in Santa Cruz?"

"You mean who is in Santa Cruz." He corrected me. "Allen Cantor. We're meeting him on the Boardwalk. His choice."

"You tell him why you want to see him?"

"Nope. Just that I wanted to ask him a few questions." We exchanged sideways glances. "He didn't even ask what they were. Allen owes me and he knows it."

"I wonder if he knows anything about Teddy Fargo," I said.

"If there's anything to know," Quinn said, "he does."

The traffic was heavier as we picked up 101, the Bayshore Freeway, and left San Francisco behind. Quinn punched a button on the satellite radio. I read the display. Sixties on Six. Probably one of Harmony's presets. Right now it was adrenaline-pumping rush-hour stuff, slipping from Jefferson Airplane into the Rolling Stones.

"I found out about Mel Racine." He had to raise his voice above Mick Jagger and the traffic so I could hear him.

"What did you find out?" I shouted back.

"Had a series of car dealerships near Santa Cruz. Then he moved up the coast to Half Moon Bay." His finger skittered over the map again. "See, right there? The bank he bought to turn into a wine storage vault is up for sale."

"Oh, yeah?" I studied the map. "By the time we leave Santa Cruz, won't the marine layer have burned off enough that we can take the coast road north to San Francisco? Looks like it goes right through Half Moon Bay. Maybe we could stop and check out that bank."

He turned to me and grinned, singing in a loud, off-key voice, imitating Mick and telling me he didn't get no satisfaction.

"'Cause I try . . . and I try," he said, leering at me.

"I guess that's a yes."

He nodded and kept singing as we wove through traffic. Usually I would have joined in. But this morning as the Porsche dodged in and out of the pea-soup marine layer, I couldn't stop wondering what was in store for us when we got to Santa Cruz and, later, Half Moon Bay.

CHAPTER 13

Once we passed the high-tech Silicon Valley corridor, Quinn turned south at Los Gatos onto Highway 17 and we began climbing through the Santa Cruz Mountains. He knew the road well enough, but the sharp zigzag turns with their blind curves as we sliced through pine and redwood fog-shrouded hills meant he needed to pay attention to his driving. Our conversation ground to a halt. When we passed a sign warning motorists to turn off the air-conditioning to prevent engine boil over, I finally asked if the road was as treacherous as it seemed.

He nodded. "Lots of accidents, especially at one underpass where drivers are so busy navigating the steep curves they don't expect a nearly horizontal switchback turn until it's too late. It's called the Valley Surprise."

My own surprise was Santa Cruz itself. Quinn started talking about it, reminiscing, actually, after we left 17 where it joined Highway 1, which ran north-south along the coast. I don't know what it was—the jaunty tilt to his chin or the sentimental softness in his voice—but I could easily imagine him as he used to be, growing up in this place that had been his idea of paradise, a well-muscled, good-looking sun god with windblown blond-flecked curls, a surfboard under one arm and a cute girl in a bikini named Tammy or Kimberly hanging on the other. The Byrds were singing "Turn, Turn, Turn" on the radio and I felt a queer tug of nostalgia for a time and place I never knew, the sun-drenched, free-spirited, live-and-let-live California of all the era-defining, generation-shaping songs that caused Penelope to become Harmony nearly half a century ago and never go back.

We'd left the mountains and the swirling marine layer behind and now were on flatter terrain, a palm- and cypress-lined street of low-rise sand-colored motels advertising cheap beach weekend rates and cable television. Quinn pulled over and reached for his phone.

I raised an eyebrow and he said, "Allen told me to call him when we were about ten minutes away from the Boardwalk."

Their conversation lasted all of ten seconds.

"Why the Boardwalk?" I asked. "Does he work there?"

"No," he said. "I don't know where he works. The Boardwalk's where the amusement park is located, too. I guess that's his way of making a joke."

I saw the looped silhouette of a roller coaster framed between a couple of palm trees and set against a hazy, blue-white sky as we drove closer to the water.

"That's the Hurricane," Quinn said. "At the other end of the park by the San Lorenzo River is the Giant Dipper, the oldest wooden roller coaster on the West Coast. It's a historic landmark now."

"How old is it?" I asked. "If it's a historic landmark."

"Old, 1907," he said. "The Boardwalk had its centenary a few years ago. The roller coaster was built in 1924. The Looff Carousel is even older—1911."

"It looks like something from an old postcard or a sepia photograph."

He smiled. "They've done a good job of keeping the vintage feel about the place. Brings in lots of families looking for something wholesome to do."

He pulled into a municipal parking lot across the street from a gaudy Moorish-style building with a toothy shark and bright red octopus painted on either side of the arched entrance and NEPTUNE'S KINGDOM written above it.

"That's the arcade," Quinn said. "We're meeting Allen at the burger place under the colonnade. I had to promise him breakfast and a beer."

I stared at him and he shrugged.

We crossed the street and walked under a sign welcoming us to the Santa Cruz Boardwalk. Framed by dusky purple mountains, Monterey Bay gleamed silvery blue, the water calm except for a froth of surf lapping at a long expanse of beach. The amusement park, on two levels, was the retro throwback Quinn had promised, with its famous carousel, along with a Ferris wheel, pirate ship, sherbet-colored sky glider cable cars disappearing into the mist down the beach—and the Giant Dipper.

"Turn right," Quinn said. "No rides for us today."

The burgundy and pale gold colonnade, with its carnival-like rows of flashing lights running along the ceiling, seemed relatively quiet for a Monday morning in the middle of summer. Only a handful of the small metal tables lining the arcade railing were occupied. Quinn picked one that had a checkerboard painted on it and we sat down on two of the low welded-on bar stools to wait. The sunlight made perfect half-moon circles of each arch on the concrete walkway, the Beatles sang "Love Me Do," and the fronds of the scalped-looking palm trees growing a few feet away in the sand rustled in the cool ocean breeze.

Quinn had taken the seat facing the Boardwalk entrance, as I'd guessed he would do. Thirty seconds later Allen Cantor came into view. I knew at once because of the tiny tightening in Quinn's eyes and the way his body tensed—like a fighter waiting for the opening bell so he could get into the ring and demolish his opponent. His gaze flicked back at me, a coded message not to turn around. I wondered, as I suspected he did, whether Cantor had been watching us from somewhere on the upper deck of the amusement park and Quinn somehow missed seeing him. Advantage, Cantor. Quinn stood up and held a hand out. I took it and he pulled me up.

"Showtime," he said under his breath.

He had never physically described Allen Cantor to me, and for some reason I'd pictured a short, wiry man with scrimshawlike tattoos, a bandy-legged swagger, and a nervous tic in one eye so that he never looked right at you. In my mind, he'd always been as sleazy as a snake-oil salesman, a liar, a cheat, a thief—so obvious that I'd often wondered why Quinn hadn't seen it coming when Allen finally got caught, even though in public I defended his innocence, saying he'd been blindsided, just like I told Mick Dunne the other day. But deep down I'd pegged Cantor as the kind of guy mothers told their daughters to keep away from because he was nothing but trouble, that one.

He was trouble, all right, but in the beautiful, dangerous way a lot of women had found irresistible. Quinn should have warned me, but I understood at once why he hadn't. Allen Cantor looked me over the way some men look at women who come into a bar alone. I couldn't stop staring back into those hypnotic blue eyes.

Physically he could have been Quinn's older brother—the same fit, taut build, same salt-and-pepper curls, though Cantor wore his hair longer, the same deep crow's-feet laugh lines around the eyes. It even looked like they'd broken their noses in the same place. But there was something in Cantor's don't-you-want-to-know-more? stare that gave me goose bumps and dared me not to look away.

"Allen," Quinn's voice was sharp. "Knock it off, will you? This isn't a singles' bar. Stop trying to put a move on her already, god-dammit."

Cantor tore his gaze from me. "Just appreciating a beautiful woman, buddy. Nothing wrong with looking."

He'd done more than that. He'd mentally undressed me.

"Keep it that way," Quinn said.

"Nice to see you, too, Quinn. What do you want? I haven't got all day."

"Oh, yeah? Where you working these days, buddy?" He empha-sized *buddy.* "Who are you making wine for?"

Cantor stood up. "Screw you, Santori. I was just trying to do you a favor because you asked. I don't need to take your crap. I'm out of here."

"No." I reached for his arm. "Please, don't go. Both of you, can you please not do this right now?"

Allen Cantor looked down at my hand on his arm and sat down. "What do you want? Lucie, isn't it?"

I removed my hand and nodded. "Yes. Quinn, are you all right?"

"Yeah." He jerked his head in a nod and looked out at the ocean. "I'm just frickin' fine."

He sat, too, but I could feel his leg shaking violently under the table. I nudged him with my knee and he stopped. Cantor noticed.

"Maybe we could all use some coffee," I said. "I'll get it."

"I'd like a beer," Cantor said. "And some eggs."

"I'll take care of this." Quinn dug in his pocket for his wallet. "That was the deal. Beer and breakfast in return for information, if you've got it."

There was an edge in his voice when he got in that last faint taunt and I glared at him. "That would be great," I said.

He walked across to the restaurant. Cantor looked at me again, steadily.

"I heard about Nic," he said. "Sorry for Quinn's loss, but she was trouble for him from the day he put the ring on her finger. You his girl now?"

He meant Nicole Martin Santori, Quinn's ex-wife, a raven-haired beauty I'd met briefly once, long after they'd split and shortly before she was killed by a jealous lover. Allen, as I recalled, had also been one of her paramours and now that I knew him, the two of them getting together seemed as inevitable as night following day.

I gave him a brittle smile. "I'm not anybody's 'girl.' "

He didn't flinch. "You should be."

Quinn set down the beer and some fries. He went back for coffees for the two of us and sat down again next to me. "Talking about the weather, are we? Your eggs and sausage will be ready in a couple of minutes."

I opened the coffee and found that Quinn had already put cream and sugar in mine.

"We'd like some help," I said to Cantor.

"Information about a winemaker who used to work in Napa. Outside Calistoga," Quinn added.

"I don't know much about that anymore," Cantor said. "Don't keep in touch with many people . . . I think that's my order over there."

He got up and walked across to the restaurant counter, picking up a bottle of ketchup. After drowning whatever was on his plate, he joined us again.

"What makes you think I'll know this dude?" he asked through a mouthful of eggs. "It is a guy, isn't it?"

I wondered how regular his meals were these days and what he did now for a living. Then I wondered why I was wondering.

I nodded. "Yes."

He looked from Quinn to me. "I get it. He's dirty, isn't he?"

"I . . . no. I mean, we don't know," I said. "He might be someone who changed his identity, is all."

"Or it might just be blowing smoke and someone got their wires crossed." Quinn shrugged. "Set Lucie up for something they want to know, asked her for a favor."

That was shrewd, making me the damsel in distress and being purposely vague about my anonymous favor. The two of them exchanged more testosterone-laced looks.

Cantor took a long swallow of beer. "Who is it?"

"Teddy Fargo. Owned a vineyard called Rose Hill up in Calistoga," Quinn said.

"Rose Hill." Cantor slapped a hand down on the table so hard it made his plate jump and shook his head, flashing a knowing smile. "Well, I'll be damned. Small world isn't it, Quinny? You know who owns it now, don't you?"

Quinn glanced sideways at me. "Brooke."

"Yup." He wiped his mouth with a paper napkin and set it on the table. "You keep in touch with her?"

"Nope. You?"

"You must be kidding. But I do keep an eye on her. Graduated top of her class from Davis. She's a smart winemaker, did it right, starting small. She wants to control everything. Not let anyone pull the wool over her eyes, the way I did with her old man." He paused, a shadow crossing his face that could have been remorse, or maybe regret. Then it was gone and his eyes glittered. "So you haven't seen her, then?"

"I said no, didn't I?" Now Quinn was the one who sounded edgy.

"Well, well," Cantor said. "Are you in for a surprise. She turned out to be quite a beauty. Guess she got all her mother's looks. A knockout, man."

"Is that so?"

Cantor drank some more beer. "You ought to pay her a visit. You know she always had a thing for you."

"I didn't notice." A slow flush stained Quinn's face. "I was married, remember?"

"Could we get back to Teddy Fargo?" I brought my hand down hard on the table and Cantor's plate jumped a little. "Before you two wander any further down memory lane and someone kills somebody."

They both gave me an astonished look, and Cantor burst out laughing.

"I like you," he said and licked his lips.

"Moving on." I held up a finger to silence Quinn before he could open his mouth. "Teddy Fargo."

"I don't know him personally. But I heard about him."

"Heard how?" Quinn asked.

"The guy was a good winemaker, really smart. He used to be a chemist or something like that before he got into wine." Cantor rattled off the facts so easily that I knew he still kept up with what was going on in Napa and Sonoma more than he had let on. "He had kind of a boutique winery. Only made a couple thousand cases a year and sold it all in his tasting room."

He paused.

"And?" Quinn said.

Cantor picked up his beer glass and stared into it, waving it back and forth.

"Want another one, Allen?"

"I wouldn't say no."

Quinn got him a second beer.

"So what else about Fargo?"

"Just a rumor."

"Goddammit, Allen, stop messing with us."

"Quinn," I said. "Please. Don't."

Cantor drank his beer, but I noticed his hand shook and he sloshed some liquid on the table. He wiped it with his fist.

"He had a little operation up in the hills behind his winery. Grew some stuff up there and apparently had the knowledge and background to get some very fine results, if you know what I mean."

"Are you talking about roses?" I asked. "As in exotic roses?"

Even Quinn flashed me a look of surprise.

Cantor laughed. "I'm talking about marijuana, honey. Supposedly the guy had quite a booming business. Growing it, selling it. He's lucky he never got busted. I figured that's why he sold his place all of a sudden and split town. Rumor is that he torched the evidence before he took off. No one's seen him or heard of him since. He vanished."

I felt like I'd been sucker punched. So Charles had been barking up the wrong tree, after all. Even if Teddy Fargo were Theo Graf— and who knew, now?—the reason he disappeared had to do with drug dealing and probably fleeing the law, not some ancient grudge that had to do with the Mandrake Society.

Quinn reached in his back pocket and pulled out his wallet again. He threw a twenty-dollar bill on the table.

"Thanks, Allen," he said. "Get yourself something else to eat. Or a couple of beers. I think we're done here."

He stood up and waited for me.

"That wasn't the information you were looking for," Cantor said to me as I got up. "Was it?"

"No," I said, "it wasn't."

CHAPTER 14

———— ⬡⬡⬡ ————

As reunions go, this one spiraled downhill and out of control before anyone realized what happened. When Quinn threw that twenty on the table, it was like tossing a live grenade into the middle of an edgy truce no one really wanted. It would take no more than the tiniest flick of a finger, the wrong look, a perceived insult, to blow it all to smithereens.

Cantor, predictably, told Quinn to take his money and shove it, but by then Quinn had disappeared into the growing crowd on the Boardwalk, as though it had suddenly become intolerable to breathe the same air as his ex-boss for one more second. Cantor stood up and came around the table so fast that I wasn't sure if he was going to go after Quinn to jam the money in his pocket because he was embarrassed, or roundhouse him because he was furious.

"Let him go. Please?" I grabbed his arm and held on. "He did this for me."

Cantor's eyes fastened on my face and he was breathing hard, but at least I had his attention.

I let go of his arm. "Thank you for coming today."

"It was worth it just to meet you, angel." He took my cane from me and leaned it against the table. "You don't need that right now. Jesus, Mary, and Joseph, you are gorgeous."

I had no intention of falling for Allen Cantor's patented and probably well-used chat-up line, even if he was turning the full wattage of his dangerous charm on me.

"Allen, don't—" If Quinn came back to find out what was taking me so long and saw Cantor standing this close to me, his body language making it obvious what was happening . . .

"He's a lucky bastard, you know that?" He kept right on devouring me with those wolfish eyes. "Bet he doesn't appreciate you the way someone as beautiful as you ought to be appreciated. Quinn never was any good with women. If you were mine, darling, you'd be on a pedestal. I'd give you everything you wanted, things you never dreamed of."

His hands slipped easily around my waist. Before I knew what he was doing, they had moved up under my breasts. He wasn't talking about chocolates and flowers, or even diamonds.

"He does appreciate me." I felt breathless, light-headed. "Take your hands off. Now."

He lifted a hand and deliberately traced his finger along the contour of my cheek. "You've slept with him. I figured as much."

My face burned. "That's none of your business."

"I wasn't asking. I know you did." He drew me closer and whispered into my hair, "Ever read the *Kama Sutra*? I have. Spend a night with me, baby. I promise it would be amazing."

"No." I jerked out of his grasp, reaching for my cane and wielding it like a club. "Come near me one more time and I'll amaze you."

I heard his taunting you-know-you-want-to laugh as I walked away, mocking me.

Quinn was sitting in the Porsche when I got to the parking lot, drumming his fingers on the steering wheel and staring straight ahead at nothing. His sharp-edged profile glinted with anger and he acted deaf, dumb, and blind to my presence.

He wasn't the only one who was mad. "Thanks for leaving me back there with Casanova." I jerked open the passenger door. "You couldn't have waited?"

He clenched and unclenched his fists. "I . . . no. I think I could have killed him. I'm sorry. He make a pass at you? Then I really would have lost it."

I'd never heard Quinn like this before. For the first time, I was scared of what he might be capable of doing, things I'd never suspected. The anger drained out of me like he'd pulled a plug.

"He was just being a macho ass. I bet he's like that with every woman he meets." I slid into the passenger seat. "By now he's probably working on getting the phone number of the cute girl who poured his beer at the restaurant, or asking her to have his baby. Besides, I can handle guys like him, especially ones who've had a few drinks. You should know that by now."

"He asked you to have his baby?" He sounded stunned.

"I said no."

It took him a second to get the joke and give me a weak grin. "What'd you do? Threaten to turn him into a eunuch with your cane?"

"Close enough. Wish I'd thought to use the word 'eunuch.' "

He burst out laughing. "Damn, I'm sorry I missed that. I'd have sold tickets."

I grinned. "Over my dead body. Do you think we can get out of here, please?"

He started the car. I reached over and turned on the radio. The Stones again. "Jumpin' Jack Flash." Quinn turned it up loud and we roared out of the parking lot.

I had to yell over the music. "Where are we going now?"

He beat his palms on the steering wheel like he was playing backup on the drums. "Half Moon Bay," he yelled back. "Taking the Pacific Coast Highway. You're gonna love it."

My hair whipped in my eyes and I brushed it away.

"Harmony's got a scarf in the glove compartment," he said. "Or there's a Giants baseball cap in back."

I took a look at the scarf, a vintage Emilio Pucci kaleidoscope design of swirling water-and-sky colors. It looked like something Marilyn Monroe or Grace Kelly would have worn, with oversized sunglasses, about fifty years ago. I folded it and put it back in the glove compartment.

"Pretty." I reached around back for the cap, pulling down the sun visor and opening the mirror.

"Suits you." He smiled as I adjusted the cap and tucked in a strand of hair.

If Quinn could have ordered up a day to dazzle me, along with the breathtaking scenery of the coast road, it would have been this one. The highway wound in and out of one pretty little bay after another, the Pacific flashing cobalt and turquoise, whitecaps crashing onto a rocky shoreline dotted with drifts of wildflowers. In some places, the heathery Santa Cruz Mountains telescoped out into the ocean, and the serpentine road cut inland so deeply that it looked like we were driving straight into the mountains. Then the highway would make a corkscrew turn and we'd wrap around another bend where the outside edge of the road fell away to a vertigo-inducing drop off a jagged cliff to the ocean below.

South of Half Moon Bay, the road curled away from the water and became farmland.

"Now where are we going?" I asked.

"The Miramar Beach Restaurant. Local landmark, been around for decades. Good food and it sits right on the edge of the water. I don't know about you, but I'm famished," he said. "After lunch we can head into town and check out Mel Racine's bank."

"Great."

"Maybe you could call the real estate agency and set up an appointment. See if he's available in about an hour or so."

"See if who's available? Did you already call? You did, didn't you? What happened?"

He shrugged, looking sheepish. "I might have tried to pry some information out of them. It's possible I kind of pissed off one half of O'Hara and Romano Estate Agents."

"Oh, brother. The old Santori charm." I pulled out my phone. "Got a phone number?"

He handed me his wallet. "On that folded piece of paper. Why don't you ask for O'Hara?"

"Why don't you let me make the call and stop micromanaging?"

Connor O'Hara had a gentle Irish lilt and an opening in his schedule for one thirty. We agreed to meet at the bank.

"You didn't even have to work for that." Quinn parked in front of the restaurant, sounding disappointed. "My luck, I got the hard-assed partner. You got the pushover."

"Says you. Or maybe I'm just naturally charming. Unlike some people."

The sand-colored Miramar was a comfortable, rambling old place with a long row of picture windows that looked out on the rocky coastline and the Pacific a few feet away. Inside, a gray-haired pianist with a ponytail played Broadway show tunes near the bar, and the restaurant bustled with the business of a lunchtime crowd. A hostess seated us by an ocean-view window and left oversized menus.

"This place is wonderful," I said. "And if that was your idea of flirting with the hostess to show me up for what I said about your lack of charm, she looked like she thought you had some weird eye tic."

Quinn pulled his sunglasses down off his head and put them on. The sun, streaming through the window, was so dazzlingly bright that I did the same. I could see my reflection in his.

"She was being discreet," he said. "I think she likes me."

"Give the waitress a big tip and keep the glasses on. Then they'll all like you."

A cute redhead showed up with a water pitcher and breadbasket and told us about the specials. I chose Seafood Louie with more Dungeness crab; Quinn took the fish and chips. We both decided to have sweet iced tea.

"This used to be a Prohibition roadhouse," Quinn said after she left. "Half Moon Bay was a great place for rumrunners to bring their illegal hooch ashore. The, uh, bordello was upstairs."

"Bordello?"

"Yup. Don't look like that. It's not a bordello now."

"I kind of figured," I said. "And I was just free-associating when you said 'bordello.' Made me think of Allen Cantor."

"What about him?"

"Not him exactly, what he said about Teddy Fargo. We're no nearer to knowing if he's Theo Graf," I said. "And if he is, it sounds like the reason he's on the lam is his little drug business. Which has nothing to do with the Mandrake Society and the deaths of Mel Racine and Paul Noble."

Quinn shrugged. "So end of story. You can still ask Brookie about the black roses, if you want to. But the drug dealing—selling and cultivating marijuana is a felony in California—is a lot more credible explanation for why the guy took off than Charles's cock-eyed idea about a forty-year-old vendetta."

Brookie. Allen said she'd had a mad crush on Quinn and that she was a knockout. I stifled envious feelings and said, "Then tell me why two members of the Mandrake Society died with those wine-glasses next to their bodies within a couple of weeks of each other."

"Coincidence?" he said. "Maybe they were as haunted by those deaths as Thiessman is. Racine was in his sixties, Charles said. That's not old, but he wasn't a spring chicken, either. As for Paul, who knows what demons tormented him that made him decide sui-cide was a better option than sticking around?"

"It's possible, I suppose. I don't know," I said as our waitress set down our seafood. "Right now I'm totally confused."

I bent my head and dug into my Seafood Louie. The timing of Charles's request and the deaths of Mel Racine and Paul Noble bothered me. After so many years of silence, why should what hap-pened to Stephen Falcone and Maggie Hilliard rise up out of the past all of a sudden? Charles thought Theo was behind all this, but who or what had provoked Theo? That is, if he was still alive and living under an alias as Teddy Fargo.

Someone else must have surfaced and vanished like a ghost.

But who was it?

Mel Racine's bank, which he'd transformed into wine storage for serious collectors needing a safe place to store their priceless bottles, was on Main Street in the historic district of Half Moon Bay. I fell in love with the romantic Spanish Mission Revival building the minute I laid eyes on it. It looked like classic early California archi-tecture with its putty-colored stucco walls, orange tile roof, and arched wooden front doors decorated with filigreed ironwork and surrounded by brightly painted ceramic tiles.

Connor O'Hara stood under the eaves in front of the massive doors, talking into his cell phone as Quinn and I parked next to a black Mercedes sporting a license plate with a realtor's logo. He was of medium height with bright red hair sticking out from under a flat tweed cap, trimmed beard, dark trousers, white dress shirt with the sleeves rolled up, and a tailored linen vest.

His eyes went to the Porsche first. Then he took stock of the two of us as we walked toward the bank, slowly focusing on me as he registered my unabashed appreciation of the elegant old building.

He shook hands with Quinn, then me. "I'm Con O'Hara. Mr. Santori, Ms. Montgomery. Welcome to the Wine Vault. We've had a lot of interest in this place, don't you know? I'm sure we'll be havin' a contract on it any day now."

I liked the lilt in his voice. He'd already checked my hand for a wedding ring. Probably trying to figure out if this was a business deal between two partners or which one of us was the potential buyer.

"It's still on the market, though, right?" Quinn asked.

"Oh, sure, sure." O'Hara pulled a round metal ring with what looked like old-fashioned jailers' keys on it and a smaller ring with half a dozen modern keys from his pocket. "This one's a wee bit special. A historic building datin' back to the early 1900s. Not often something as fine as this comes available."

"I suppose that explains why the seller is asking so much more than the assessed value of the property?" Quinn asked.

I pretended to study the patterns in the glazed ceramic tile. We were supposed to be casual lookers, not acting like we might actually purchase the place.

"I believe we'll get it." O'Hara unlocked the front door with one of the jail keys. I felt a rush of cool air like the building had been holding its breath.

If potential buyers had besieged Mel Racine's bank, they must have floated through here on a magic carpet. Dust motes hung suspended like fine silt in the dim sunlight filtering through two small, high windows. Shadows cast by the grillwork made a graceful design on the marble floor. I brushed my fingers across the back of a saddle-colored leather sofa that had been pulled up to a glass coffee table and felt grit.

"The former owner used the upstairs as a gathering place to host wine tastings and the like," O'Hara said. "Set up a small kitchenette in the back and turned the counter where folks did their banking into a bar. He liked to feature a different wine at each of the tellers' windows. Clever, wasn't it?"

Quinn nodded, hands behind his back, as he wandered around the large room, peering behind the counter to check out the kitchenette setup. A moment later, O'Hara and I heard the ding of a cash register drawer popping open next to one of the tellers' windows.

"He loves toys," I said to O'Hara. "He's just a kid at heart."

"Where's the vault?" Quinn shot me a dirty look that O'Hara couldn't see. "I understand the owner redid it as high-end wine storage."

"That he did." O'Hara grinned. "You'd not be guessing the place has such a large basement as it does, would you? Perfect temperature to store wine, and the adobe foundation keeps it nice and cool."

Two closed doors were on the other side of the room. I pointed to them. "Do you get to the basement through one of those?"

He nodded. "The one on the left leads to the corridor where the offices are located. The stairway to the vault and another storage area is through the door on the right."

"Can we see the vault, please?" Quinn asked.

O'Hara pulled out the jail keys again. "Course you can. Right this way."

I leaned on my cane. "Do you mind terribly if I stay up here? The stairs . . . I'm sorry . . . I don't feel up to . . . maybe I could check out the office space while you two have a look at the vault?"

O'Hara looked alarmed. "Can I get you a glass of water or something, Ms. Montgomery? There's a sink in the kitchenette and I'm sure I can find a glass in one of the cupboards. There's no elevator, I'm afraid."

"No, no, I'll be fine. Take your time. Quinn, you'll tell me all about it?"

"You bet, sweetheart. Just take it easy, okay? I don't want you to overdo it." He gave O'Hara a knowing look. "The little woman doesn't know when she's pushed herself too hard."

The little woman was going to kick him in the shins as soon as we left the bank and O'Hara disappeared.

"Are the offices unlocked?" I asked.

"I'll take care of that for ye."

He opened the door on the left and began matching keys to doors.

"Keep him downstairs as long as you can," I said under my breath to Quinn. "Stall, do anything. Talk to him about collecting expensive wine."

"Look, Nancy Drew, I'll do what I can, but it's not like I'm touring Fort Knox. It's a damn vault. Four walls, floor, ceiling . . ."

"You know, you could be a little more supportive—"

"Everything all right, folks?" O'Hara asked.

"Fine," we said in unison.

"Grand." He made a sweeping gesture toward the door. "All right, then, after you, Mr. Santori." To me he added, "Sorry, Ms. Montgomery, but there are still items from the owner in those offices. The place is a bit of a mess, I'm afraid."

Hallelujah. Now if I just had enough time to look around while Quinn chatted up O'Hara in the vault.

"No apology necessary," I said. "I'll just have a quick peek at everything."

He nodded and they clattered down the stairs. A minute later I heard the clank of a metal door opening followed by Quinn's amazed whistle and his voice, indistinct but nevertheless sounding impressed. The vault must be quite a place. I pulled my phone out of my purse and checked the time. One forty-five. I'd give them five minutes; if Quinn got garrulous and O'Hara was intrigued by cases of wine that cost more than his Mercedes, maybe ten minutes.

The three rooms off the small corridor with its arched ceiling, wrought-iron sconces, and whitewashed walls all had the same fusty, abandoned look about them, as though the occupants had left temporarily, expecting to return but never did. I glanced into each of them, beginning with the smallest, which was nearest to the outside door.

It had been used as an office supply depot—computer paper, printer cartridges, envelopes, invoice forms, a carton of lightbulbs—everything stacked on the floor or piled pell-mell on an otherwise unused desk. Another office belonged to a secretary, judging by the desktop computer bristling with sticky note phone numbers tacked to the monitor, a multiline telephone, and an overflowing in-box. Surprisingly, there were no personal effects, no family photo or calendar with circled dates or corny newspaper cartoons tucked under the desktop glass. Probably removed before the place went on the market. My heart sank. What if Mel Racine had a wife or kids who'd come in and cleared out his personal things, and all that was left was just paperwork related to the Wine Vault?

The largest office had obviously been his, the walls lined with framed posters of vintage cars—Vauxhall, Bugatti, Citroën—as well as brochures and catalogs from his dealerships piled like snowdrifts on a credenza across from his desk. He, too, had a full in-box. I rifled through it, but everything appeared to belong to the wine storage business and his tasting events—leases, catalogs for auctions, wine price lists, an old issue of *Decanter,* a couple of copies of *Wine Spectator.* No family photos or memorabilia on his desk, either, except for an expensive silver-framed portrait of an Irish setter with JENNY written in calligraphy on the mat, and a small hand-painted oval frame with a candid snapshot that could have been Jenny or another dog.

I checked my phone again. One forty-nine. I'd been counting on Mel to have pictures from his old life hanging in his office as Charles had done. All he had was two photos of his dog sitting on his desk. I pulled open his top right-hand desk drawer, stifling my guilty feelings. As it turned out, I needn't have felt bad. Nothing but the usual desk junk in that drawer and the two others below it.

The top drawer was locked. I looked around the room for a place to hide a small key and hoped O'Hara didn't have it swinging from a key ring. Where—?

One fifty-three. I lifted the blotter and there it was. The drawer, predictably, stuck and I had to yank it open. It banged into the desk chair and my heart thudded against my rib cage. Downstairs had gone quiet all of a sudden. Had Quinn and O'Hara heard the noise and figured I tripped over something in my weary state and fell over? Were they on their way upstairs to check on me?

I went through the top drawer as quickly as I could with fumbling hands. My time was running out. The envelope was all the way in the back, taped to the top of the desk. I unstuck it and pulled out half a dozen faded color photographs. And there they were: the Mandrake Society.

It must have been one of their parties at the beach house, possibly at sunset. The colors had gone a little orangey after so many years, but the rich warm light burnished the five of them like beautiful bronzed statues. They could have been posing for a magazine cover shoot or a Christmas card photo of the perfect family, sitting on sand-rumpled towels and sprawled in beach chairs with the flat horizon line separating the cobalt ocean and the sunlight-and-cloud-threaded sky behind them. What shocked me was how young they were. Charles had said so, but I hadn't taken in the fact that they were kids, barely out of college.

They'd been a close-knit group, tactile and comfortable with one another, changing the order of who stood or sat next to, or on, whom, but always arms draped over shoulders, someone's legs in someone's lap, one of the girls tucked into a protective embrace with one or two of the guys. I couldn't stop staring; they didn't look cold and heartless despite Charles's sybaritic depiction of their drinking and sexual habits. In fact, they looked enviably happy and carefree, as though their futures were something wonderful they held in the palms of their hands.

I wondered when it all changed.

Instinctively I knew who was who, somewhat by process of elimination. I recognized Paul Noble well enough to pick him out. He had the same sharp features, but back then his hair had been dark and glossy and he'd been a lot slimmer and fitter. Mel had to be the one with sandy blond hair and horn-rimmed glasses, looking somewhat professorial and bookish. Theo Graf was the oldest of the group by a number of years and the only one not wearing a bathing suit. Instead, he had on a pair of bleached jeans and a tie-dyed Woodstock T-shirt. Maggie was the dark-haired beauty with an upturned nose and radiant smile. In one photo she sat on Theo's lap clowning around; the camera had caught them both in profile, heads thrown back in laughter, arms twined around each other. That made Vivian the perky blonde, petite and a little pudgy.

Quinn's easygoing baritone and O'Hara's higher-pitched tenor floated up the stairs and I nearly dropped the photos. It sounded like they were wrapping up the tour. For a moment, I was tempted to shove the pictures back in the envelope and stick it in my purse. Who would know now, anyway? Instead I turned on my camera phone and quickly photographed them one by one. These were not my pictures. They were someone else's sweet memories. Already I felt like a grave robber.

O'Hara slammed the vault door shut and I jumped. His voice and Quinn's grew louder, along with the sound of quick footsteps on the stairs. I taped the envelope back where I'd found it and pulled my hand away. My fingertips brushed something glossy that seemed to have gotten stuck between the drawer and the desk. I tugged on it. More photos, two of them.

These hadn't been with the others and they were completely different. A school yearbook picture of a young man dressed in a tuxedo. His features seemed somehow off-kilter, or unaligned, and he looked askance at the photographer. I turned the picture over, though I already knew it was Stephen Falcone. He had printed his name in irregular uphill letters and the date: September 1967.

The second picture was blackmail, pure and simple. Maggie Hilliard and Charles Thiessman making love outdoors somewhere. After seeing the photos in the hunting lodge the other night, I recognized Charles, even in profile. The two of them were lying on what looked like a daybed on a sunporch or balcony and obviously unaware of the photo being taken since they were in the middle of having sex. Maggie was half sitting, half lying against a couple of pillows with Charles on top of her, fondling her breasts. I turned the explicit picture over. My face felt hot, as though I'd been the one to catch them in the act.

So that's what Charles had left out of his story. Maggie, who was supposedly Theo's girlfriend, was also having an affair with Charles. Had Theo known? If he'd seen this picture, he did. I wondered who had taken it, but it was probably another member of the Mandrake Society.

Charles said he didn't spend time with them at the Pontiac Island cottage, but the wicker furniture and the blurred background in that photo looked sort of beachy. Had Charles been there the night Maggie died, and lied about that, as well?

I heard Quinn's muffled voice shout my name. "Where are you?"

"Here! I'm coming!"

If O'Hara caught me rifling through Mel Racine's desk . . . I swept up the photos and put them in my purse, along with my phone, and joined Con O'Hara and Quinn.

There was no going back from here.

CHAPTER 15

———∞∞∞———

"What'd you find?" Quinn said after we'd decoupled from O'Hara and were back in the Porsche. "Obviously it's something. You've gone quiet ever since we left the bank."

"Photographs of the Mandrake Society," I said. "I took pictures of the pictures. They're on my phone."

We were on the Pacific Coast Highway heading north, the sunlight now softer, filtered through a thin haze of clouds. From here I could no longer see the water. This time I hadn't put on the Giants cap and Quinn hadn't turned on the music. Whatever giddy sense of adventure we'd been caught up in earlier in the day had vanished, just like the ocean. We drove past fields and farmland baked by the summer sun and arid from months with no rain, the colors faded and dusty: subdued greens, golds, browns, and tans.

"What else?" he said. "You keep looking at your purse like you're waiting for a bomb to go off inside."

How did he know?

"A picture of Stephen Falcone, the kid who died during the Mandrake Society's field tests."

"And? Something else is really bugging you."

"Never take me to Vegas and let me play poker. I'll lose everything."

He laughed. "So what is it?"

"A picture of Charles Thiessman having sex with Maggie Hilliard.

I'm sure they didn't know anyone was taking that picture since they were sort of . . . busy."

"Those pictures on your phone with the others?" He used that lazy, laconic tone of voice that meant we both knew he already knew the answer. It always put me on the defensive.

"There wasn't time. You and O'Hara came up the stairs like someone was chasing the pair of you, so I nicked them. Now I wish I hadn't. They weren't mine to take. They were Mel Racine's. He'd tucked them all the way in the back of his top desk drawer. Which he'd locked."

Quinn gave a one-shoulder shrug of indifference.

"Well," he said, "you figure if Racine had any family, they would have already cleaned out whatever they wanted. The vault was empty, so someone had been in there taking care of business. My guess is that whoever buys the building will trash all that stuff anyway. So it's not exactly like you stole the pictures. You just helped with the cleanup."

"I didn't borrow them." I twisted and untwisted the shoulder strap to my purse. "But you have a point. Whatever is still there is going straight into some Dumpster when someone finally buys the building."

The ocean had slipped back into view. We were only about fifteen miles from San Francisco and Quinn was driving like he had a destination in mind.

"I thought we'd have a drink at the Cliff House," he said. "We'll be there in about twenty minutes. I wouldn't mind looking at those photos, if that's okay with you?"

"I dragged you into this, didn't I? Of course it's okay."

"Story of you and me." His voice was light, teasing. "You're always dragging me into something."

That was the nearest we'd come to bringing up what had been hanging over us since yesterday: whether or not I'd succeed in dragging him back into my life. Back to Virginia.

"I'll ignore that." I matched his bantering tone and changed the subject. "Tell me about the Cliff House. Is it another famous landmark?"

"They call it 'the place where San Francisco begins.' It's perched on a promontory cantilevered out over the Pacific. Not too far below the Golden Gate," he said. "There's been a restaurant there since the 1860s. It kept getting wiped out by fires, and one time an abandoned schooner full of dynamite blew up on the rocks underneath and just missed blasting the building into the ocean."

"Sounds like quite a place. You really are a good tour guide, you know that?"

"Don't look so surprised. Told you I was."

"Then tell me the real reason you left California for Virginia. They're totally different and it's so obvious you love it here."

He straightened his arms on the steering wheel and leaned back against the seat. It looked like he was flexing stiff muscles, but I knew he'd gone tense.

"After what Allen did, I had to get out."

"California's a big state," I said. "As for making wine, you've got Oregon, Washington State, New York. All of them have more wineries than we do, and you could easily have stayed on the West Coast. Not to mention all the states that produce more wine than Virginia does."

"I wanted something different," he said. "I liked the experimenting that was happening there, how much the industry was booming, thriving. The fact that Virginia is getting a reputation as a hot wine-tourism destination. It's been kind of cool to be on the cutting edge of something like that."

"It's a much smaller pond," I said.

"Actually, it's minuscule in terms of total U.S. wine production. California accounts for ninety percent all by itself. Nine more percent—in other words, ninety-nine percent—comes from the three other states you just mentioned." He held up fingers as he ticked off each one. "New York, Washington, and Oregon. Everyone else is fighting for a market share of the remaining one percent. That includes Virginia."

I knew those numbers, knew where we stood, but it still shocked me to hear him rattle them off like that. Until now I had never considered that his private tug-of-war between California and Virginia had been about leaving the Eden of American winemaking with its worldwide reputation to come to a place that many people still didn't even know grew grapes, hot tourism destination notwithstanding.

So Virginia was "first in wine" because we made it two years after colonists arrived in Jamestown and discovered native grapes, big fat deal. California was the largest, as in ball-out-of-the-park-home-run size, and I wondered, though he'd never admitted it to me, if Quinn still equated that primacy and clout with being the best. And whether the glamorous cachet and storied history of California wine country, which to most of the world meant Napa and Sonoma, where he was from, were really what he missed after he moved to Virginia.

"Well, we may be small, but we're damn good," I said.

We were finally back in the city, catching red lights at almost every intersection. I saw signs for the San Francisco Zoo and then, abruptly, the ocean was directly in front of us as if we were going to drive straight into it. Quinn turned right at the edge of the beach and we followed the coast up a long, steep hill.

"Don't be so defensive," he said. "I wasn't criticizing."

"I'm not."

But it was like what Mark Twain said about his wife and swearing: Quinn had the words right, but not the tune. He'd sounded halfhearted, and I wondered yet again if he'd been subtly signaling his intent to stay here and I'd been resolutely trying to ignore it.

He reached over and squeezed my hand. "We're almost there. Enjoy the view. We can talk business another time."

I saw the rooftop sign for the Cliff House before the long, low white building came into view. We rounded a corner and all of a sudden it was right there, sitting perilously close to where the traffic whizzed past, tucked into a sharp elbow curve as the road spiraled upward. Anything that came downhill in the opposite direction probably needed to slam on the brakes for that wicked turn or else end up in the dining room. A dozen or so cars were parked in front of the restaurant, jammed in at angles like bad teeth.

"Damn," Quinn said. "I didn't think it would be so crowded at this hour. We'll find a spot up the hill."

"Where are we?" I asked as we drove past a sprawling wooded park.

"A place called Land's End."

He did a neat job of parallel parking in a space that should have required a shoehorn. We walked back down the steep sidewalk to the restaurant. A large stone ruin filled with water sat at the edge of the sea below us.

"It looks like an old swimming pool," I said.

"That's the Sutro Baths," he said. "Dates back to the early days of the Cliff House. It was supposed to rival something a Roman emperor would have built. Now it has a reputation as a kind of mystical place, especially at the end of the day when you can see the setting sun and the lights from inside the restaurant reflected in the water. It makes the baths look like a cauldron of fire. You see photographers here all the time taking pictures of cloud formations or seagulls flying into the marine layer—the lighting's pretty amazing."

I stared at the dark, placid pool, the broken lines of stone, and the tumble of rocks to the shore, and imagined flaming water and wide-winged birds soaring in the mist over the Pacific Ocean.

"It must be beautiful. Are the baths off-limits, or can you go down there and explore?"

"Oh, you can check it out," he said, "but there's a sign in a bunch of languages warning that you could get thrown off the rocks and die if you're in the wrong place when a wave comes crashing in."

I shuddered, but he'd spoken in such a matter-of-fact way I knew it was firsthand information. "You know that because you've been there."

He flashed a smug grin and held open the door to the restaurant. "Of course."

A waitress dressed in black brought us to a corner bistro table on a balcony lounge overlooking a two-story restaurant in the new part of the building. Already the shades on the floor-to-ceiling windows had been lowered to screen the fierce late-afternoon sunlight, which glinted like polished mirror off the Pacific, and streamed into the all-white room with its vaulted ceiling and modern steal-beamed architecture.

Quinn ordered mojitos for us and asked for them to be made with rum rather than Mexican tequila. After the waitress left, I got my phone out of my purse and handed it to him. He pulled his reading glasses from his shirt pocket and turned his back to the window, squinting in the bright light as he stared at the little screen, flicking through each of the photographs.

"They seem to be good friends, real close," he said. "Looks like these were taken at a summer beach get-together."

"Charles said they spent weekends together at a cottage on Pontiac Island. That's where Maggie came up with their name. The Mandrake Society. He made it sound like they did everything as a group, including socializing."

"Well, with the super-top-secret clearances they must have had, at least they were hanging out with people who were involved in the same project," he said. "At that level, it's need to know only. You can't even blab to your reflection in the mirror without worrying about a security breach."

I took the phone and scrolled through the photos as he had done. "They genuinely liked each other," I said. "Look at their body language and how comfortable everyone is with everyone else. I'll bet they had some good times together."

"Until it all fell apart," Quinn said.

"Their breakup must have been spectacular if they scattered to the winds after Stephen Falcone died and Maggie was killed in that car crash."

Our waitress set down our mojitos and a dish of salted nuts.

He touched his glass to mine. "I'm glad you came to San Francisco."

"Me, too. Thanks for a fabulous tour."

He dunked his mint leaves into his glass and squirted lime into his drink. I copied him.

"I didn't know you liked mojitos," I said. "I can't remember the last time I had one."

"I read somewhere it was Hemingway's favorite drink in Key West. I also read he drank whatever was on the table until he was under it." He shrugged. "It seems like a mojito kind of day."

He sat back and watched me as though he were contemplating something, or perhaps waiting for an answer to one of the unspoken questions that hung in the air between us. I couldn't go down that road right now. All the warning signs were there for this to come to grief if we pushed it.

We'd come this far. Why ruin everything?

"Back to the pictures," I said.

He sipped his drink. "You have the floor. We were talking about a breakup, I believe?"

"Of the Mandrake Society."

He grinned and I went on. "After they split up, everyone went their own way. Maggie was dead and Theo thought the others conspired to tamper with her car and cause her accident. That meant Mel, Paul, Vivian. And Charles."

Quinn set his drink down and made circles on the table with it like he was trying to work this out. "Especially Charles. Based on everything you said, Theo held him more accountable than anyone else."

"I wonder if Theo knew about the affair? Or maybe he guessed," I said.

He stopped moving his glass around. "How long after Stephen died was Maggie killed?"

"You mean like days or weeks?" I asked and he nodded. "I don't know, and Charles didn't specify. But after Stephen died, his sister—I think her name was Elinor—showed up. That's what seemed to freak everyone out."

"What happened to Elinor?"

"Charles paid her off and told her that Stephen was a patriot. Said he saved her from a lifetime of caring for her disabled brother, who wouldn't amount to much anyway, not to mention all the bills she wouldn't have for his medical expenses. Unquote."

I shrugged and drank my mojito. I still felt the same cold fury I'd felt that night in the lodge, remembering the matter-of-fact way Charles had tossed off that remark.

"God, that's sick," Quinn said. "Except I suppose we need to remember that was forty years ago. Those were the days when you stuck people like that in closets and tried to forget about them."

" 'People like that.' It breaks my heart." I fished in my purse for the last two photos and pulled out the one of Stephen Falcone, setting it on the table for Quinn to see. "That's Stephen. Look at him. He has such kind eyes. And a sweet smile. I bet he really trusted everyone. Never thought anyone would do anything to hurt him."

Quinn picked up the photo, his lips pressed together. "I'm sorry, Lucie," he said.

I took the final photo, the blackmail photo, and slid it in front of him. "And now here's this."

Even Quinn reddened, staring at the raw sexuality of a man and woman utterly engrossed in making love when they believed no one was watching.

He cleared his throat. "Wonder who took it."

"We can eliminate two people right off the bat," I said. "These two. It must have been someone else among the Fearsome Fivesome."

"Sixsome."

"Huh?"

"Charles was part of this group, too." He tapped his finger on the edge of the photo. "There were six of them, counting Charles. What do you bet he took the photos on your phone?"

"It could have been a timer," I said. "And he said he wasn't a member of the Mandrake Society. He was married, though not to Juliette back then. Said he didn't like their drinking and disdained what he called their 'sexual experimenting.' "

"He doesn't look too disdainful doing what he's doing there."

My turn to blush. "Why would he lie about being part of the group? About"—I indicated the picture—"that."

"Maybe he had a rich-but-jealous wife and he didn't want her finding out he was screwing a gorgeous twentysomething hot chick, in case she decided to divorce him and leave him penniless."

"That sounds like a plot from one of Thelma Johnson's soap operas."

Unexpectedly, his eyes softened and he sounded wistful. "Good old Thelma. I miss getting coffee in the General Store in the morning with her and the Romeos. Finding out what's going on in the world."

"That can be remedied." I tried to keep my voice light.

He sighed. "Yeah, I know. You've only dropped two million hints." He slid the photo over to me. "Back to the matter at hand. What's your explanation for this, since you don't seem to like mine?"

"I didn't say I didn't like it," I said. "But I wish I knew more about Maggie Hilliard. She's the one who gave the group their name and then had those wineglasses made for everyone. So she's into bonding, weekend parties at the beach. Kind of like a family."

"Then why would she betray her boyfriend by having sex with another member of the group? Especially the father figure."

"Ugh, that almost sounds like incest when you put it like that."

Our waitress stopped by. "Another round, folks?"

Quinn glanced at me and we both shook our heads. "We're fine with these," he said. "Thanks."

She set down the bill and left.

Quinn indicated the picture of Maggie and Charles. " 'Incest' is a pretty strong word, if you ask me. Though Maggie doesn't exactly come across as a wholesome all-American girl, into group hugs and singing 'Kumbaya' with the rest of the campers when she's doing this with a married guy old enough to be her father."

I turned the photograph over.

"Except she was the one—apparently the only one—who felt so much remorse about Stephen that she wanted to come clean about covering up his death."

"Returning to a distasteful subject, she had sexual relationships with two men she worked with at the same time. That can't have done much for group dynamics," he said.

"Unless she was coerced," I said. "What if Charles lusted after her and promised to protect the Mandrake Society if she cooperated? So being a good team player, she went to bed with him. Maybe she figured they'd be discreet since he was married and she was involved with Theo. Counted on the others never finding out about it."

"Yeah, well, throw that theory out the window because someone did find out," Quinn said. "And decided to record them in flagrante delicto. Wonder who it was. And why."

"Two reasons: blackmail or jealousy." I ticked them off on my fingers. "Maybe both."

"That's why. What about who?"

"You don't take a picture like this unless you intend to do something with it. Someone meant to use this photo to influence—or blackmail—either Maggie or Charles. Or hurt Theo. Again that leaves Mel, Paul, and Vivian."

"My money's on Vivian," Quinn said. "It seems like a female thing. What do you bet she was jealous of our girl Maggie who was having good-time sex with not one but two guys who worked together?"

"Mel had the photograph," I said.

"Maybe Vivian made copies and put 'em in her Christmas cards to the rest of the gang."

"Now you're being crude."

"I notice you didn't dispute that I could be right."

"Okay, multiple copies," I said. "But when did the others see this photo? At the time? After Maggie was dead, or long after they were disbanded?"

"Does it matter?"

"Of course it does. Charles implied that Theo believed—but couldn't prove—that Maggie driving off that pier and drowning wasn't an accident. So I'm betting Theo didn't know about the affair, because if he did, you'd have to wonder about a lovers' quarrel between him and Maggie."

"Meaning Theo might have tampered with her car in a jealous rage?"

"Yes, except Charles said Theo accused him and the others of doing something to shut Maggie up about Stephen. That's when he threatened to make them all pay for her death. So I guess we can eliminate Theo." I frowned. "Wonder what made him doubt the drunk-driving explanation?"

"I don't know, but it leaves us with the Usual Suspects. One or all of whom might have had a motive for murder." Quinn tipped his glass and drank, rattling the ice cubes. "Vivian, Mel, and Paul. And we can't discount Charles, either."

"Everybody's dead," I said. "Except Charles."

For a long moment, neither of us spoke.

"What if Charles engineered Maggie's accident?" I said finally.

The thought had been flitting uneasily through my mind all afternoon, ever since I found that photograph. If Charles bore some responsibility for Maggie's death, played some role, it changed everything.

"How?" Quinn asked.

"I don't know. If he did, the police never figured it out." I shrugged. "Maybe I'm grasping at straws."

"If he did, that could explain why he wants to know if Theo is still alive. Maybe Charles is worried Theo finally learned something after all this time that can tie him to Maggie's death." He paused. "There's no statute of limitations on murder, you know."

"No," I said. "There isn't, is there?"

"You'd better watch it, Lucie. I know we're just speculating, but if any of this is true, you're dealing with a guy with no conscience."

"I know," I said. "And if it's true, then it would make Charles a murderer."

CHAPTER 16

⎯⎯⎯⎯⎯⎯⎯

Quinn paid the bill and we walked up the hill to the Porsche. Low cumulus clouds piling up in great heaps like meringues scudded across the sky over the Pacific. Underlit by the sun, they were the color of an old bruise. Above they exploded in soft gold that faded to creamy yellow, like the skies on my French grandmother's prayer cards portraying the Blessed Virgin ascending to heaven.

"I have an idea," Quinn said.

"What?"

"We ought to get an early start tomorrow. It could be a long day in Napa."

I glanced at him. "Yes, I suppose it could."

"So . . . well, I was thinking." He seemed to be frowning at his feet. "How about if you checked out of the hotel now and spent the night on the houseboat with me? Sausalito's already on the other side of the Bay, so we could beat all the city traffic and head straight up from there."

"It would save time, wouldn't it?" My heart raced. "I guess it makes sense."

Was he asking me to spend the night with him in his bed, or was this really just about traffic and getting an early start?

"I'm not sure what makes sense now." His voice was quiet in my ear as he pulled me close, burying his face in my hair. "Especially about us."

I closed my eyes. "Me neither, Quinn. But I know what I want. I want you back in my life. What about you? What do you want?"

If I pushed too hard, I knew I risked losing him. Quinn was like that, afraid to commit, afraid of getting tied down . . . but at least, at the very least, he owed me an honest answer to that question after everything we'd been through together.

"What do I want?" He blew out a long, soft breath. "Tonight I want it to be like it was that first night."

I felt like he'd knocked me sideways. I wanted to say, "And tomorrow? What about tomorrow and the day after that and the next and the next . . . ?" But I didn't, because I couldn't. There would be no talk of the future, no declaration of our feelings, no discussion about whether he would be coming back to Virginia for good.

Tonight there would just be us and it would have to be enough, for now and maybe forever, until I could pick up the pieces of my life and move on, if that's how we ended it.

I leaned on my cane for support and kissed his cheek. "It won't take me long to pack my things."

The drive to Sausalito, as lights winked on across San Francisco on a surprisingly clear summer evening, was intoxicating. What lay ahead once we got there thrummed between us, alternately thrilling and scaring me. I pushed Charles, and whatever dark secret the survivors of the Mandrake Society had harbored, to the farthest recesses of my mind as we drove across the Golden Gate Bridge, its enormous red-orange piers rising up out of the night sky, majestic and imposing. In the distance, the Bay Bridge sparkled like a diamond necklace, and the city itself was a graceful, ethereal kingdom of glittering lights.

The houseboat was located in a marina just beyond the town, off Bridgeway on Gate 5 ½ Road. I hadn't known what to expect. I had pictured a large room, somewhat primitive and rustic, that served as the living, dining, and sleeping area with some clever rearranging of modular, vaguely uncomfortable wooden furniture with thin beach-type cushions. Instead, it was a luxurious little jewel, with the neat efficiency of a puzzle whose seams fit together so perfectly they disappeared.

I don't remember much about when we first got there, except a blurred recollection of scented roses blooming on a floating patio, the creak of wooden stairs under our footsteps, a lavender front door, water lapping against the sides of the gently rocking boat. Then we were inside, with soft light shining from a seashell-decorated lamp and Harmony's strong, primitive paintings—something tribal, Tahiti, Bora Bora, the Amazon—hanging on pale yellow walls. Quinn led me down a narrow corridor lined with fitted doors, behind which I assumed she carefully stored clothes or linens. Neither of us spoke until we got to the master bedroom, with its king-sized platform bed and lights from the marina slatting into the darkness through the blinds of a large window. He jerked the cord shut with a quick move and then we tumbled onto the bed, sharp sighs and little cries as we undressed—I heard the rip of fabric—and devoured each other with dizzy, desperate fury.

If this was going to be our last time, I knew that tonight—the way his hands moved over me, our bruised mouths, the pressure of his body on mine, how we fit so perfectly together—would be branded on my skin, our whispered words tattooed onto my heart and into my memory. In years to come I knew remembering this night would fill me with a breathless ache triggered by some small thing when I least expected it—a sea breeze light as a caress across my cheek, a boat rocking like a cradle in a sweet lullaby, faint shafts of moonlight making animal stripes on bare skin, a tangle of bed-sheets that smelled of musk and sweat and passion.

When we were finally finished, he pulled me into his arms and we clung to each other for a long time, listening to the settling creaks and groans of the boat against the quiet sound of our breathing, our heartbeats finding a rhythm together, in the dark liquid stillness.

After a while he murmured, "I'm starved. I think it's past ten o'clock."

I turned on my side so I could see his profile. "Sex always does that to you."

"I'm also predictable." I could feel him smiling in the dark.

"Want me to cook? I presume this place has a kitchen. I can fix eggs and bacon or whatever you've got around. Though of course knowing you that would be a six-pack and a bag of chips."

I sat up and stretched lazily as he leaned across me to turn on a candlestick lamp on a bedside table. His tongue deliberately grazed my breasts and I shivered. In the golden shadows he looked tousled and content. For a long moment we stared at each other without speaking.

Finally he brushed the tip of my nose with his finger and the moment passed. "On a boat it's called a galley. Yeah, there is one and it's pretty amazing. And I'll ignore that remark about my culinary habits."

We were back on familiar territory. "So what *is* in your fridge?"

"This and that." He grinned. "How about ordering Chinese? I know this great place. I never did take you to Chinatown. In San Francisco that's practically a sacrilege."

He pulled on a pair of jeans and rummaged through a built-in armoire for a shirt that had our vineyard logo on it. My heart did a slow flip-flop. I started to reach for my underwear when he said, "I've got something for you to wear."

At home I'd often worn his clothes after we made love. Usually it was one of his favorite Hawaiian shirts or an old sweatshirt that came down around my knees, something that wrapped me in his scent and the memory of being together. But now he was opening a different armoire, this one for hanging clothes. There was nothing in it except a long silk robe.

"I, uh, saw this one day at one of those artisan street festivals we have here." He held out the robe. "The, um, colors reminded me of you. I was going to give it to you when I came back to Virginia. I thought it would go nice with your hair." By now he was stammering. "At least I hope it does."

Last year for Christmas he gave me a wine aerator—an expensive wine aerator, but a wine aerator nonetheless. We'd always kept our gifts minimal and somewhat impersonal. And as for noticing what colors I wore, the work we did was dirty and messy, so more often than not he saw me in old jeans and wine-spattered T-shirts or sweatshirts that looked like I'd been shot multiple times.

The robe was lovely, intimate, sexy. I took it from him and held it against my body. It fell in graceful folds of peach, yellow, celadon, and cream, so soft it seemed to melt in my hands.

"If you don't like it, you don't have to keep—"

"Oh, Quinn, it's *beautiful*. I love it!"

"Really?"

"Yes!" I threw my arms around him, crushing the robe between us. "Thank you!"

I slipped into it and wound the sash around my waist, tying a bow and turning around to show off to him. "What do you think?"

He smiled as I caught his arm for balance. "I think I have good taste."

There was a mirror inside the armoire door. I stood in front of it and admired myself. "I look gorgeous."

"Yeah, you do." He laughed and caught my hand. "Come on, gorgeous, I'll call for Chinese. There's a bottle of Sauvignon Blanc chilling in the fridge."

I raised an eyebrow. "For us?"

He ignored the astonished look on my face. He'd planned this evening, every last detail, ever since yesterday.

"Unless you want to invite some of the neighbors in. They're pretty cool, actually."

"Another time," I said. "Tonight's ours."

"I thought you might say that," he said and led me down a narrow spiral staircase to the lower level.

The galley kitchen had a sliding glass door that opened to the flower-filled patio, which I could now see ran the length of the boat. While Quinn found the phone number for the restaurant, I let myself outside and leaned on the railing to watch the dark silhouettes of low, boxy rows of houseboats while the little floating pier shifted gently with the current. From somewhere nearby I heard an explosion of laughter, the tinkle of china, the drone of television voices. The glow from San Francisco was a soft halo in the night sky below a fingernail-shaped moon. The only additional light came from the windows of the other boats, warm golden squares or porthole circles, as comforting and welcoming as old friends. In the kitchen, Quinn's voice rose and fell on the phone.

He joined me a moment later, holding two glasses of wine. "I was thinking," he said. "Harmony's got a great little office, real compact, hooked up with wireless and everything. She's even got a photo printer, for her art."

"You want to print the photos of the Mandrake Society on my phone?" I said as he nodded. "What about a connector cable?"

"She's pretty geeky for an artist," he said. "I bet she's got one that works."

We took our wine with us to the living room where a small modular home office was tucked into a corner. I sat on a brushed suede sofa and admired more of Harmony's artwork—Quinn said all the sculpture and the paintings in this room had been done by friends—while he did things to her computer and printer, producing a slightly blurry set of images of the photos.

"You should have lifted the originals while you were at it," he said later, as we sat on bar stools in the sleek polished-aluminum-and-black-granite kitchen, surrounded by cartons of kung pao chicken, moo shu pork, and beef with snow peas. "These are kind of out of focus."

He'd lined up the half dozen reproduced pictures of the Mandrake Society along the counter wall next to where we sat. By tacit mutual agreement, the school photo of Stephen Falcone and the shot of Maggie and Charles lay next to them facedown.

"You know I already feel bad about the two I did pinch. As for the others, I was in a rush. It was the best I could do under the circumstances." I pointed to the little photo gallery with my chopsticks. "At least we know what everyone looked like. I wonder if we'd recognize Theo Graf after all this time, if he really is alive."

"We could look on the Internet," Quinn said. "We didn't even think about that when we were printing the pictures. Come on. Bring your dinner and let's see."

There was nothing. We searched for half an hour. While Fargo's name popped up here and there on assorted wine blogs and community calendars in Calistoga or Napa Valley, no one had gotten a photo of him accepting an award for one of his wines, standing in a grinning lineup of winemakers at the county fair, or a random private photo that had been posted on some website.

"Jeez," Quinn said. "How'd he manage to stay undercover like that for so long?"

"Practice. You know, we should have guessed that Charles would already have done this search," I said. "And come up empty-handed, just like we did. If there were any photos, he'd probably know better than anybody if Fargo and Graf were the same person. He wouldn't be sending me on this weird black rose mission."

We were back in the kitchen, cleaning up after dinner. Quinn poured the last of the Sauvignon Blanc into our glasses.

"Not necessarily. What if Fargo had surgery? Maybe he was in a car accident in Austria just like Charles said, but the paper got it wrong and he survived. Now he looks totally different."

"Maybe." It sounded far-fetched, but anything was possible, especially with this secretive group. "There's just too much we don't know."

"Yeah, and the only person who does know might be playing fast and loose with the truth. Charles could have made up a bunch of stuff and you'd never know," he said. "I wonder what he's hiding."

"His affair with Maggie, for one thing."

"You think he might have been embarrassed to admit that with your grandfather there?"

"Pépé's French. The French invented love and all its various nuances," I said.

"The Italians invented love," he corrected me. "We know how to do passion, baby. The kinky stuff, meaning all the various nuances, came from you French."

"The Italians invented beautiful leather shoes and jackets and purses. And pizza," I said, and he laughed. "Getting back to our conversation: Charles, who is neither French nor Italian, doesn't seem like the embarrassed type. You know, the more I think of it, the more I think the affair was relevant to Maggie's death."

"How?" Quinn folded his arms across his chest.

"That's what I can't figure out. Maybe she broke it off or threatened to tell his wife because he kept pursuing her. Maybe he was a jilted lover with a badly bruised ego. Any of the above. But I'll bet you if we ever find out what really happened, Charles Thiessman will have played some role in Maggie Hilliard's death."

Quinn hooted. "I don't see how that could be. The others were there that night at their booze party. If he did something, they'd *know*."

"Maybe they were covering up for him."

"Because he covered up for them about Stephen?"

"Why not? A Faustian pact."

He thought about that a moment. "Or consider this: Maybe they were all in it together. Don't forget, Maggie wanted to come clean about Stephen. That would give all of them a motive to keep their mouths shut."

"Oh, my God." My eyes widened. "You mean like Agatha Christie? *Murder on the Orient Express*? They all did it?"

He nodded. "If one hangs, they all hang together. Which would explain Charles knowing where in the world the others were living, what their new careers were. Shared culpability for manslaughter, maybe even murder. That's what kept them in line."

"Everyone but Theo," I said. "The now possibly undead Theo Graf."

"Something's kind of funny about Theo," Quinn said. "Changing his name—if that's what he did. And going off the grid. I'm not sure he gets a free pass on this, either."

"Maybe we'll find out more about him tomorrow when we meet Brooke," I said. "The plan for Mick to buy her wine and us vetting the blend is still on."

"Maybe you should just do the wine deal and forget the rest," he said. "Why get in the middle of it anymore, especially the way it's turning out? Let Charles and Theo—if he's still alive—sort out their own skeletons in the closet."

"I can't." I picked up Stephen Falcone's photo and turned it over, setting it on the counter in front of him. "Charles talked about Stephen like he was a lab rat in an experiment. He was a *person,* Quinn, and his death troubled Maggie so much that she wanted to tell the truth about what happened, regardless of the consequences."

Quinn stared at Stephen's photo, a muscle tightening in his jaw.

"Okay," he said. "Then do what you have to do."

He stood up and paced in the little kitchen. "God, I'd love a cigar right now. You've got me all stirred up, you know that? But if I light up, Harmony'd know and she'd kill me for stinking up the place."

I reached for my cane and stood, too. "Forget the cigar. I have a better idea for stirring you up."

He stopped pacing and stared at me, a slow smile lighting his eyes. "Is that a threat or a promise?"

"You'll just have to find out, Mr. Italian-Who-Thinks-He-Invented-Love."

He leaned my cane against the counter and took me in his arms. "You won't be needing that, Ms. Kinky-Nuance. At least not for the rest of tonight. I'm expecting you to live up to your French reputation."

"Bet on it."

He led me upstairs to the bedroom. From somewhere on the boat, a clock with a lovely clear chime rang twice.

"You look beautiful in this light." He pulled on the bow to my robe, untying it. The soft silk slipped off my shoulders and the robe dropped to the floor in a puddle.

I closed my eyes and let Quinn lay me back down on the bed, his hands moving over me sure and strong. But for the rest of the night, as our bodies rose and fell in the old, familiar rhythm, I knew—I could feel it—that the face of Stephen Falcone now haunted him as much as it haunted me.

Stephen probably hadn't asked for much in this world. Charles may have paid off his sister, but I suspected there had been a threat attached to that payoff, something he'd been able to hold over her head—a warning about violating national security or some super-secret hoo-ha she would be too scared to question—just as he'd done to the members of the Mandrake Society. Blood money wasn't justice.

Maybe it was time Stephen Falcone got justice.

CHAPTER 17

When I opened my eyes the next morning, Quinn was already awake, propped on an elbow watching me. He ran the back of his finger down my cheek.

"Morning, sleepyhead," he said.

"How long have you been up?"

"Not long. I was just making sure you were still breathing. Last night was pretty intense. That Italian thing, you know."

I grinned and stretched, and he kissed me. "Could you remind me again?"

This time it was gentle, unrushed . . . nostalgic. Afterward Harmony's tiny shower was practically too small to fit two people, but we managed.

As it turned out he did have bacon and eggs in the refrigerator—more advance planning—and I fixed it while he made his usual brand of coffee. If they were ever looking for a "green" fuel with enough kick to blast the space shuttle into orbit, someone from NASA needed to contact Quinn.

I packed my small suitcase, carefully folding the silk robe, while he cleaned up and then we were back in the Porsche, driving through a pea-soup marine layer.

"Is it going to rain?" I asked as he drove down Bridgeway and we left Sausalito, now nearly invisible in the fog, behind. San Francisco could have been swallowed up by the Pacific overnight; there was no trace of it.

"Yup," he said. "In November. Don't worry, in a few hours it will burn off like it does every day and the weather will be sunny, clear, and California perfect."

"Always?"

He gave me a slant-eyed look. "Unless there's a wildfire somewhere."

"That sounds scary."

"It is."

We drove north following the curve of San Pablo Bay and took Highway 121 toward Sonoma. After a while, Quinn turned east, which eventually brought us to the main north-south highway through the Napa Valley.

"We'll take this up to Calistoga," Quinn said. "Highway 29 is the main drag. You'll see all the legendary places like Martini, Mondavi, Inglenook, Beaulieu—the first-generation wineries that really got us started, put us on the map."

"Great." I smiled and willed myself to stop thinking about whether he was sending me another coded message that he wasn't coming back to Virginia when he talked about "us."

If Quinn noticed that I seemed subdued, he didn't let on and kept going with his cheerful travelogue.

"When we get up near Calistoga, we'll cut across the mountains and drop down into Sonoma Valley near Santa Rosa. There's a place I want to show you. It's the long way, but I want you to see Napa," he said. "After that we'll double back to Brooke's winery. It's on the Silverado Trail, just below Calistoga. A bunch of terrific wineries but the Trail doesn't get the high tourist traffic 29 does."

"Sounds like a lot of driving."

"Not really. The entire Napa Valley is only thirty-five miles long and about four miles wide, so it's not that big," he said. "Bigger than Sonoma Valley, though."

"Is this the famous rivalry between Napa and Sonoma surfacing?"

He grinned. "Sonoma's jealous of Napa. That's the rivalry."

"Really?"

"Yeah, really."

A truck hauling two tankers with white and red wineglasses

painted on them passed us on the other side of the road. Wherever I looked there were acres of vines as far as I could see bounded by the rugged, deeply folded Mayacamas Mountains to my left and the less steep Vaca Range on my right. As we drove through the town of Napa and continued through Yountville, Rutherford, St. Helena, heading north, the storied vineyards flashed by as Quinn promised—a who's who of California winemaking royalty.

Eighties tunes blared on the radio, the music Quinn grew up with. The Police, "Every Breath You Take." I leaned back against the seat, listening to him sing in his warbly baritone and watching the mountains grow grander and more imposing.

Quinn's surprise was a pilgrimage to the oldest vineyard in Sonoma Valley, a historic site. Gianni Bellini had been a major force in the first wave of Italian immigrants who settled here, along with Louis M. Martini and Cesare Mondavi. Three generations of Bellinis owned Gianni's far-flung holdings, which included land next to the Russian River, an estate near Mount St. Helena in Napa Valley, and his pride and joy: this vineyard on the slopes of the Mayacamas in Sonoma County. A decade ago Gianni's grandchildren, who lived and worked in San Francisco, Paris, and Hong Kong, sold it all to Pépé's friend Robert Sanábria.

Quinn seemed to know the place well, driving past the sign indicating that this was private property as though it were meant for real trespassers and not us. The paved road wound around the side of a mountain and cut through immaculately terraced acres of vines before turning to dirt and gravel. Quinn stopped and put the top up on the Porsche to protect against the swirling red dust that coated the car until it turned rust colored. When the road ran out, he parked on a grassy hilltop overlooking the valley. The Sonoma Mountains bracketed the vast, sweeping view of overlapping vine-covered hills and crisscrossing mountains, which grew lighter as they receded and faded into the sky.

We stood next to each other without touching on the crest of that hill with only the sound of the whistling wind behind us and the chirping of birds somewhere in the trees.

"Quite a view, isn't it?" he said finally. "Can't you just imagine Gianni getting off the boat from Italy a hundred and fifty years ago and seeing this place, standing right here? Dreaming about the promise of what this land could be?"

I nodded and the knot in my stomach tightened. That he loved it here was clear, this land with its big skies, fertile valleys, and rugged mountains. That he belonged here was becoming even clearer. It was the reason he'd brought me to this place: to show me, so he wouldn't have to tell me.

"It's magnificent," I said.

"I knew you'd fall in love with it."

My heart felt like he'd attached a stone to it. "Yes."

"There's one more stop," he said. "Something else I want you to see."

We took the corkscrew road down the mountain until he made a sharp left onto another road that led to an abandoned-looking fieldstone building set in a clearing surrounded by woods.

"Gianni's original winery," he said.

Quinn helped me climb down steep steps past a weed-filled garden. Above the arched stone lintel, the year 1886 had been carved into a piece of rose-colored granite.

"Should we be doing this?" I asked.

"It's okay," he said. "Sanábria's vineyard manager is a good buddy of mine. I come here a lot."

He lifted a heavy wooden latch and pushed open the door, flipping on the lights. Inside, the old winery looked bigger than it had from the outside. A few bare bulbs glowed like small moons among the crossbeams, casting murky shadows on the wide plank floor. Someone had attached rows of white Christmas lights to the exposed studs along the walls.

In the dim light, the sepia-tinted room smelled of history and ghost barrels of fermenting wine. For a moment I almost heard voices laughing and shouting and cursing in Italian, a few notes of Verdi sung with gusto. Quinn leaned against a wooden pillar in the middle of the barn, hands in his jeans pockets, and watched me.

"What do you think?" His voice echoed off the rafters.

"I think it's fantastic," I said.

He smiled. "Me, too."

"I wonder what it was like to make wine back then, before everything was mechanized. Maybe they didn't even have electricity or refrigeration when they built this place."

He looked up at the ceiling. "There's another floor above us that was probably used for crushing and fermentation. They would have been able to take advantage of gravity to drain the wine off the skins into settling tanks down here. That huge door you saw on the upper level was possibly the way they got rid of the pumice. Just shoveled it out to the ground and carted it off."

I pointed to the Christmas lights. "Someone still uses this place."

"Tastings for special clients. My winemaker friend got married here. Stuff like that. Eventually they'd like to get it on the National Register of Historic Places."

"It would be wonderful to get married here. I'll bet it was really romantic."

It slipped out, an easy response to his comment about his friend's wedding. But Quinn's reaction—stunned silence—was like a curtain slamming down between us. He realized it, just as I did.

"Yeah, they had a nice ceremony. Real pretty." His voice was flat, deadpan.

"Oh, come on, Quinn. It was just a simple remark. I wasn't implying anything."

"I didn't say you were."

"Then why are you acting like I yelled 'fire' in a crowded room, and you're looking for the nearest exit?"

"Now you're the one reading into things."

"I'm not."

It ended right there in the old winery, the magic of the past two days. We were like guests who overstayed their welcome at a party, forgetting to leave while everyone was having a good time. A gust of wind blew through the open doorway, skittering a puddle of dry leaves across the floor. Quinn roused himself from his post.

"We should get going," he said. "What time is Brooke expecting us?"

"When we get there," I said. "Mick told me she was pretty laid-back about it. She gave him her cell number and said I should call before I wanted to come. She'd be there."

"Then let's grab lunch in Calistoga," he said. "You can call her from there."

We barely spoke on the drive back to Napa. But when he turned off Petrified Forest Road onto 29, I spotted a sign that said ROBERT LOUIS STEVENSON STATE PARK, 9 MILES.

"What's that?"

"Stevenson spent time near Calistoga back in the late 1800s," he said. "I thought you knew the story. The park is on the site of an abandoned mine where he camped out one summer. Spent his honeymoon there, with a married woman he'd fallen in love with, after she got divorced, of course. He wrote a book about it. *The Silverado Squatters.* Talked about the Napa wine he drank, calling it 'bottled poetry.' You know that quote."

"I didn't realize this was the place," I said. "And I'd forgotten it was his honeymoon."

He gave me another look like I'd just lighted the fuse to a stick of dynamite.

"Maybe we should change the subject. Maybe I should call Brooke." I got out my phone and thumbed through the contacts.

He pulled into a parking space on the main street of Calistoga in front of a restaurant called Café Sarafornia. "You did tell her I'm coming, didn't you?"

"I didn't tell her anything. I haven't talked to her yet. Mick made the arrangements. I told you that."

"So she has no clue?"

"No, she doesn't. Why, is it going to be a problem? She might not sell me the wine if you're involved?"

I shouldn't have baited him like that, but he asked for it. He got out of the car and slammed the door.

"Don't do that," I said. "Don't slam the door like that. And if you want to go with me, fine. If you don't, I'll get a cab and go myself."

I picked up my cane as he opened my door.

"This isn't the big city, sweetheart. You don't just step out into the street and wait for a taxi to pull over." His voice was curt.

"Don't worry, I'll figure it out, just like I always do," I said. "If you're going to walk out on me."

I didn't say "again," but I might as well have done.

"That was low," he said. "And if you don't want me to come along, it's no skin off my nose."

"You know, I don't care what you do anymore. You don't want to commit to this, either, suit yourself."

"What 'either'?"

"You know damn well what 'either.' I'm talking about everything. Us. The vineyard. Virginia. All of it." By now I was practically shouting at him.

An elderly couple passing by swiveled their heads and gave me reproachful looks like I'd been talking in the middle of the church sermon. I lowered my voice. "I'm done asking, okay? Do whatever you want, but just make up your damn mind and let me get on with my life."

"What the—?"

"I'm calling Brooke." I punched the button to my phone. "And telling her I'll be there and maybe I'll have someone else with me, or not."

He clenched his jaw and I knew he was biting back something that would only throw more gasoline on the fire.

"Fine," he said. "I'll come. But don't blame me if this blows up when she sees me and shows us the door."

"I thought she had a mad crush on you."

He shot a look at me and something dark simmered behind his eyes. "Yeah," he said, finally. "She did."

Brooke Hennessey's vineyard was easy to spot from the main road, even without the hand-painted sign. On either side of the gated entrance a pair of Don Juan rosebushes bloomed profusely, their espaliered masses of velvety red flowers brilliant against a white brick wall. Quinn turned down a drive lined with silvery-green olive trees that ended in a small, new-looking parking lot. A fresh coat of white paint gleamed on a post-and-board fence separating the parking lot from an orchard of apple and peach trees.

We hadn't said more than ten words to each other during and after lunch, but Quinn could have warned me about the winery. It was hidden around a bend at the bottom of a hill, masked by a pathway lined with wrought-iron arches graced by pastel climbing roses twining through them. The building looked like a miniature castle that had been plucked from old Europe, or a fairy tale. The mottled stone façade with its mossy crenellated parapet, multiple turrets, and two gargoyles leering at us from weathered corbels startled me so much that I stopped walking and stared at it.

"A change from your classic California mission architecture, huh?" he said.

If we were going to get through this meeting, we at least needed to be speaking to each other even though the lunchtime tension still hung in the air between us, thick as fog.

"You've been here before?" I was polite, but we had clearly drawn boundary lines.

"Nope. I've heard about it. Everybody around here knows it. Built by an eccentric guy with a trust fund and a taste for the slightly weird and offbeat. I think his family owned railroads in Canada. He blew through all his money before he ever finished the main house—that place is a real doozy. Kind of Gaudí meets Disney. The stories went that it had doors on the upper levels that opened to absolutely nothing and staircases that ended in midair since the workers just stopped construction from one day to the next," he said. "For years it was an abandoned ruin that kids used as a place to get high or have sex. Then about ten years ago someone from the Central Coast bought the property and planted vines. They must have sold to Fargo, who, in turn, sold to Brooke."

"What happened to the house with the doors and stairs to nowhere? Was it ever finished?"

He shrugged and held the door. "I guess we'll find out when you ask for the nickel tour, won't we?"

I walked past him and said coolly over my shoulder, "Yes, I guess we will."

Brooke Hennessey looked up from doing paperwork at a bar on the other side of the room when she heard us come in. A shaft of light from an open leaded glass window lit her profile so that she looked like the medieval princess who inhabited the castle—heavy brows, dark long-lashed eyes, exquisite cheekbones, an aquiline nose, a serious mouth.

"Can I help you—?"

Her gaze shifted from me to Quinn and her hand flew to her throat.

Allen Cantor hadn't been kidding about Brooke being a knock-out. She was tall and slender, dressed in well-fitted black shorts that showed off long, tanned legs and a white T-shirt with a deep V-neck that hugged willowy curves. For a moment I could have sworn she was the younger sister of Quinn's beautiful ex-wife, Nicole.

I heard Quinn breathe "whew" next to me as Brooke flew across the room and threw herself in his arms.

"Quinn! Where have you been? Oh, my God, it's been ages. I've missed you so much."

Quinn's arms went around her like he was afraid she was going to break. So much for worrying about his presence screwing up this deal. Finally, he disentangled himself and introduced me.

Brooke blinked as she looked from Quinn to me, taking stock of my cane.

"You're the one who called just now," she said. "Lucie Montgomery. You're from Virginia." She turned to Quinn. "That's where you went when you left. You two know each other?"

"I've been the winemaker at Lucie's vineyard for the past few years," he said.

Brooke's mouth fell open and, for a second, her guard came down and I saw the old hurt in her eyes, how painful his departure must have been for her.

"Why didn't you call me?" Her voice held a quiet note of reproach. "I had no idea you were coming. How long are you going to be in California?"

I wondered how he planned to answer that.

"It's kind of complicated." He looked uncomfortable. "Hey, Brookie, do you think it would be possible to taste that Cab?"

She smiled at the affectionate use of the nickname, though the abruptness of the request seemed to take her aback.

"Sure, no problem. It's downstairs in the barrel room, of course. Or, as I like to call it, the dungeon." Her eyes flickered to my cane. "There's no elevator, only stairs. Is that, I mean—?"

"I can handle stairs. And dungeons."

"If you're sure."

It almost sounded like she wished I'd said I couldn't join them.

We'd reversed roles, Quinn and I, good cop, bad cop. Brooke was so captivated by him, so glad to see him again, that he probably could get a tour of her underwear drawer, if he'd asked. I had my doubts what she'd say if I inquired about Teddy Fargo's off-limits-to-the-public gardens. Quinn was going to have to finesse this for us.

The wine was good—very good—just as Charles had promised. Neither Quinn nor I said anything, but it couldn't have been Brooke's. Teddy Fargo—Theo Graf—had made it. I wondered why it hadn't crossed my mind before now.

It didn't take us long to figure out the blend we wanted. Brooke's eyes darted between the two of us and I caught the tiny flare of surprise as she realized how well we knew each other, how easily we slipped into a private, coded way of communicating that had been honed over the past four years.

After the paperwork was done, Quinn asked for a tour of the rest of the vineyard.

"I was hoping you'd ask." She flashed a flirty smile at him.

Her bright red four-seater all-terrain vehicle was out by the crush pad. I got in back before anyone could say anything, so Quinn climbed in the passenger seat next to Brooke. She started the engine and gave us an overview of her land, much of which was woods stretching up the steep slopes of the hills behind the winery. The Gaudí-style castle, still unfinished, sat at the end of a road that branched off behind the orchard. Her home was a small stone cottage that would have been intended for a groundskeeper in grander days.

The vines—she had only six acres, planted in Cab, Zinfandel, Chardonnay, and Sauvignon Blanc—were terraced on stepped fields that surrounded the winery on three sides. Her vineyard was small and compact, but as Allen Cantor had said, that's how she wanted it. I kept silent while she and Quinn talked about her trellising system, what she was doing for canopy management, her hopes for this year's harvest. She was tight for start-up money, which was obvious; otherwise she wouldn't have been selling her wine.

"The guy who owned the place before me was into organic pesticides." She turned the steering wheel and swung the ATV down the Zinfandel block. "I'm following what he did, though it drives my dad nuts. But, hey, there's no REI or PHI. It's better for the grapes, better for the environment."

REI stood for reentry interval, the amount of time after spraying before anyone could work safely in the vineyard; PHI was preharvest interval. Same thing. You couldn't harvest grapes that were still coated with a potentially lethal pesticide, so PHI was critical: no spraying of toxic substances permitted a certain number of weeks before harvest. The time interval depended on the product.

I knew that Quinn's eyes were rolling up into the back of his head as Brooke talked about organic spraying. He and I had the same discussion, regular as clockwork, every year: Organic pesticides may be better for people, but they aren't effective at killing pests or fungus, especially with the climate we have in Virginia. So decide what you want, he'd say to me. A decimated crop because we sprayed the vines with nontoxic *Bacillus thuringiensis,* an organic product that didn't require wearing masks or hazmat gear, or a guaranteed fruitful harvest because we suited up and used a heavy-duty pesticide that would really do the job, REI and PHI notwithstanding.

But Brooke had nudged open the door when she mentioned the previous owner, Teddy Fargo, and that was all I needed.

"So what did your predecessor use?" I asked. "Bt?"

"Yes," she said over her shoulder. "He was into some other stuff, too. Not just for the grapes, but for the gardens, especially the roses."

"Did any of it work?" Quinn asked. "Don't tell me he was one of those New Age weirdos who put bull semen in animal horns and planted them under the vines?"

I wanted to poke him for being ornery and changing the subject, but he wasn't sitting close enough so that I could do it unobtrusively.

"How'd you guess?" she asked. "You bury them at night during a full moon. After the ritual naked dance through the vineyard."

"You know, I've been thinking about trying that," I said.

Quinn looked incredulous. "You're not serious?"

Brooke caught my eye and grinned.

He caught on, finally. "All right, very funny. Both of you."

"You started it," she said. "You're just like Daddy. An unbeliever."

"Bull crap. That stuff's voodoo, say what you want. You got six acres, Brookie. How much naked dancing and planting under the full moon are you willing to do?"

She took a corner too fast—I think on purpose—and hit the brakes. Quinn and I grabbed on to our seats. "Six acres' worth. Eventually."

I needed to reroute the conversation back to Fargo. "I'm interested in what else the former owner used. Even if Mr. Skeptic here isn't."

"There used to be a greenhouse up there." Brooke pointed to one of the hills behind the vines.

"Where?" I asked. "It looks like nothing but woods and scrub."

"There's a dirt road that winds around behind those madrones if you follow the contours of the hill," she said. "It was private, out of sight. I think Ted was into crop modification, but he didn't want to experiment near the vines. He had a separate garden away from everything else."

"Experiment?" Quinn said. "What kind of crops?"

"I have no idea."

"Brookie, there are rumors the guy was growing marijuana here."

Her eyes flashed. "There's not a single marijuana plant anywhere on this property, okay?"

"Someone told me he grew black roses," I said. "Did he ever say anything about that?"

For a long moment she was silent. "I don't think so," she said finally. "I've seen everything that he left behind."

"What do you mean 'that he left behind'?" I said. Allen Cantor said Fargo destroyed anything to do with his drug business.

"What's with you two?" Brooke stopped the ATV and turned around and glared at me. Then her gaze swung back to Quinn. "Why so many questions about Ted? What's going on?"

"Do you know him?" I asked.

She drummed her fingers on the steering wheel. "I bought this place from him, didn't I? What do you think?"

"Where is he now?" Quinn said.

"Is he in trouble?" She folded her arms across her chest and looked stonily at Quinn. "What is this, a drug sting? Are you guys working undercover for DEA?"

We'd pushed too hard. I tried to make a joke out of it. "If we were, we obviously aren't very good at it, are we? Look how fast you made us."

"Come on, Brooke." Quinn touched her arm. "We're just wondering if you know where he is. He's gone missing ever since he sold you this place."

"Why do you care? Does he owe you money?"

Quinn cut a look in my direction. "No, he doesn't. And it's kind of a complicated story."

"Go on."

"I'm sorry," I said. "We can't."

Brooke stared out at the place where Fargo's greenhouse had been.

"He told me that if anyone came around asking about him that I'd be smart to keep my mouth shut. I thought he was kidding, but I guess I was wrong." Her voice wavered and she looked into Quinn's eyes. "I wasn't expecting the person who asked to be you."

Quinn rubbed her shoulder like he was comforting a child. "You know about the drugs, don't you, kiddo? He was a dealer and he grew the stuff right here."

"I don't know. Maybe. He burned some fields and cleaned out the greenhouse and the lab before he left. Then he tore down those places, too."

I sat up straight. This was the first I'd heard about a laboratory.

"Why did he have a lab? What did he do there?" I asked.

"It's where he made the pesticides. What did you think? That it was a meth lab?" She sounded irritated.

"God, no."

"The only drug I heard about was weed," she said. "One of these days they're going to legalize it in California. There are people who say alcohol is worse. I'm not going to judge what he did, but I'm no dealer and I don't grow it."

"What about the burned field? What was there?" Quinn said.

"Presumably his marijuana crop. He put barbed wire around that field; it wasn't much land, half an acre, and nailed up KEEP OUT signs. Warned me not to go near it or let my dog or any animal near there," she said.

"Did he say why?" Quinn asked.

"Told me he was worried about some of the stuff he'd experimented with. He wasn't sure about the REI. Said it could be a really long time."

That didn't make sense.

"But why worry about that if he was using organic pesticides on the vines and gardens?" I said.

Brooke gave an impatient flick of her hand and started the ATV. "Look," she said, "I don't need to be cross-examined by either of you. Whatever Ted did or grew or experimented with, it's all gone now. Legal, illegal, whatever. You can't see where it was from here and it was on private property. So what the hell? Are we done now?"

There was no point asking her if we could see where the lab and greenhouse had been, or even the field with its barbed-wire fence and KEEP OUT signs. No one spoke as she drove us back to the Porsche.

"I'm sure Mick Dunne will be in touch with you in the next day or two about the wine," I said.

"Fine." She'd clammed up.

I caught Quinn's eye. "I'll wait in the car."

I got into the Porsche and heard his voice, low and soothing, talking to Brooke. I didn't catch what he said, or her murmured replies, but he seemed to be comforting her and she was still upset. Finally, he put a hand on her shoulder again and she nodded.

"Be seein' you," he said and kissed her forehead.

He didn't say anything to me until we were back on the Silverado Trail.

"She's worked up. We shouldn't have gone at her like that."

"I'm sorry. I know she is. But it does sound like Teddy Fargo could have been Theo Graf, don't you think?"

He shrugged. "No black roses."

"The guy had a lab where he made pesticides."

"The guy was into drugs. A lab comes in useful. Saying he used it as a place to make pesticides for his garden could be just to keep people off his back."

"Then he disappears and tells her not to talk to anyone about him?"

"I repeat. Drugs." He gave me an ominous look. "What are you going to tell Charles? All he wanted to know was whether there were any black roses and now you know the answer is no."

"I don't know what I'm going to tell him," I said. "This has gone down a whole different road from what we expected."

"I think it's over." Quinn spoke with finality. "Charles was barking up the wrong tree. Let it go. If Fargo, or whoever he is, finds out Brooke talked to us about his little side business and his cash crop, and you get Charles and some of his spook friends involved—"

He left that remark hanging on purpose, but I knew what he meant. Leave it alone. Walk away.

I nodded, but we both knew that was no longer possible; I needed to finish this. Wherever it led, whatever the consequences.

Even if it included losing Quinn.

CHAPTER 18

⎯⎯ ⬢⬢⬢ ⎯⎯

We didn't talk about Brooke or Charles or Teddy Fargo for the rest of the trip to Robert Sanábria's guesthouse, which took all of ten minutes. The private drive off Highway 29 was so well screened from view that Quinn missed the turn and had to double back; then we nearly drove past the cottage, which was at the end of a small cul-de-sac. The rustic house with its weathered gray shingle roof and ivy-covered chimney was shaded by a giant redwood whose enormous branches enveloped the place like we were in a tree house. Quinn parked under a portico of logs and rough-hewn beams that was long enough for another car to pull in behind us.

"Bet this was a Prohibition roadhouse, the way it's so well camouflaged in the woods," he said. "It's close to the highway but tucked far enough away so the cops wouldn't see any lights or cars."

"Pépé told me Robert lives at the top of the hill at the end of this private road," I said.

"Yeah, it's supposed to be quite a place."

He set my suitcase next to the front door.

"I'll call you after you get back to Virginia," he said. "Make sure the rest of the trip went okay."

I nodded. "I'll see you in a few weeks for harvest."

He looked as uncomfortable as I felt.

"Yeah, we'll talk about dates and all that stuff."

"Great."

"See you then."

"Quinn—" I touched his arm.

"What?"

"I'm sorry about what happened today. I don't want it to ruin the rest of the trip, everything we did together."

"I understand."

I closed my eyes and wished he'd said he agreed or it hadn't spoiled anything or not to worry. He sounded so formal and closed to me, a stranger. I tried not to think about last night in his bed or the shower together this morning as he bent and brushed my cheek with his lips.

"Tell Charles he got it wrong about Fargo when you get home," he said as he got in the car.

"What about Maggie Hilliard and Stephen Falcone?"

"They've got nothing to do with Fargo." His eyes locked on mine, a challenge. "Even if he is Theo Graf, which we don't know and now won't. You said yourself that Charles admitted Graf was gone by the time Maggie's car went off the bridge, and he wasn't at the lab the day Stephen died."

"I know that."

"But you're still going to ask him about Maggie and Stephen, aren't you? Now that you know about that affair."

"Yes."

"Dammit, Lucie, you don't have to."

I thought about the photo of Stephen. His smile and the trust in his eyes.

"I think I do."

If I'd never seen that picture, maybe I'd agree with Quinn right now. But I had. Whatever Quinn and I were on the verge of repairing in our relationship was about to break apart one more time.

His voice was harsh. "You're not going to change anything. It won't bring them back."

"I know nothing will bring them back, but I still think it matters. *They* matter."

He lifted his hands off the steering wheel, and for a moment I thought we were at the beginning of another soul-wrenching argument. Then he let them fall and hit the wheel with an exasperated finality before he started the engine.

He kept his eyes straight ahead as he drove out of the portico and snaked back in front of the cottage to the main driveway. I caught a glimpse of his angry, unyielding profile and heard him gun the engine, on purpose, as he roared out onto the highway.

Then he was gone.

I picked up my suitcase and went inside Robert Sanábria's guest cottage. Large and airy, it smelled faintly of lemony furniture polish and woodsmoke. Soft tree-filtered light flickered through a picture window and made patterns like moving water on the polished hardwood floor and scattered tribal carpets. The centerpiece of the room was a stone fireplace that nearly filled an entire wall; the mantel held pillar candles melted to various heights, framed photographs, and a dried-flower arrangement. The furniture was large, masculine, and comfortable looking. A gold tinsel ball, probably left over from Christmas, hung from a chandelier in the middle of the ceiling, spinning lazily when it caught a draft of air from the open front door. A grape-colored doormat at my feet read, WE SERVE ONLY THE FINEST CALIFORNIA WINES. *DID YOU BRING ANY?*

Pépé had left me a note on the coffee table; he was up at the main house having drinks with Robert and I was invited to join them. Otherwise, the three of us were dining together at seven P.M. at a restaurant in Calistoga.

I found my bedroom, a cozy room in the back of the cottage with windows on two sides overlooking a small garden. Right now I didn't feel like having drinks or dining with anyone. I threw myself on the king-sized bed and lay there.

The next thing I knew, my grandfather was shaking my shoulder, waking me from a deep sleep.

The dinner with Pépé and Robert Sanábria passed in a merry-go-round blur of conversation, fabulous food, and even more fabulous wine. We went to the restaurant in the Mount View Hotel, a sleek and elegant place where the staff greeted Robert as an old friend.

He was about twenty years younger than Pépé, in his early

sixties, soft-spoken, and unpretentious. I liked the jaunty way he swung a bottle of his own private reserve Cab between his fingers as we walked into the dining room and the respect the waiter showed as he took it away to open it and let it breathe before our dinner. Robert gave me a slow, mischievous wink, deliberately and delightfully flirting as we sat down, and thereafter proceeded to charm me for the rest of the evening. Pépé and I had not yet spoken about Charles or Teddy Fargo. By the time we finished our appetizers, even that last tense scene with Quinn receded like a dream whose details had grown cloudy in my mind.

We lingered over dinner, talking and laughing as the restaurant reverberated with the noisy chatter of arriving dinner guests who knew Robert and one another, calling greetings, stopping by our table to be introduced. Robert took care of ordering as the waiters effortlessly slid little plates of fish and meat and vegetables in front of the three of us; my wineglass was never empty.

We had brandy back at the cottage, though by then I was more than a little tipsy. In a moment of recklessness I went into my bedroom on the pretext of getting a sweater and called Quinn. I shouldn't have done it; it was stupid and I knew it. His phone went to voice mail and I left a goofy, inebriated message that I couldn't remember ten minutes later.

I slept as soon as my head touched the pillow—in French we call it "sleeping on both ears"—as though I'd been drugged. When I woke at five thirty to my phone alarm going off, Pépé was already moving about in the bathroom. I sat up, with a hazy memory of Robert promising that his housekeeper would bring breakfast down from the big house at six, and then his limousine would be at the cottage door at six thirty to take us to the airport.

My grandfather is not a morning person—though he's not grumpy, a conversation consists mostly of monosyllabic grunts—and I was still tired from the past two whirlwind days. So we padded around the cottage in silence, getting dressed and packing our bags, until a young woman showed up at the front door with a picnic basket containing a plate of steaming-hot scones with fresh butter and homemade blackberry jam, and a thermos of jasmine tea from Robert's favorite tea shop in Chinatown.

The limo came at six thirty sharp. Robert followed the driver down in a Jeep to say goodbye. He and my grandfather embraced, and then he turned to me, bending in for a kiss. The damp chill of the early morning fog clung to him, mingled with cypressy cologne, and his lips were cold on my cheeks.

"Take care of him, Lucie," he said in my ear.

He stood on the front steps and watched the big car pull away from the portico, catching my eye and flashing a thumbs-up, just before we turned the corner and he vanished from view as the red-wood forest swallowed up the big car.

I leaned my head on my grandfather's shoulder and slept. The next thing I knew it was light outside and we were at the airport. My phone rang as a porter took our bags from the limousine driver. I glanced at the display: Mick Dunne. He hadn't wasted any time. I slipped the phone into my purse, letting it go to voice mail.

We got to the gate an hour before the flight was scheduled to leave. I got Pépé settled far enough away from a blaring television that he could resume reading the thick document he'd started in the limo, no doubt given to him by someone at the Bohemian Grove, and told him I'd find two ridiculously expensive cups of coffee for us somewhere on the concourse.

I got in a long line at a place called SFO Java and called Mick.

"How did it go? What'd you think of the wine?" he said.

"You'll be happy. It's very good. Quinn and I agreed on the blend yesterday. You just need to call Brooke Hennessey and set it up."

"If it's that good, maybe she'd be willing to sell more than we agreed on," he said.

"Ask her."

"Be a love and take care of it for me, will you?"

"I don't think—"

"Damn, there's my other line. Look, darling, it's a chap I've been trying to reach for two days. He's calling from London and I've got to take this. Ring me back after you speak with Brooke, all right?"

He hung up and I moved to the front of the coffee line. While I waited for two cafés au lait, I found Brooke's number and called.

She answered after a few rings, sounding sleepy. " 'Lo?"

"Brooke, it's Lucie Montgomery. I'm sorry, is this a bad time?"

"No . . . wait, hang on a second, will you? I just need to throw on a pair of jeans."

"You can call me back—"

I heard the male voice in the background asking something, then her giggle and a murmured reply.

"Two cafés au lait." Someone called my order and set the coffees on the bar.

I felt like I couldn't breathe. "Sorry, I've got to go. My flight's leaving and I've got to get back to the gate. Mick Dunne will call you to sort this out."

I disconnected before she could reply and grabbed the cardboard carton with the coffees, nearly tipping one of them over as I did. A man next to me reached out and saved the cup just in time.

"You all right?" he asked.

"Yes, fine. Thank you so much." I stuffed a bunch of napkins into the carton and fled.

The male voice on the other end of the receiver had been muffled, but of course I recognized it.

Quinn.

CHAPTER 19

———⌀⌀⌀———

I didn't even make it to the gate when my phone rang again. This time it was Quinn. I had no intention of taking that call. Not now, not ever.

He hated commitment, any commitment, so he had done what he always did when he felt the walls closing in. Found some sweet young nymph and had a quick roll in the hay to prove he was still free and unfettered. I knew all his girlfriends; he always picked someone who wanted to have fun without getting serious. No strings attached, no hard feelings when it ended.

The phone beeped that I had a message. Pépé looked up from his reading and I handed him his coffee.

"*Quelque chose ne va pas, chérie?*" he asked. "*Tu as l'air troublée.*"

"Nothing's wrong," I said. "I'm fine. I spilled one of the coffees, so it was a mess. That's all."

He nodded and went back to his papers. I walked over to the window where I watched our plane pull up to the gate and deleted the message without listening to it. Then I drank my coffee and waited to board our flight back to Virginia.

Pépé and I finally talked about Teddy Fargo on the plane, cocooned in the relative privacy of our first-class seats, our quiet voices inaudible to anyone sitting near us above the noise of the engines. My grandfather pressed his hands together in front of his lips as though he were praying as I took out the blurry photographs of the Man-drake Society and laid them on his tray table.

I waited while he studied them, wondering what he'd finally say, since I'd colored way outside the lines, bringing Quinn in on this, tracking down Allen, and searching Mel Racine's wine vault.

"Whoever this guy was—Fargo or Graf—apparently he was into drugs. He was growing marijuana in the hills behind his vineyard and he was dealing," I said. "That's why he disappeared. Charles got it all wrong."

"But Charles was right that Teddy Fargo was Theo Graf, wasn't he?"

"I don't know. I'm not sure."

"You are sure. I can tell. You just don't have proof, any more than Charles did."

I pulled out the last two photos.

"Stephen Falcone." I set down the yearbook portrait.

My grandfather focused on it, nodding.

"And this one." I placed the explicit photo in front of him. "Charles never said a word about his affair with Maggie Hilliard, who was Theo's girlfriend. I wonder why he lied about it. I also wonder if he lied about being at the beach house the night she died."

Pépé's expression shifted from shock to disgust. He flipped over the picture and shoved it to a corner of the tray table.

"Where did you get that?" His voice was sharp. "Juliette must never see it."

"Mel Racine had it."

"You took it to blackmail Charles?"

I blushed. "I took it because it proves he lied."

"And what do you expect to do with it?"

"I'm not sure," I said. "But I think Charles lied about a lot of things."

"Such as?"

"Such as, if he was keeping track of everyone in the Mandrake Society, wouldn't he know that Teddy Graf disappeared because of the drugs? Especially if he thought Graf was really Theo?"

"Maybe he didn't know about the drugs." My grandfather still sounded angry. "As for why he said nothing, Charles operates on a need-to-know basis with everyone, including his wife. Surely you've figured that out by now?"

"Please, Pépé, don't shoot the messenger. Whose side are you on?"

"Yours," he said, "but I am thinking in the same calculated manner Charles would."

"I'd like to know why he lied about the affair with Maggie. It would have been useful to know he was involved with Theo's girlfriend before he sent me off to California to check out whether Theo was still alive and living under an alias."

"It probably never occurred to him you'd find out about it."

"Well, I did."

"Charles's womanizing, his *petites amies,* has always been an open secret. It destroyed his first marriage. Juliette knew about it, but she believed she could change him, and, of course, she was wrong. His infidelities hurt her deeply, even if he is discreet."

Charles was discreet, all right. A private lodge in the woods and a groundskeeper who drove guests home after hours and kept his mouth shut.

"You don't like him, do you?" I said.

"He is the husband of a very dear friend. If I want to see her, I have to spend time with him, *n'est-ce pas?*"

He'd avoided the question. But that was Pépé, a gentleman who would never behave improperly toward another man's wife, who believed in the sanctity of marriage, that the traditional vows—for better or worse, 'til death do us part—meant what they meant.

A flight attendant set down our menus and began taking drink orders for the first-class passengers at the front of the cabin. I scooped up the photos and tucked them into my purse.

"Since I presume you are going to show Charles this photo, or at least make him aware of it, suppose he admits the affair with Maggie?" Pépé said. "What of it?"

"I'm betting he knows what really happened the night she died."

Pépé steepled his fingers and I wished I could read his mind. So far our conversation had been like a lawyer gently cross-examining a nervous witness, giving no hint that the hammer was about to come down.

"And you believe he will make a confession to you? Lucie, don't be naïve." He leaned back in his seat. "He won't say a word."

The rebuff stung, even if it was probably true. "If Charles had any culpability in Maggie's death, he's managed to get away with it a very long time. I think he's worried Theo discovered something that could incriminate him and the truth will finally come out," I said.

"Theo is gone and Charles won't talk. Nothing will come out." Pépé sounded just like Quinn. "You don't need to get involved. And you haven't told me why you are so sure this man Fargo is Theo Graf."

"Teddy Fargo had training as a chemist. He set up a lab where Brooke said he made his own organic pesticides."

"You saw it?"

"No. When he left, he destroyed it and a greenhouse. He also burned a field and put barbed wire around it. What do you bet he grew marijuana on that land?"

"What did I tell you? You can't prove anything, not even the drugs."

"No."

"Then forget about it, *ma belle*. It's finished. Why bother now, after all this time?"

"Because if Maggie had lived she would have made sure Stephen Falcone's death wasn't swept under the carpet. After she died no one was left to speak up for him anymore. Charles erased Stephen like he was a lab experiment gone wrong."

My voice cracked and Pépé laid a hand on my arm. Now I was the one who was angry. "People who are handicapped don't get a break in life, you know? You're treated as less than a whole person, not quite good enough because you're deformed or, if you're mentally disabled, you're slow and stupid. Or your behavior is bizarre. Somehow it's your fault, or else you're too dumb to realize how different you are so people think they can talk in front of you the way they talk in front of a pet. You don't have emotions or feelings like 'normal' people—"

I couldn't stop talking, trying to make him understand the harsh twilight universe of the disabled where everyone rushes past you—all those perfect people—and you just can't keep up, though you want to so badly. Stephen's world wasn't my world exactly, and my very minor disability paled in comparison to what he lived with, but I understood it well enough to be outraged at how he had been taken advantage of and used.

Pépé covered my hand with his. *"Chérie,"* he murmured. "It's okay."

My voice had grown steadily louder and more ragged. The woman across the aisle glanced up from her copy of *Cosmopolitan,* a look of surprise and annoyance flashing across her face. Any moment I was going to start crying like a child for someone I never knew who died more than four decades ago. It was crazy.

Pépé pulled a neatly folded linen handkerchief out of his pocket and handed it to me. I dabbed my eyes and blew my nose.

"All right, tomorrow we'll call Charles," my grandfather said, in the voice he used when I was a child who'd skinned my knee or been tormented by Eli and his friends, "and pay him a visit. I can stay on for an extra day or two until this is resolved."

"Something to drink? Sir? Miss?" Our flight attendant stood next to us.

"Champagne," Pépé said. "For two."

It was just past noon Pacific time; three hours later at home.

"Why champagne?" I asked.

"Because, as Napoleon said, in victory you deserve champagne and in defeat you need it," he said. "After what you just told me, I believe a glass of champagne would be a good idea, though I can't decide whether it's because we deserve it or we need it."

"Maybe a little bit of both," I said. "Either way, it's still a good idea."

But it was Charles who called first. He didn't waste any time, phoning Pépé the next morning as we were finishing breakfast on the veranda. I was on my third cup of coffee, lounging in the glider and still groggy from so little sleep the last few days. My grandfather had astonished me by rising before noon. He sat across from me, smoking a Gauloise in the love seat where he could watch the mountains change color as the early-morning sky deepened behind them.

I heard the faint buzz of his cell phone vibrating. He pulled it from his pocket, frowned at the display, and answered. I knew at once who it was by the tightening of his lips. Their conversation, in French, lasted less than a minute.

My grandfather disconnected and said in a disgusted voice, *"Quelle cochonnerie."*

"What do you mean, 'what rubbish'? Are you talking about Charles?"

"I don't understand him. He agreed to join us for a drink at five o'clock this evening at the Goose Creek Inn, only because I insisted on a face-to-face meeting. He can't stay long because he and Juliette are attending a political fund-raiser in Georgetown."

I raised an eyebrow and sipped my coffee. "That's awfully cocky of him. I would have thought he'd want another clandestine meeting in his lodge as soon as possible."

"Actually, he didn't want a meeting at all."

Pépé lit another Gauloise with sharp, jerky motions. It took me a moment to realize he was really angry.

"You're kidding? What did he say?"

"He asked how the trip to the Bohemian Grove went and whether we had a good time in California."

"That's it? Nothing about Teddy Fargo?"

"He said, 'Oh, that. Don't give it another thought, Luc.' Like it was something *I* was concerned about. What a nerve he has."

I was stunned. "What's going on?"

He blew out a cloud of smoke. "I guess that's what we're going to find out later today."

He was still upset. I opened my mouth to say something that would calm him down, but from inside the house I heard footsteps clattering down the grand staircase, followed by Eli's deep voice and Hope's giggles and squeals. Pépé met my eyes, a tacit agreement. End of conversation.

"Daddy, Daddy! *Noooo!* I don't want to walk. Carry me. Now!"

Eli laughed and there were more happy shrieks from Hope as the screen door banged and the two of them came outside. He was carrying Hope dangled over his shoulder; my brother unshaved and tousle headed, his daughter's long, dark hair swirling around her like a cloud, baby doll pretty in pink shorts and a ruffled top. Her chubby hands clutched his shirt.

Pépé stubbed out his cigarette at once, a smile creasing his face, and I held up my arms for my niece.

Eli and Hope had moved in while we were in California. When we got home last night just after midnight, I'd been startled to find her rocking horse in the middle of the foyer—I thought a fox had gotten inside until I turned on the light—and the contents of a doll-house had been strewn throughout the room. The child herself was snug in her new room where she'd been asleep for hours, but Eli had come padding downstairs in a pair of shorts and a Virginia Tech T-shirt to join us for a nightcap.

"Here," Eli said to me now, flopping Hope onto my lap. "I've got a delivery for you. A sack of potatoes. Watch out, though. It wiggles."

"Da-*dee*! I'm not a sack of 'tatoes, am I, Aunt Woozy?"

"No, you most certainly are not." I hugged her tight, kissing her soft cheek and rocking the glider back and forth with my good foot. "Give Beppy a kiss, too, angel. We missed you when we were in California."

She jumped up and obeyed.

"You two are up early," Eli said. "What's up, Wooze?"

I made a face at him. "There's coffee in the pot for you, sun-shine. Frankie must have dropped off croissants for our break-fast late yesterday because they were fresh, unless you went by Thelma's?"

"Uh, you can thank Frankie," he said, coloring a little. "We, uh, had a couple with our dinner. Last night was the first time we actu-ally ate here."

"I hope you got takeout. I don't think there was much in the fridge."

"I found some mac and cheese in a box in the pantry."

"Good Lord, you didn't! I was going to throw that stuff out. Did you check the sell-by date? Frankie and I cleaned out the kitchen in the winery last week. Everything in that box was Quinn's. It looked like he was getting ready for the aftermath of Armageddon with all the provisions he had stored there. Most of it was junk food."

"I guess that explains the ten packages of beef jerky and all those boxes of toaster pastries."

"What," Pépé asked, "is a beef jerky?"

"Dried, cut-up shoe leather," I said. "Comes in different flavors to disguise the actual taste."

"It's guy food," Eli told him. "Women don't appreciate it. I bet it doesn't have a sell-by date, either. It's good for years."

"Right, and it probably doesn't break down in landfills if you ever throw it out. It'll be around in the next millennium when aliens land on Earth to study the extinct human race, which died out from a diet of hydrogenated fat, processed white flour, and refined sugar."

Eli rolled his eyes. "I take it you won't mind if I move Quinn's box into the carriage house? I've nearly got the place set up as an office. You have no idea how long I can keep going at one in the morning with a couple of Twinkies, a can of Red Bull, and a package of chipotle-flavored beef jerky."

"Gross, that's just so gross, Eli, but be my guest." Hope left Pépé's side and came back over to climb onto the glider. I stroked her hair and pulled her to me. "What are you going to do today, sweet pea?"

"Play with Daddy," she said, smiling. "And my dolls."

Eli scooped her up. "First we're going to have breakfast," he said. "And then Daddy will play with you. But after that, I have a new friend for you. Her name is Jasmine. You're gonna like her, honey. She'll play with you this afternoon while Daddy has a meeting for his work. Okay?"

Eli caught my surprised look. "Hey, Luce, chill, okay? I talked to Jasmine and she agreed to babysit if she was free. Cheaper than day care, and she's a sweet kid. I think it will work out fine."

"Uh-huh. My, what big teeth you have, Grandpa. You could have asked me to babysit."

"You were in California."

"I'm here now."

"It's all worked out with Jasmine," he said. "She's babysitting for a couple of hours this afternoon before her shift at the Inn. Tomorrow she's going to be here from two o'clock on to set up for that Hundred-Mile dinner you and Dominique have got going on, so she said Hope can spend some time with her while I check on a job site. She might help me out on the weekend, too. After that, we'll see how it goes."

He sounded huffy and a little self-righteous. Eli and I knew each other so well we could practically finish each other's sentences. How it was going to go was that next he'd be asking Jasmine on a date. I'd seen the way he looked at her the other night at the dance. He'd been captivated.

"Daddy, what's wrong?" Hope asked. "You look all puffed-up, like a fishy."

She made a face like she was about to explode. Eli's eyes skittered across my face and I managed not to burst out laughing.

"A puffed-up fish? You don't say? Uh, sweetie, how about some breakfast, a nice toaster pastry? There might be some chocolate ones." He glared at me. "No comments from the peanut gallery, okay? We'll have the food pyramid discussion another time."

I made a face like a fish breathing in and out, then zipped my finger across my lips. He gave me another martyred look as the screen door slammed behind them, Hope's happy singsong chatter and Eli's patient answers receding until it was just Pépé and me again.

"*Elle est adorable,*" he said. "*Un trésor.*"

"She is adorable," I said. "I'm glad they're living here now, even if there are times when Eli and I want to kill each other like we did when we were kids."

He smiled. "Jasmine—the pretty, dark-haired girl who was helping Dominique at Charles's and Juliette's party?"

"Yes."

"Why don't you want her to babysit Hope?"

"I think I'm more worried about her babysitting Eli . . . which is what I think he has in mind, ultimately."

Pépé laughed. "Maybe you should let him make that decision for himself."

It wasn't often my grandfather pulled me in line.

"Fair enough." I shrugged. "I've talked to her for probably a total of fifteen minutes so it's not like I know her well. Dominique thinks the world of her, and I guess she'll be at the Inn this afternoon when we meet Charles."

Pépé sat back against the cushions of the love seat and stared at the long, low sweep of the Blue Ridge, exhaling dragon-fire smoke.

"Charles," he said, finally. "He has always been a vain man with a monstrous ego. But I have managed to overlook that—we all have our flaws—because he is also intelligent and very shrewd. He was an excellent ambassador for your country. And, of course, he's Juliette's husband."

"You care for her a lot, don't you?"

He nodded without looking at me. "She's not herself these days. I am worried about her."

"I can tell."

"You know, I once thought I'd do anything for her. All she had to do was ask. But now there's one thing I won't do."

"What's that?" I asked.

He turned to me with eyes full of pain. "Save Charles."

CHAPTER 20

---✺✺✺---

The Goose Creek Inn is tucked away like a secret in an L-shaped wooded bend on Foxcroft Road, next to the creek that gave the place its name. A rambling, half-timbered building surrounded by native flowering cherry trees and dogwoods, the front entrance has a tranquil Japanese garden with a small waterfall, a terrace framed by flower-filled border gardens, and an ivy-covered springhouse that is a favorite of wedding photographers. At night it is an enchanted jewel, with its graceful low profile and the surrounding trees limned by twinkling white lights like hundreds of tiny stars.

Pépé and I arrived half an hour before we were due to meet Charles so Dominique and I could go over some last-minute items before tomorrow's One-Hundred-Mile dinner. On Sunday, the day we flew to California, the *Washington Tribune* ran a front-page story in the Metro section about the economic benefits of shopping locally—focusing on our dinner that showcased only farms, dairies, and small businesses that grew or produced food within a one-hundred-mile radius of the vineyard. Kit had tipped me off about the piece, written by a colleague, but she hadn't warned me that it would feature us so prominently. Since then, Frankie told me, the phone had rung off the hook and tickets for the dinner were snapped up by Monday at noon.

My cousin led us to a table overlooking Goose Creek, now a thready trickle in a cracked streambed. Earlier in the day the wind had changed direction, wringing the humidity out of the air so that it was pleasant enough to sit outside. The annual summer serenade of the cicadas had bloomed into a full-fledged symphony in the few days since we'd been gone, and somewhere two tree frogs called to each other. A waiter brought out a tray with four glasses and a chilled bottle of white in a cooler.

When he pulled out the bottle I saw the label: California Sauvignon Blanc. I must have looked startled because Dominique said, "What's wrong, Lucie? Would you prefer something else? *Un verre de rouge?*"

"No, thanks; white's fine."

Why had that spooked me? Dominique knew nothing about my own bottle of wine being found next to Paul Noble's body, nothing about the Mandrake Society or Charles's setup, and what I'd been up to in California. Maybe it was just the coincidence and my nerves about the impending meeting with Charles.

"Jasmine will be out in a minute," Dominique said as the waiter filled three of the glasses. "She and Gilles are taking care of an emergency for a retirement party we've got here tonight. The two of them have been running around like children with their heads cut off."

"Oh, gosh, in that case don't bother her. I just wanted to give you the latest ticket sales information to make sure we agree on numbers and go over the menu one more time. Frankie told me you changed two dishes because some things weren't available anymore from a couple of the farmers."

"That's right," she said, "but we could have discussed this over the phone, you know. Not that I'm not glad to see the two of you."

"I know, but we're meeting Charles Thiessman at five for a quick drink. He wanted to hear about the California trip since he's the one who arranged Pépé's talk, then he's got to dash off to D.C."

Dominique's eyes widened in surprise. "Why didn't you wait until tomorrow when you'll have more time to talk? We're buying heaps of vegetables from Juliette's garden. She told me they're both planning to be at the dinner, especially because Pépé will still be in town. How odd that Charles didn't mention it."

I avoided looking at Pépé. Obviously he'd found time to call Juliette and let her know he'd postponed his trip home to Paris.

"I'm sure it slipped his mind." My grandfather calmly picked up his wine and drank. "Juliette's always been the one to take care of their social calendar. Charles probably forgot."

Dominique flipped open an overstuffed planner and pulled her cigarettes out of a pocket. "I suppose you're right. She's terribly organized but he seems a bit . . . not *there* sometimes."

It didn't take long to go over the dinner plans. My cousin was born with an ambitious list of goals to accomplish right out of the womb, and she'd remained an overachieving perfectionist ever since. She and I had finally found a way to work well together professionally—the Inn catered all the vineyard's parties and events—once I learned that getting her to relinquish control or delegate responsibility was probably a tougher sell than if Moses had asked God to reconsider one of the commandments. What surprised me was that she seemed to have ceded some of her power to Jasmine. I'd thought blood was blood and I'd be the first one she'd trust, but Jasmine must have done a hell of a job impressing Dominique to pull that off.

She was stubbing a cigarette butt into an ashtray when the waiter led Charles to our table. He was dressed country-club casual: kelly green Bermuda shorts, pink polo shirt, and boat shoes with no socks, so I guessed he'd need to go home to change before driving into D.C. for his fancy party. He really did expect this to be a quick-and-dirty chat.

For a moment he looked nonplussed to see the three of us sitting there, but Dominique jumped up and set the empty wine bottle and cooler on a tray.

"Please, have a seat. I was just leaving." She picked up her planner and slid the ashtray onto the tray. "Luc and Lucie told me they were expecting you, Charles. How nice to see you again. Please, all of you, order whatever you want; it's on the house. Thomas, will you take care of everyone and get them drinks? Oh, and Charles, I'll see you and Juliette tomorrow at the One-Hundred-Mile dinner, of course."

Charles clearly had no idea what she was talking about, but he put on a game face and nodded. "We'll try to drop by for a bit if we can."

Dominique froze until she caught my wink and didn't-we-tell-you look. "Please do," she said.

Charles sat down and we ordered—sparkling water for Charles and me, another glass of white wine for Pépé.

"I heard about your talk at the Grove, Luc," Charles said. "Bravo. You got kudos from everyone. Tough crowd to impress."

"You're very kind."

"Not at all. I mean it." Charles smiled and leaned back in his seat, crossing one leg over the other, a foot ticking back and forth like an overwound clock. "And, Lucie, I heard you made a deal with Brooke Hennessey. Sounds like everything went well."

"Checking up on us, I see?" I smiled back at him.

"I would be derelict in my duty if I didn't make sure it all worked out, wouldn't I?"

Thomas appeared with our drinks and vanished.

"I suppose you would."

Charles squeezed the lime from the rim of his glass into his fizzy water and said, without looking up, "Well, I'm glad you both had a good time."

"What happened, Charles?"

He picked up his glass. "What are you talking about?"

"What happened that you no longer seem interested in knowing whether Teddy Fargo is really Theo Graf? Or whether there were black roses growing at Rose Hill Vineyard?"

His smile was tolerant, almost patronizing. "How astute of you to pick up on that. The day before yesterday Teddy Fargo was shot to death in a warehouse in the Tenderloin district of San Francisco. Apparently a drug deal that went bad. I guess he moved on to the lifestyle of better living through chemicals." He rattled the ice cubes in his glass. "What a pity."

Neither Pépé nor I saw that one coming. I was speechless.

"So were there any?" Charles asked in a friendly tone.

Game, set, and match to him. What a bastard, not to say a word about Fargo's death until now. "Pardon? Were there any what?"

"Black roses. Were there black roses at his vineyard?"

"No," I said, "there weren't."

He finished off his drink in one long gulp. "It doesn't matter. It was still Theo. I know it was."

He stood up. "Thanks for your time. I hope you both had a good trip. I guess we're done here. Luc, see you on your next visit to the States. Or maybe Juliette and I will hop over to Paris sometime in the fall and we'll get together there. She missed seeing you when we were there over the winter, but I seem to recall that you were in Russia."

"Forgive me." I pulled the envelope with the photos out of my purse and set it on the table. "But we're not exactly done."

"Sit down, Charles," Pépé said. "Please."

Charles's eyes went immediately to the envelope. He looked at Pépé and me with the high-strung wariness of a cornered animal sensing a predator. "Juliette's waiting. I hope this won't take long."

He made a fuss about sitting down again, but at least he sat. Looking back, I'm pretty sure he already knew the ground had shifted, that the secret pact of silence he had enforced for so many decades was beginning to implode from the weight of years of guilt just when he'd almost gotten away with it for good. His eyes kept flicking to the envelope. I picked it up.

"Now that Theo Graf, or Teddy Fargo, is dead," I said, "you're the only one left who knows about the Mandrake Society."

A long pause while Charles assessed what cards I might be holding, if this was perhaps a colossal bluff. Finally he said in a cool, dry voice, "That's not entirely true. Now the two of you know about it as well."

It sounded faintly like a threat.

"While I was out in California," I said, "I found out that Mel Racine's wine vault was for sale down in Half Moon Bay, so I dropped by to see it."

He didn't need to know about Quinn. I took out the beach pictures of the gang and laid them on the table. "These were in his office."

Charles's jaw went slack with shock and his hand trembled as he picked them up one by one, holding each photo like something fragile that might disintegrate and blow away on the soft summer breeze.

"My God." His voice was barely a whisper.

"Did you take these pictures?" I asked.

He nodded, still staring at the photos. "With Vivian's camera.

She was the group photographer, but that day she asked me to take a couple of photos of all five of them. We were celebrating Maggie's birthday that weekend. She turned twenty-four."

"There were two more pictures among Mel's things. Not with these."

Charles looked up, and for a moment I'm sure he was expecting more the-way-we-were happy family snaps. Then I set them down in front of him, one at a time. First, Stephen's yearbook picture. Then the shot of him having sex with Maggie. I heard his intake of breath, like a sharp pain gripped him somewhere near his heart.

"How dare you?" His mouth compressed into a thin line and two vivid red spots flared on his cheeks. "You have no business—"

"No, Charles," Pépé said. "You set up my granddaughter, sending her on this errand of yours after inventing a story that suited your purposes. You made it her business."

"Why did you lie about your relationship with Maggie Hilliard?" I asked.

"I don't need to explain anything and I believe that concludes—"

Something seemed odd about his reaction. It took a moment until I figured it out.

"You've seen that photo before," I interrupted him. "The one of you and Maggie. You weren't shocked when you saw it, just by the fact that I had it—and that I found it in Mel's office." He didn't answer, so I kept going. "If Mel had a copy, who else did? Besides you, that is."

Charles folded his arms across his chest. "How the hell would I know who else had a copy?"

He was lying, but I let it pass for now.

"Who sent you this photo?" I asked. "Vivian took it, didn't she? You just said she was the group photographer."

He rested an elbow on the arm of his chair and laid two fingers across his mouth. I couldn't tell if it meant he wasn't going to talk or if he was trying to figure out how to play this based on what Pépé and I now knew.

"Excuse me, Lucie?"

We'd been so absorbed in our little drama I hadn't seen Jasmine Nouri walk across the terrace until she was standing in front of us, the friendly smile on her face fading as she seemed to realize she had stumbled into the middle of an angry private conversation.

"I beg your pardon," she said. "I thought I was supposed to meet Dominique here with you. Forgive me for being late. I guess I missed the meeting. And I apologize for intruding."

Pépé leaned forward resting an arm on the table so it covered the photographs. "No intrusion at all, my dear. We were just talking."

"Don't worry, it wasn't a real meeting. We were just wrapping up some last-minute details for tomorrow," I said.

"I see. I'll, um, check with Dominique." She took a step backward. "Can I bring anyone another drink?"

"I think we're fine," Pépé said. "Ambassador Thiessman needs to leave shortly."

"Of course. Nice to see you all again." She ducked her head goodbye and fled.

There was a moment of stunned silence before Pépé said, "She didn't see anything."

"Maybe she heard something." Charles sounded irritable.

"If she did, out of context it means nothing," my grandfather said.

"Juliette has no idea—" he began.

"No one is going to say anything to Juliette," I said. "And you were about to tell us who sent you the photographs, Charles. And who else has copies—that you know of."

He gave me a disgusted look. We both knew he hadn't been about to say anything. "They came in the mail."

"When?" Pépé asked.

"Around Christmas. The postmark was smeared. I have no idea where they were sent from."

"Did Paul Noble get photos as well?"

He glared at me without speaking.

"Is that why he killed himself?" I said. "Because someone decided to bring up Maggie's and Stephen's deaths after all this time when he assumed they had been forgotten?"

"He didn't confide in me," Charles said, "before he put the rope around his neck."

Pépé and I exchanged glances.

"But you did talk to him," Pépé said. "Or else you wouldn't have known he also got the photographs."

He sat there, stone-faced.

I'd had it. "Oh, for God's sake, Charles, don't you have a party in D.C. that you'd like to get to before Labor Day? Can we quit playing twenty questions? Who sent the pictures? Theo?"

He said with some disdain, "That's my guess."

"So you sent me to California to check out Teddy Fargo."

He waved a hand tiredly. "Yes, brilliant. You get a gold medal."

I ignored that. "Where did Teddy, or Theo, get them, then? Why would he hang on to them for all this time and send them to you, Mel, and Paul all of a sudden?"

"I imagine Vivian took the photo," he said. "So the picture would have originally been in her possession, don't you think?"

"But she died of a heart attack last winter, didn't she?" I asked.

"Yes, that's right. Look, none of this matters now anyway. So why don't we just forget it, all right?"

"What I don't understand," my grandfather said, "is why Vivian kept that photograph a secret for all these years."

"I have no idea," Charles said. "As I was saying, it no longer matters—"

"I know why," I said.

"What are you talking about?" Charles's voice was cold.

"I know why Vivian never showed anyone that photograph. Obviously your affair with Maggie had to be kept secret because she was Theo's girlfriend and you were married."

"What of it?" He sounded dismissive, but he watched me warily.

"Once Maggie died, if Theo saw that photo he'd have one more reason to suspect that her death wasn't an accident. Isn't that why your first wife divorced you? Because of your affairs? You couldn't afford to have this come out in the paper after Maggie drowned," I said. "You were there the night she died, weren't you?"

"No."

"I think you're lying."

"You don't know what you're talking about."

"Vivian, Mel, and Paul knew what really happened that night, didn't they? Did you leave with Maggie in her car? Maybe the others helped you cover up Maggie's death, stage it as an accident, in return for your promise that nothing would happen to them because of Stephen's death?"

Charles stood up, towering over me, his face blotchy and mottled with rage. "This conversation is *over*. Everyone involved is *dead*. It's finished, do you understand? Continue to pursue it—and that includes you, Luc, old friend—and I will see to it that you are very sorry indeed."

His angry footfalls receded on the flagstone, followed by a car door slamming and the whine of an engine as he roared out of the parking lot.

Pépé picked up his wine and downed what was left in the glass in one gulp. "You certainly got him stirred up, *chérie*."

"I'll bet he knows what happened to Maggie," I said. "And that her death was no accident."

"As I said yesterday, there's nothing you can do to prove it, Lucie," Pépé said.

"Oh, I wouldn't be too sure about that," I said. "You know what they say: When you want to dig up dirt, go find a worm."

"And where do you plan to find this worm?" he asked.

I don't know why the idea hadn't occurred to me until just now.

"Where else?" I said. "In a garden."

CHAPTER 21

———∞∞∞———

Pépé was uncharacteristically irritable on the drive home from the Inn so I dropped the subject of Charles until later that evening when we were sitting outside on the veranda after dinner. The idea to visit Noah Seely, an old family friend and one of the Romeos, at his eponymous garden center had been rattling around in my head ever since yesterday when we got home from the airport. Indirectly, I had Quinn to thank for it. He'd left another message on the answering machine at home. I saw the flashing light the moment I walked through the front door.

"I need to talk to you. Call me or else."

Two nights ago Quinn and I had been together. The next night he'd traded me for Brooke. I punched Delete harder than I needed to, knocking over the mail that had accumulated on the hall table while I was away.

Noah's slick-looking brochure had landed on top of the pile of bills, catalogs, and credit card offers that skidded across the floor. It was chock-full of news about what he'd been doing on behalf of the good people in our part of the Commonwealth of Virginia as our newly elected state senator in Richmond. There was also a survey, because my opinion mattered to him. I'd set it on the table to fill out later, but that brochure jogged something in my memory this afternoon as we left the Inn after the meeting with Charles.

During World War II, Noah had worked as a government

researcher before joining the family business. He'd been in intelligence. It was a long shot, but maybe he knew Charles back then.

I brought it up with Pépé as we were finishing off another bottle
of wine and watching the moonrise over the mountains.

I couldn't recall ever seeing my grandfather drunk—he could
hold his liquor better than anyone I knew—but tonight he'd set out
to get good and stewed and I left him to it. Hope was upstairs asleep
and Eli had gone out to the carriage house to finish some drawings
for a client, so the two of us sat there, while the flickering candlelight from the hurricane lamps cast a viscous glow over us like a
spell as Pépé smoked cigarette after cigarette, refilling his wineglass
as soon as it was empty. Later he switched to cognac. I quit keeping
pace with him long before then.

"Maybe Noah knew some of the members of the Mandrake
Society," I said. "He was also involved in the kind of hush-hush
medical research they were."

"Lucie, when you're part of the intelligence community, the
unbreakable rule you learn from day one is that everything is absolutely need to know," he said. "Even if Noah had the same top-secret
clearance Charles and the others did, you don't discuss your latest
project in the staff cafeteria over lunch. In English, it's called SCI,
sensitive compartmented information."

"Fair enough, but I don't care who you are and how many
walled-off secrets you keep, who is sleeping with whom—especially
if one of the people involved is married—is definitely fodder for
gossip. And that does get discussed in the cafeteria or around the
office coffeepot or in the bar after work."

"It was a long time ago." He stared into his wineglass. "And you
can be sure Charles did his absolute best to keep it quiet. Even Theo
didn't know about him and Maggie."

The wine was making him morose, melancholy.

"It's worth asking Noah."

"If you like."

He was lost in his own thoughts, barely aware of my presence.

I dropped the subject and went to bed at midnight, planting a
kiss on his head and telling him with as much tact as I could that I
hoped he wouldn't be up too late. At two I came back downstairs to

check on him. From the doorway I could see his elongated shadow in the diminished light of the guttering candles and the white curl of smoke from yet another Gauloise. A glass clinked against another glass and I knew he was probably pouring more cognac. I nearly went outside to try to coax him into calling it a night, but I wasn't sure I could bear seeing him as anything less than my strong, resolute grandfather—not shattered and grieving as he was now. Not for Charles, for whom I think he now had nothing but angry contempt, but for Juliette whom he loved but couldn't—wouldn't—tell her what he knew about her husband.

Much later I heard the creaky treads on the spiral staircase—only Eli, Mia, and I knew how to avoid the noisy ones, a skill honed as teenagers sneaking in or out after our curfews—and the faint crack the walnut banister made when someone leaned too heavily on it, as he slowly climbed the stairs in the dark. I lifted my head off my pillow so I could see the clock on my bedside table: four fifteen. Then I heard the click of his bedroom door closing, and not even the thinnest blade of light shining through the cracks into the hall.

After that, silence.

I drove over to Seely's Garden Center Friday morning first thing after breakfast, hoping to catch Noah in his rabbit-warren office in the alcove behind the customer service desk. Later he'd probably join up with the Romeos for lunch or happy hour at one of their many watering holes, and in between he'd drop by a senior citizens' center or visit some local business in his post-retirement job as our state senator. But I needed to talk to him when he was alone, not knee-deep in Romeos or constituents.

Virginia is a state that invokes the death penalty, and I'm not going to go into the politics and morality of how and why my home state—the place I grew up in and love fiercer than anywhere on earth—got there; it just is what it is. Noah was staunchly against capital punishment; an integral part of his campaign platform had been his promise to work to get it revoked in the Commonwealth.

I didn't find out the real reason behind his passion and commitment until a couple of the Romeos explained it one night in the bar of the Goose Creek Inn. During the war, Noah's research had involved testing the effectiveness of newly discovered antibiotics on human subjects. It later came out that some of the "volunteers"—prisoners and inmates in mental institutions—had been deliberately infected with awful diseases and, in the case of sexually transmitted diseases like syphilis, prostitutes had been used in the government's service.

Noah finally couldn't take it anymore—playing God and sacrificing one life to save others was wrong to him, whatever the noble motivation, so he left to take over the nursery from his father, a world of plants and trees and flowers that grew and flourished with the seasons, things that lived and brought beauty and pleasure. At Christmas, he dressed up as Santa Claus for as long as anyone could remember. Everyone under the age of fifty who lived in Atoka, Middleburg, and Leesburg, including Eli, Mia, me, and now Hope, had sat on his lap as a child, confiding our wished-for gifts, promising we'd been good all year.

Seely's Garden Center is a sprawling, luxurious place located at the intersection of Sam Fred Road and the Snickersville Turnpike in Middleburg, not far from where Goose Creek continues its meandering path toward the Potomac River. Even at nine o'clock in the morning, it was alive and busy with a few early-bird customers and staff taking care of the ritual morning chores of watering and dead-heading bedding plants, weeding display gardens, and sweeping the flagstone patios and walkways.

The main building looked like a cross between a log cabin and a barn, a big airy place that smelled of the tang of fertilizer and the steamy, vaguely tropical odor of hundreds of hothouse plants in the large adjacent greenhouse. A young girl working at a cash register told me Noah was in his office doing paperwork. His door was ajar so I knocked.

"Come!"

He pushed up a pair of reading glasses so they rested on his tanned, bald head and sat back in his chair as I walked in. "Lucie, my dear, how nice to see you. It's been awhile. What can I do for you?"

Noah and my mother had worked closely together many years ago when she set out to restore the blighted gardens at Highland

House, and later when she tackled more substantial landscaping projects at the vineyard and the Ruins. With the tens of thousands of dollars we'd spent at Seely's over the years, anytime anyone in my family or a vineyard employee came by, we got VIP treatment. But asking Noah to talk about the painful subject of his involvement in carrying out gruesome lab experiments on prisoners, albeit in the name of medical advancement that would prevent future deaths and suffering, wasn't the same as asking for advice on the color palette for the summer flowers in the courtyard.

There was no point being coy with Noah, and I hadn't rehearsed how I was going to bring this up, anyway.

"I got your latest brochure about the spring legislative session in Richmond," I said.

He sat up and folded his hands on top of what looked like a daunting pile of constituent mail and paperwork spread out across his old metal desk. Noah's office was even more cluttered than it had been when he ran the nursery full-time, with stacks of papers heaped in a semicircle on the floor around him and shoved into empty corners on the tiered shelf where he grew his prize collection of African violets.

"You fill out that survey, you hear? I presume you want to talk about my vote on the transportation bill?" he asked. "Believe me, I've been hearing about it."

I smiled. "I'll fill it out and no, it's nothing like that. I came to ask if you knew Charles Thiessman when you both worked for the government."

I waited for his reaction, which I figured could range from telling me he didn't discuss that period of his life anymore, so mind my own business, to stunned silence.

"I did," he said, after a moment. "Why in the world do you want to know?"

"Because I thought you might know some of the people he worked with."

"Care to be more specific?"

"A woman named Maggie Hilliard. She died in a car accident a little over forty years ago."

He didn't say anything at first, just stared at me—or maybe

through me—with a faraway, glassy-eyed look like an old movie reel he'd forgotten about had started playing in his head.

"How did you hear about Maggie Hilliard?"

Not a direct answer to the question, but an answer. And more than I'd hoped for.

"Charles told me about her."

"Really? And what did he say?"

"That she was part of a team of biochemists working on a classified project and he was their supervisor."

Noah pushed back his chair. At least one of the wheels needed oil. "Take a walk with me."

I followed him down a back corridor to the staff break room.

"I could use an extra jolt of caffeine this morning. Don't tell my cardiologist or she'll kill me before this stuff does," he said, patting his Santa belly. "Care for a cup of coffee?"

"Sure, thanks."

He gave me a to-go cup and poured two coffees from a half-full pot, adding a healthy dollop of chocolate-flavored creamer to his and a couple of sugars. I expected that we'd have our chat at the conference table in the middle of the room, but instead he unlocked a door that opened directly onto the back terrace. Under a large metal awning, massed pots of flowers were grouped by color on stepped shelves or spilled out of planters that hung from the rafters above our heads.

"Come on." Noah reached over and deadheaded a scarlet and purple fuchsia as we walked through the pavilion, tossing the spent blossoms in a trash can. Old habits obviously died hard. "Hope you don't mind a little walk."

He took me to the back lot where hundreds of slender young trees with their root balls wrapped in burlap formed a small, well-organized forest. The wind was soft and warm; the early morning sunlight made shifting patterns of light and dark through the fretwork canopy of the trees. We stopped in the middle of a small grove of pink and white dogwood.

"Make you a deal. I'll tell you what I can about what Maggie Hilliard was working on if you tell me what you know about what happened to her—and Charles Thiessman. I still can't go into detail, but there's plenty of stuff in the public domain that you could find out on the Internet, if you knew where to look."

"Why do you want to know about Maggie?" I asked.

"Why else? Your basic human curiosity." He took the lid off his coffee and swirled the cup around. "There were loads of rumors about that car accident. No one ever found out if any of them were true. Charles kept his yap shut all these years and so did the rest of that group of rebels working for him. I don't know how he did it."

"Wasn't keeping quiet about things the nature of your business?" I asked.

He smiled. "Of course it was. But hell, Charles could have sold the Sovs the combination to the nuclear codes and gotten away with it. He was like Teflon, nothing stuck to him. If he's finally willing to open up about what happened to that girl, I'd like to know."

"This needs to stay just between us, Noah. Please don't say anything to anybody."

He rolled his eyes. "First, I have some practice keeping secrets. Second, there aren't too many anybodies left to tell after forty years. And third, when have I ever let you down?"

"I didn't get that sled I wanted for Christmas when I was ten."

He grinned. "Once. Big deal. And I'm sure there was a very good reason, young lady."

I laughed. "Okay, fair enough."

"Ladies first," he said. "Please enlighten me. What did Charles tell you about Maggie's accident?"

I sipped my coffee. "He said she left a party drunk one night and drove her car off the bridge to Pontiac Island and drowned."

"Huh. The papers said that. That's nothing new."

"She was . . . romantically involved with Charles when it happened."

"As in having sex?"

My face turned red. "Yes."

"Want to tell me how you know?"

"A photograph."

"How interesting. Sets up the possibility of blackmail."

"Not at the time. The only person who knew about the photograph appears to have been the person who took it. That is, until very recently when the photo resurfaced. And now there's no one left to blackmail, so it's sort of moot."

"I see. Well, either way, it explains a lot, though I can't say I'm surprised at Charles going after Maggie Hilliard. He had a reputation as a skirt chaser and she was a knockout," he said. "Still, it's curious. She was supposed to be pretty tight with one of the other scientists. Rumor was she was sleeping with the guy who ran the project. It was a bigger deal in those days, people went to some trouble to keep that kind of thing quiet. His name was Graf. Theo Graf. Hell of a smart guy, really brilliant. Tore him up something awful when she died. I heard he had a huge row with Thiessman and they nearly came to blows. Then he was gone, and soon after that everyone involved in that project left, too."

"According to Charles, Theo Graf didn't know about him and Maggie."

Noah shrugged. "You wonder. Anyway, that crowd was a bunch of rogues, working on something that should have been shut down after Nixon signed the order stopping all biological and chemical weapons research. It was one thing to be conducting experiments on weaponizing anthrax in wartime when you knew the Japanese and Germans were doing it, but how the hell could you justify it to a bunch of politicians and the American public in peacetime? Obviously not everyone agreed with the president—it was still the Cold War—and Charles found the right people willing to look the other way. The U.S. didn't sign the international treaty outlawing that stuff for good until 1972."

" 'Weaponizing' it?" I said, stunned. "Charles's group was working on developing an anthrax bomb?"

"A bomb is one way to do it, but there are others," he said. "His gang was working the other side of the coin, ways to neutralize it—trying to improve the anthrax vaccine we developed during the war. Before Nixon shut everything down, the biowarfare crowd tested more than twenty strains of the anthrax bacterium trying to determine which were the deadliest. Then they'd stage mock attacks, see how far it could spread, that kind of thing. What they found out was that it could spread pretty damn far, maybe even as deadly as a nuclear blast. As a result they wanted a better, more effective vaccine."

Mock attacks with anthrax that had the devastating potential of another Hiroshima or Nagasaki. I shuddered. "How did you know what they were doing?"

Noah gave me a long look that made me wish I hadn't asked. "I worked as a researcher for the public health service. Our mandate was different. We were working to *save* lives from some of the worst, most wretched diseases in the world. Those guys were military. What they developed were new and creative ways to use bacteria, germs, chemicals, things in nature, or stuff they created in test tubes as weapons. It was a different mission." He paused. "Of course we had our ethical lapses, too. Things we did in the name of research."

He pressed his lips together and fingered the leaves on a small pink dogwood. I wondered how much his old ghosts still haunted him, what his involvement had been in the experiments where people had been infected unknowingly or against their will.

"The world's such a scary place now," I said. "You try not to think about it, but it's always on the news or they ratchet up the terrorism level at the airport or someone puts a bomb in some clever new place. Why did we have to weaponize anthrax to begin with? Look at that sick person who sent it through the mail and killed those postal workers in Washington after 9/11. All it takes is some lunatic with a test tube and a grudge—"

Noah scuffed a toe of his work boot, digging a small hole in the dirt. "Lucie, you can find anthrax bacteria living in the soil naturally—you don't always need a test tube and a lab. Not everywhere, mind you. But it's out there and it's part of nature. And a smart scientist could replicate it without too much trouble."

"Please tell me you're not serious."

" 'Fraid so." He finished the last of his coffee and crushed the cardboard cup with his big hands. "You use *Bacillus thuringiensis* on your grapes. I know you do since you buy it from me."

"We try. It doesn't do much against some pests, so we resort to the more toxic sprays, unfortunately."

"You know Bt comes from the same family of bacteria that causes anthrax, don't you?" he said.

"That's right, it does." I stared at him. "Oh, come on, Noah!

You're not saying someone could take Bt and produce anthrax by making it . . . what's the term . . . mutate?"

"So far that's never happened, either in a lab or in nature. But with modern technology and a bit of luck, you could take the toxin-producing genes from anthrax and transfer them into Bt. So you'd get a Bt that could cause anthrax."

"Surely that's not very easy."

"Not for your average bear, no. But a scientist who knew what he was doing could find the necessary gene sequences on the Internet and reproduce them in the laboratory. It's a fairly common way to study genes and it should work just as well with toxin genes. You use short segments of a strand of DNA called oligonucleotide primers to replicate the gene from a fragment." He shrugged. "Order the primers online and do a PCR—sorry, polymerase chain reaction—meaning you make more of it. Then you clone those genes into a plasmid, put it in Bt, and voilà, you've got Bt that could be as lethal as anthrax."

"Maggie and the scientists she worked with were replicating anthrax bacteria?" I asked. "Making it multiply?"

"Let's just leave it that they understood the process." He folded his arms across his chest to let me know that was all he planned to say.

"All right, whatever they did or didn't do, they needed animals or, better still, humans who were infected in order to test the vaccine. Or they themselves needed to infect rats or sheep or people since anthrax isn't one of those diseases with a long survival rate where you can round up a test group."

"It's true you need to do field tests to find out if something is effective or not."

Had Stephen Falcone died from coming in contact with anthrax because he'd agreed to be tested for the vaccine? How could he have understood what he'd agreed to do?

"Isn't that incredibly risky, if we're talking about real people? Not to mention life-threatening for anyone who volunteers?"

"Of course it's risky, but the point is to administer the vaccine quickly enough for it to be effective."

"And how fast is 'quickly enough'?" I asked. "Did they also experiment to see how long they could wait before it was too late?"

Noah's face darkened. "Sorry, Lucie, we really have reached the end of the line about what I can discuss."

We stared at each other.

"What do they call that?" I said. "A nondenial denial?"

"I'll walk you back to the parking lot." He wasn't going to back down.

I shrugged. "Okay. Thanks for your time."

"I've got one final question for you," he said. "About Maggie. The newspapers reported exactly what you said Charles told you—the car she was driving went off a bridge into the water off Pontiac Island. She'd been drinking and she shouldn't have been behind the wheel."

"That's right." We'd already discussed this.

"It wasn't her car. Couldn't have been," he said. "Didn't Charles ever mention that Maggie didn't drive, didn't know how to, didn't have a license because she grew up in Manhattan?"

"No."

"Well, there's your problem right there." Noah made a clicking sound of disapproval with his tongue. "You ask me, someone else had to be in the car with her that night, even if the police never found any evidence to prove it—the car'd been underwater for hours, anyway. She didn't drive off the bridge herself because she was too drunk. I think the driver managed to escape but left her there and she died. Either he or she was too scared to report what happened, too drunk, or it was deliberate. Jealousy can be a powerful motivator, my dear, enough to make someone take leave of his senses if he'd been drinking. Wouldn't be the first time a person was pushed too far when there was a love triangle." He broke a small dead branch off the dogwood.

I felt like he'd knocked the wind out of me. "You think it was Charles?"

"I don't know. Maybe she did get in that car and take off. We're talking about a semiprivate island, not the streets of D.C. The police never charged Charles with anything, so I could be all wet. Or maybe I'm right and Charles Thiessman got away with that, too. I told you, Lucie. The guy is made of Teflon."

CHAPTER 22

───⊗⊗⊗───

I headed through the now-busy parking lot and thought about what Noah had said—or implied. If Maggie's death wasn't an accident, Noah seemed to believe the love triangle among her, Theo, and Charles could be motive enough for murder. That implicated Charles and, just as a complete wild card, maybe Theo had returned to the island after storming out of the beach house, found Maggie behind the wheel, and they quarreled. Throw in Vivian, who apparently had been so jealous of Maggie she spied on her tryst with Charles and captured it on film, and the list of possible suspects was longer than the list of those who were innocent or, so far, uninvolved: Mel and Paul.

Except Paul's death seemed to be somehow tied in with the Mandrake Society—the wineglass deliberately placed next to his body—and the same glass had also been at the scene where Mel died, reportedly of a heart attack. One wineglass and one dead body is someone haunted by the past; two starts to sound like a creepy pattern, too unusual a coincidence not to be relevant to what happened to Stephen Falcone, who I now suspected died of exposure to anthrax.

I had learned plenty from Noah about the research Charles's group had been doing, and that explained why it had been so critical to keep Stephen's death quiet. But Noah had also revealed the tantalizing fact that Maggie didn't know how to drive a car—though she wouldn't have been the first person in the world to get behind the wheel and drive drunk without a license, especially if she was upset enough. The police must have believed that latter theory or someone would have been arrested or charged with something. I wondered whose car she'd taken.

I got into the Mini, opened my phone, and called Kit. She answered midway through the second ring.

"Do I know you? Who is this? Wait—don't tell me. Lucie Some-thing-or-other. You own that vineyard."

"I was only gone four days, not four years."

"You could have called."

"I am calling."

"I meant before."

"Before what? I got in Wednesday at midnight. It's Friday morn-ing. What's going on? You sound like the eighth dwarf. Crabby."

"Sorry. I was here last night until midnight. And the night before. And the night before."

"You can't go on like this."

"You're telling me. If you divide my salary by the number of hours I live in my office, I'm practically paying them to let me work here."

"Maybe you should find another job."

"Yeah, well, I'm worried about that, too," she said. "That one of these days I might be job hunting."

"You think they'll fire you? Who else would work her heart out the way you do?"

"Some child straight out of college who will toil for a third of my pay and be grateful."

"The child won't have your experience."

"The bosses won't care. It's the bean counters who are driving this thing, Luce."

"Jeez, now *I'm* depressed."

"Yeah, well try being me."

I heard a deep sigh and then the sucking sound of a straw at the bottom of a glass. "Moving on," she said. "What's up? How was California? See Quinn?"

"California was fine, I saw Quinn, and I need a favor," I said. "Pretty please?"

"Wow, that was fast. Thanks for dishing," she said as her computer dinged that she had e-mail. "I know how this works, you know. You want me to say yes before you tell me what it is."

"You are so suspicious. It's just an archive search of a couple of old news stories."

"Huh. That sounds harmless. Which old stories?"

"A woman who died in a car accident forty years ago. Drunk driving. Maggie Hilliard, probably Margaret Hilliard. She drove off the bridge to Pontiac Island and drowned. It might have been fairly sensational. And second—this one I'm not sure about—can you find anything about an autistic man named Stephen Falcone who disappeared, say, six months or so before her accident? Might be less than six months. He might have lived locally. He had a sister, Elinor. She might have reported him to the police when he took off."

"That's a lot of 'mights.' You're only looking for the story about him going missing?" she asked. "Anybody find him?"

"Yeah," I said. "Maggie Hilliard, among other people. He died a few months later. You won't find anything on that."

"All right, I'll look. But you're going to have to connect the dots between these two when I see you. You got me all curious."

"Me, too. That's why I was wondering if there was anything in the press back then. The only person still alive who knew them might be lying about what happened to one or both of them."

"And that would be?"

"Charles Thiessman."

"Are you kidding me? Ambassador Charles Thiessman?" I heard her chair creak and the click of computer keys.

"Yup."

"What are you saying, Luce?"

"Nothing yet. I could be completely wrong about this."

Kit's computer keys continued clicking. Finally she said, "This is going to take some time. Can you be more specific on your dates or a time line?"

"Try looking during the months of June, July, and August in 1970 for Maggie Hilliard. She was at a beach house party the night it happened. Sounds like summer to me."

More clicking. I finished the lukewarm water from my water bottle, set it back in the cup holder, and waited.

"Nope, nothing." Kit's desk chair creaked and her e-mail bell went off again. I heard her mutter something and she said, "Look, my managing editor is about to go nuclear about something, so I gotta go. He has this thing about business hours being the time we ought to be doing work."

"Oh, gosh, I didn't mean to get you in trouble."

"Don't worry, I do that just fine all by myself. Look, if I find anything, I'll bring it to the dinner tonight," she said. "Thank God we digitized our archives so at least I don't have to squint at microfilm."

"Tonight?"

She must have heard the disappointment in my voice. "It happened forty years ago, Luce. Why so urgent all of a sudden? What's going on?"

"I'll tell you when I see you. It's way too long to go into now."

"I'll do some poking around on my lunch hour, okay?" She sighed. "I never go out anymore. Just stuck at my desk all the time. I may as well do something interesting . . . aw, jeez, there's my boss e-mailing again. I'd better go. I'll call you later if I get any hits."

I stopped by the General Store on my way home from Seely's to pick up a few items—milk, peanut butter, and bread, as well as whatever was left in Thelma's baked goods case after the Romeos swept through like a plague of locusts for their daily fix of doughnuts, coffee, and gossip. Eli had an appetite that reminded me of a Hoover vacuum, and even Hope, a delicate little angel who looked as though she ate like a bird, inhaled food like there was a hole in the bottom of her shoe.

Thelma liked to boast that she had more variety on her shelves than even the most upscale grocery store in the region, which happened to be true since none of those places carried ammunition, camping equipment, bloodworms, fireworks (in season), chain saw replacement parts, and two kinds of hoof polish. As for food, she stocked the emergency staples, or as she liked to say, the essential white stuff you needed to survive the white stuff of a blizzard: milk, bread, and toilet paper. But the currency that had kept her clients loyal for five decades was her single-handed talent for turning our little country store into a throbbing nerve center of information about every who, what, where, why, and when that went on in two counties. Over the years, she'd cultivated a far-flung network of sources—anyone who walked through her door—and refined her interviewing technique so that she'd either surprise out of you what she wanted to know, or scare you until you told her.

The Christmas sleigh bells Thelma used as a low-tech security system jingled and a blast of frigid air-conditioning hit me as I walked inside. The parking lot had been empty, but it sounded like a party in the back room, which meant she was already engrossed in one of her beloved soap operas or a game show.

She yelled, "I'm coming," in her reedy voice and a moment later stood in the doorway, making an entrance with the dramatic timing of a venerable leading lady appearing on stage and the verve of a teenager who liked showing more skin than fabric. Her face lit up when she saw me and I knew that meant I was about to be squeezed for the details of my grandfather's visit and—if she'd heard about it—how it had gone between Quinn and me in California.

"Why, Lucille! Speak of the devil." She adjusted her thick trifocals and smoothed wrinkles out of a brilliant canary yellow knit dress that looked like it had shrunk a size or two in the dryer. "I was just talking about you a little while ago."

It was too late to say that she was out of what I needed. She'd seen my hand, still on the doorknob, so she knew I hadn't even set foot in the store. I could feel the wagons circling around me.

"Really? Who were you talking to?"

"One or two of the Romeos. Someone said you and Luc went out to California for a few days. Did you patch things up with Quinn? You did see him, of course? And come on in, child. You're standing in that doorway like you grew roots."

"How did you . . . ?" There was no point conning her. She knew. "I mean, well, yes, Quinn and I saw each other."

She clacked across the room in stiletto mules that matched her dress, a sly smile on her face. "Oh, I just put two and two together when I heard about you going to California. You know me, Lucille, and that special seventh sense I've got for knowing things before people tell me." She tapped her forehead with a bony finger. "It's called extraterrestrial perception."

"You always say that."

"Yes, indeedy." She walked over to a table where three coffeepots were lined up in a tidy row and straightened the "Regular," "Decaf," and "Fancy" signs that hung above them. "How about a nice cup of java? We could talk a little."

"Thanks, but I just stopped by to get a few groceries and those three blueberry muffins you've got left."

"Deary me, I should have wrapped one of those muffins and put it away," she said. "You can have two of 'em. The other one's for the Thiessmans' gardener. He said he'd drop by this afternoon. The poor man looked falling-down tired when he showed up this morning. I felt so sorry that I opened up early, just for him."

She stood there, hands on hips, regarding me. Thelma had extraterrestrial perception, all right. I wondered how much she knew about Charles using Juliette's gardener as a late-night chauffeur for guests at his lodge, and my own firsthand experience being driven home half sloshed with Pépé in the wee small hours of the morning. Maybe Thelma was baiting me—again.

Who cared? I wanted to know what she knew.

"Come to think of it, that coffee does smell good and I'm still tired from the trip. What's today's Fancy? I think I've got time for a quick cup."

"Course you do. And it's Bean There, Done That. That'll perk you up." She reached for a Styrofoam cup. "Make yourself to home, Lucille."

I took the coffee after she fixed it and sat in a spindle-back rocker across from the one she always sat in.

"Juliette Thiessman is selling Dominique a lot of produce from her garden for our dinner tonight. I guess that's why her gardener's working overtime." I concentrated on stirring my coffee.

Thelma settled herself in her rocking chair and straightened a pile of soap opera and gossip magazines on a little table next to her. "Oh, he's working extra hours, all right. But it's not hoeing and weeding. It's that little side business he's got goin' on for Charles."

I bumped the stirrer too hard against the cup and nearly sloshed hot coffee on my lap. "What business would that be?"

"Well, of course he's never said, but you tell me what to think when a man shows up in my store first thing in the morning smelling like he just took a bath in a vat of perfume?"

"Uh . . . I don't know."

"He's driving Charles's girlfriends home, that's what. After Charles finishes having his way with them in that little love nest he's got in the woods. At first I thought the perfume was Juliette's. Then I remembered what my grandmamma, a wise and proper lady, always said: A woman should pick one special fragrance to be her unmistakable scent for life and that's how a man will remember her. Men find it very erratic, you know. Sort of a . . . turn on."

She plucked at imaginary lint on her dress. Her cheeks had gone pink.

I'd heard that before, too—about the erotic and sensual power of scent, especially a woman's signature perfume—when I worked as a translator at the perfume museum in Grasse, France, before I came home to run the vineyard. But right now I didn't know what to say to Thelma because I had a feeling she knew more about my relationship with Charles than she let on—and this was another setup to see if I'd spill any information.

I sipped my coffee. "It does sound very romantic, though it's hard to wear perfume with what I do all day. Really screws things up when you're trying to make wine."

"Don't you see, Lucille?" She sounded frustrated that I had missed the point. "That's how I *knew*!"

Now I'd lost her. "Knew what?"

"That it wasn't Juliette who'd been in the car. Juliette wears Chanel Number 5. Trust me, I've got a nose like a bloodhound. In fact, all the Johnson women have very keen oligarchy systems." She touched a finger to the side of her nose. "That poor man comes in here regular as rain for a morning cup of coffee just reeking of Dior or Ralph Lawrence or whatever the latest one was wearing. It's just about killed Juliette, don't you know?"

I sat up in my chair. "Juliette knows about this?"

"Lordy!" Thelma waved a hand at me. "She's known for ages."

"How do you know she knows?"

"When a man's cheating on his wife the way Charles cheats on Juliette, she knows. Lately I've been thinking that it's finally getting to her, after all this time," she said. "Wouldn't surprise me if she broke down and did something about it."

"Like what? You don't mean something violent?"

"There are other options, Lucille, that are less . . . drastic." Thelma shrugged. "Maybe she'll leave him."

"Did she say that?"

"Not to me. But something's weighing on her mind." Thelma jumped up and bustled over to the glass-fronted cabinet where she kept the bakery items. She picked up a white towel and began rubbing imaginary spots on the glass. "I think she's found somebody new herself."

I heard the catch in her throat, a tiny quiver. Then the room grew quiet, except for the rushing sound of the air-conditioning system and an indistinct squawking from the television in the back room. I held my cup with both hands and rocked in my chair, taking in what she'd just said. The old wood creaked, sounding like a baby animal crying. I stopped rocking.

"I heard she and your grandfather are very old and special friends," she said in a sad, quiet voice. "That she knew Luc's wife, your grandmother, way back when in Paris."

"Yes," I said, "that's true."

It was an open secret that Thelma had a mad crush on Pépé. The likelihood of them ever getting together was about the same as the sun colliding with the moon, but my gallant grandfather had taken her to dinner at the Inn the last time he was in town, charming her with the European politesse and old-fashioned chivalry he showed every woman, being especially kind to a lonely spinster whose relationships with men had always ended in heartbreak and disaster, until she finally found vicarious comfort in her soap opera hunks.

"Well, he is available," she said. "And he's quite a catch."

"My grandfather is an honorable man. She's a married woman."

"There's a remedy for that, child. It's called divorce," she said. "And who could blame Juliette what with Charles having lovers coming and going all the time?"

"I think you're wrong, Thelma. Pépé's one great love was my grandmother. That's why he never remarried. And I don't think he ever will."

"Someday when you're my age," she said, "you'll realize that just simple companionship is more than enough. They could still be together and he wouldn't have to marry her. She never gave up her French citizenship, so she could go back and live there easy as you please."

I finished my coffee and stood up. I didn't want to think about the consequences of what she was saying. Pépé cared for Juliette, that I knew. And, okay, Juliette was a little in love with my grandfather. But what Thelma was implying, that there was some romantic liaison between them that went beyond the very proper behavior I'd witnessed at their party last week, was ridiculous—had I been that blind?

"What do you need, child?" Thelma took my coffee cup and put it in the trash.

I needed to think she was wrong, that her theory was way off base. "Pardon?"

"Besides the muffins. You said you needed a few things."

"Oh. Milk, bread, peanut butter."

She wrapped my muffins while I got the items and paid her.

"My grandfather respects Juliette as an old and dear friend," I said as she walked me to the door. "He's fond of her, but not in the way you think."

Thelma's smile was tinged with sympathy and regret. "You're his granddaughter. The man's been alone for more than thirty years. Let me tell you something, Lucille. Juliette Thiessman is a strong-willed woman. If she wants your grandfather, she'll get him. You can bet the farm on that."

She adjusted her glasses, blinking hard, and I couldn't tell if she was holding back tears. Then she squared her shoulders and patted my arm. "I do run on sometimes, don't I?"

"Not at all," I said. "Anyway, I guess it's not up to either one of us what they do, is it?"

"Nope." She glanced at her watch, back to her old brisk self. "Lordy, will you look at the time? I'm missing *Tomorrow Ever After*.

I just love that show. The people are just so *real,* you know? And Shay's about to propose to Amber."

"Oh, gosh. You don't want to miss that."

"Oh, honey, it's television. This is July. They won't finish their candlelight dinner on his yacht until sometime in August. Then he'll take her to his bedroom."

"Then he asks her?"

"No. They'll argue—she's very temperamental—and carry on until she finally tells him she's pregnant. He'll pop the question by Labor Day."

I grinned. "You'd better get back so you don't miss any of it."

"I just love Shay," she said. "He deserves better than Amber. It's not his baby, you see. But he's an honorable man and he'll take care of her because he's a gentleman. Toodle-oo, Lucille."

The sleigh bells rang as I closed the door. An honorable man and a gentleman: Had she been talking about Shay or my grandfather?

My phone rang as I was putting the groceries in the Mini.

"Hey," Kit said. "Pay dirt."

"You found something in the archives?" I felt breathless. "Maggie's accident?"

"Sorry, not that. And definitely nothing about Stephen Falcone going missing."

"Then what?"

"I got to thinking about his sister, since you said he might have lived locally. Call me lazy, but I took the easy route after I couldn't find anything right away in the archives. I looked up Elinor Falcone on the Internet phone number lookup site. It's an unusual name."

"And?"

"Got a pencil or pen?"

"Give me a second." I fumbled in my purse as my heart pounded against my ribs. "Okay, shoot."

"There's an Elinor Falcone, age sounds about right, still living in D.C. Brookland, to be precise. Maybe you want to go pay her a visit?" She gave me the address and phone number.

I looked at my watch. "I can be there in about an hour."

CHAPTER 23

I raced home to drop off the groceries, since I didn't want to drive into Washington with a gallon of milk in my car on a sultry summer day. As I pulled into the circular driveway, Eli walked out the front door balancing a plate with a towering deli sandwich, a large bottle of Coke, and a bag of chips big enough to get lost in.

"What's up?" he said. "You look kind of frazzled. I just took a break to make lunch."

"I picked up some things at Thelma's. Where's Hope?"

"At the Ruins with Jasmine and Dominique. They're getting ready for tonight."

I got out of the car and grabbed the groceries. "I've got to get this stuff inside. See you later."

"You're running like you stole something, Luce. What's going on? The girls have got things under control."

"I'm sure they do . . . uh, actually I've got an errand in town. I might be a little late."

He frowned. "I thought that's where you just came from."

"I mean D.C."

He cocked an eyebrow. "You're driving all the way to D.C.? Why?"

"I need to see someone. Won't take long." I held up the bag. "Better get the milk in the fridge."

He looked puzzled by the brush-off, but he didn't push it. "Yeah, sure. See you later."

★ ★ ★

It took me an hour and a half to get into Washington, thanks to a highway-paving project that funneled traffic to a single lane and slowed it to a crawl. By the time I crossed the Potomac over the Teddy Roosevelt Bridge and drove down Constitution Avenue toward the Capitol, the temperature gauge in my car read 105 degrees. In the hazy humidity and blinding sunlight, the Federal Reserve, the Commerce Department, and the Archives seemed to shimmer. Cars, tourists, and even the occasional crazy jogger along the Mall moved with slow motion torpor.

I didn't know the Brookland area well, except that it was where Catholic University was located, off North Capitol Street and Michigan Avenue. There is an intrinsic logic to how Washington is laid out. A medallion under the crypt in the Capitol Rotunda is the geographic center of a city that originally was intended to be a perfect square—though it isn't—and from there, four quadrants radiate away from it as northeast, northwest, southeast, and southwest. Within each quadrant, alphabet streets run east-west and numbered streets are north-south in a large grid. What throws off the simplicity are the state-named streets, which cut diagonally across this symmetry and the circles—Dupont, Logan, Thomas, et cetera—which can really screw you up if you don't know what you're doing.

Still, it wasn't too hard to figure out where Elinor Falcone lived. The alphabet streets had moved into two-syllable words by the time I drove past the bright blue mosaic-domed Shrine of the Immaculate Conception, so it was clear that Lawrence Street was between Kearney and Monroe and 13th Street was a block beyond 12th.

The university hadn't overrun the local community, so there was a mixture of college bars and restaurants, and a corridor of thriving businesses on 12th Street. The surrounding neighborhood of wood, stucco, and brick bungalow homes looked like they dated back to the 1920s or thereabouts.

Elinor lived in the middle of the 1300 block of Lawrence Street in a well-looked-after tan stucco Craftsman-style home. Half a dozen steps led up to a wide front porch with heavy tapered columns, a white railing, and a low-pitched roof. I parked across the street and got out of my car. A frail, white-haired woman sitting in a wheelchair on the porch watched me as I made my way between two closely parked cars and started up her front walk.

"What do you want?" Her high-pitched voice was querulous. "No soliciting allowed here."

"I'm not soliciting," I said. "I'm looking for Elinor Falcone. Would that be you, ma'am?"

I saw her hands drop to the brakes of her wheelchair and she called over her shoulder. "Alice? Can you come here?"

The front screen door banged open and a graceful African-American woman in her fifties wearing a short pink apron over red shorts and a white sleeveless top came outside.

"You all right, Miss Elinor?" she asked. She gave me a wary look. "May I help you?"

"My name is Lucie Montgomery," I said. "I was hoping to have a word with Elinor Falcone. I've just driven here from Atoka, Virginia."

"Where's that? Roanoke?"

I smiled. "Not that far. Just past Middleburg in western Loudoun County. I won't take more than a couple of minutes, I promise."

Alice's hand strayed protectively to the back of the wheelchair. "And what do you want to talk to her about?" she asked. "That you've come all this way."

"Her brother Stephen."

Elinor gave a faint cry and Alice placed both hands on the old woman's shoulders, bending down to murmur in her ear. When she stood up, her face was impassive.

"That won't be possible. You should leave now."

"Please." I looked directly at Elinor. "Someone else might have died because of what happened to Stephen. I know it was a long time ago, and I don't mean to upset you, Miss Elinor, but could I please ask you a couple of questions?"

Elinor's eyes locked on mine as she sized me up. I held my breath. If she wouldn't talk, there was no one else left to ask.

"Why do you want to know what happened? Are you kin to the other person who died?"

"No, ma'am, no relation. I think I know what happened to your brother and I just want you to tell me if I'm right or not."

"Go on."

"What I know is that he agreed to take money in return for participating in an experimental drug study for a new vaccine. But they had to infect him with the disease first and he died before they gave him the antidote."

"So you know everything." Her voice was harsh. "You've been talking to the other girl, haven't you?"

I moved closer to the stairs. "What other girl?"

"Stay where you are."

I held my ground. "I don't know who you mean. And I haven't been talking to anyone."

"She showed up one day, just like you did. I don't remember when it was. Last winter, I think. No, wait. It was Thanksgiving."

Elinor glanced at Alice, who said, "You may as well come up here so we don't have to be shouting to the whole neighborhood about it."

I climbed the stairs, feeling their eyes on me.

"What happened to you?" Elinor asked when I stood across from her. "Awful young to be using a cane."

Up close, her deep-set eyes looked haunted and her downturned mouth looked like she hadn't known much happiness. I glanced at Alice, whose face revealed nothing, though she continued to watch me like a mother hovering over a delicate child.

"A car accident," I said. "And you?"

"MS."

"I'm so sorry."

"It's terminal, as you probably know," she said. "I have good days and bad, but now it's come to this." She lifted a hand and I wondered if "this" meant the wheelchair, or her life in general. "Before I tell you any more, I want to know why you're here."

"Because Stephen's death shouldn't have been covered up like he never existed."

"It had to be that way," she said in a flat, dull voice. "The man who talked to me told me I couldn't say anything about it. He called himself Mr. Smith. John Smith. Believe that and I'll sell you the Shrine for a good price. He said I had to tell people that Stephen ran away. He gave me money and, God help me, I took it."

John Smith. Charles hadn't been very creative. Maybe he didn't care if Elinor knew it was a fake name.

"What about the girl who came to visit you? Who was she? How did she know how to find you?"

"Because of her aunt's diaries," she said. "That's how she knew. Came across them in her mother's house after her mother passed last year."

"Was her aunt . . . autistic, like your brother?"

"Good Lord, no. Her aunt was one of the researchers. Turns out I knew her, too. I met her, by chance, when I went to the park in Adams Morgan where a lot of homeless people slept rough. It was one of the places where they recruited volunteers. Easy pickings when your home is a cardboard box. A friend of Stephen's told me where to go." I waited as Elinor rubbed her forehead with a hand, trying to recall details of a meeting forty years ago. "I had to find out what happened to him, you see. So this woman, a girl, actually, took my name and address and said she'd see what she could do. I could tell she was upset. The next thing I knew John Smith came to see me and offered me money. I presumed they worked together." She looked up at Alice. "Molly, wasn't it? Molly Harris?"

"No, dear," Alice said. "Molly Harris is one of the church ladies who come to visit sometimes. Her name was Maggie."

"Maggie Hilliard," I said.

I'd figured it had to be Maggie or Vivian. What I hadn't guessed was that Maggie had a niece who had tracked Elinor down. Recently.

"Yes, that's right."

"Why did Maggie Hilliard's niece come to see you?"

"She had questions, same as you," she said. "She told me her aunt wanted the human testing to stop until they did more research after what happened to Stephen. No one else at the laboratory wanted to do that, so she threatened to tell the truth. That's why they killed her."

Elinor said it in such a matter-of-fact manner that at first I didn't think I'd heard right.

"That's why who killed who?"

"Why, Maggie, of course. The others killed her. They covered up her death like they did with Stephen."

"The others being the other researchers in the program?"

"That's right."

My head was spinning. "How do you know this?"

"I read it in her diary. Maggie's niece brought it with her, thought I could explain some things. Maggie wrote that her boss threatened to do something if she talked," Elinor said. "She was scared of him and he was . . . well, infatuated with her. So she played along, let him flirt with her. He told her that if she cooperated, he'd take care of her. He said what they were doing was important work and they needed to think of the greater good, not dwell on a minor setback."

"I'm so sorry." The "minor setback" had been Stephen. "Did Maggie mention any names—who these other people were?"

"Not in the diary. That's what the niece was trying to find out. Except for Stephen—Maggie had a yearbook photo of him with his name on it and our address. Guess she wrote that down after she met me. The others she called by names of characters in fairy tales. Probably to protect their real identities." Elinor lifted a weary shoulder. "What help could I be? The only one I knew was John Smith. Presumably the boss."

"What did she call the boss in her diary?"

Her mouth twisted in an ironic smile. "The Pied Piper."

That fit.

"So how did the niece figure out that the others killed her aunt? Maggie obviously couldn't have written about it."

"She found a letter with some other papers. From a woman who lived in Paris."

My mouth felt dry. "Vivian Kalman."

"You seem to know quite a lot, Miss Montgomery. It was an apology. Vague, but the gist of it was that Vivian claimed she had nothing to do with Maggie's death, never wanted to go along with the cover-up. Said she'd been forced to do it. She asked for forgiveness." Another small shrug. "Sounds like an admission of guilt to me."

"Did Vivian say anything else in that letter? Anything about how Maggie died, for example?"

"Nothing. Only that 'the others' were still alive so she couldn't talk about it."

Elinor bent over in her wheelchair, seized by a coughing fit, something deep and rheumy. Alice reached in her apron pocket and pulled out a tissue.

"You're exerting yourself too much, dear. Let me get your medicine. That bronchitis doesn't sound good at all. I need to get you to the doctor." She placed the tissue in Elinor's shaking hand.

Elinor waved her away, still hacking. Finally the spasm passed. "I see too many doctors. They're all quacks. Let me finish here."

Alice flashed a warning look at me. "She shouldn't be doing this."

"I know, but please—?"

"Where was I?" Elinor was still wheezing.

"Vivian asking Maggie's sister to forgive her."

"Yes, that's right." Her voice grew stronger. "She wrote they'd been drinking, all six of them were stinking drunk. It didn't excuse what they did, but no one was in their right mind. And she knew that they genuinely did try to save Maggie when they went back to the pier, but by then it was too late."

"Six of them?"

"Yes, that's right. Six."

So Charles had been there that night after all.

Another coughing spasm shook Elinor.

"Miss Elinor, I'm taking you inside right now." Alice unlocked the brakes on the wheelchair. To me, she said, "Please leave. It's enough."

"I . . . of course. Just two more questions. Please, do you know the niece's name? What happened to her?"

Alice whispered something to Elinor, who nodded as she wiped under each eye with her finger.

"Wait a second," Alice said. The screen door banged as she went inside the house. A moment later she was back holding a scrap of paper.

"Why don't you talk to her yourself?" she said. "If you could find us, I'm sure you could find her. Unless she stayed in France."

"Pardon?"

"She came through Washington on her way to Paris. Flew here from Oregon, just to see Miss Elinor. Told us she was leaving for Paris that night. She has family there. She also planned to look up Vivian, if she was still alive."

Alice handed me the paper and I read the name and a Paris address—though I knew already who it was the moment she said the niece was from Oregon.

Maggie Hilliard's niece was Jasmine Nouri.

CHAPTER 24

———⦚⦚⦚———

I called Eli the second I got back to my car after thanking Elinor and Alice for their time. Jasmine was babysitting Hope. She had no reason to suspect I knew anything about who she really was, and I sure as hell didn't want to alarm her or tip my hand. But right now she was the last person I wanted to be looking after my three-year-old niece.

Eli's phone went to voice mail and I left a terse message to call me. I thought about calling Dominique, but she was probably with Jasmine and Hope. What could I say that wouldn't raise a red flag, especially if Jasmine was standing right there next to her?

I drove back to Atoka as fast as I dared, but it was Friday and the summer rush-hour exodus from the steamy city had started early. The first thing I intended to do was to find Hope and bring her home, if Eli hadn't already picked her up.

After that, I didn't have a plan. Especially since I still had no proof of anything, just a lot of speculation based on what Elinor had said. Jasmine had flown to Paris and, if I guessed correctly, she'd probably managed to track down Vivian Kalman. Within the next nine months, Vivian, Mel, and Paul all died. Vivian and Mel of heart attacks; Paul, an apparent suicide.

Maybe Vivian had given up the names of the other members of the Mandrake Society and Jasmine had visited the rest of her aunt's former colleagues. At a minimum, she might have gotten that compromising photo of Maggie and Charles from Vivian, who had taken it. Plus she found Stephen's yearbook photo in Maggie's diary. Jasmine could have mailed the pictures to the others as the warning shot across the bow that the secrets and lies surrounding those two deaths had returned to haunt them all, and Charles had automatically assumed Theo was the one who had sent them.

But why would Jasmine do it? Why would she want revenge for the death of an aunt she never knew? Could she have committed murder that was passed off as a natural death—more than once—and gotten away with it? And how did Theo fit in? He was dead now, too, though his death seemed unrelated to any of this—a drug deal gone bad in San Francisco.

It was just before four when I turned off Atoka Road and flew past the stone pillars at the vineyard entrance on Sycamore Lane. My head throbbed with a tension headache and my jaw ached from clenching it. I drove straight to the Ruins.

Dominique was there, giving orders to half a dozen people setting up folding chairs, laying out tablecloths and place settings, and generally getting ready for tonight's sell-out event. Jasmine and Hope were nowhere in sight.

My cousin saw me heading toward her. "Thank God you're here. I could use a hand. We haven't given ourselves enough rope and I'm about to hang myself."

"Where's Hope?" I asked.

"Pardon?"

"Hope. Where is she? Is she still with Jasmine?"

Dominique waved a distracted hand. "I don't know. I think so."

"Where's Jasmine?"

"She might have gone back to the house to look for Eli. Juliette called and said she'd finished the floral centerpieces so Jasmine was going to head over to the Thiessmans' to pick them up."

Charles. The only remaining member of the Mandrake Society. Jasmine had ingratiated herself with Juliette, gaining easy and unquestioned access to their home and grounds. She'd done it in spite of Charles's famously reclusive reputation—how clever. No one would ever suspect her if he were to have, say, an unexpected heart attack like a couple of his ex-colleagues had done. Who would possibly connect the dots between Charles, Vivian, Paul, and Mel—

since Charles himself had done such a stellar job of erasing any information that could link them all to one another?

And what about Theo?

"Can you cover for me?" I said. "I'll be back."

She looked puzzled. "Where are you going?"

"To the house," I said. "Then to the Thiessmans', if that's where Hope is."

"Lucie, what's going on?"

"Nothing. I just, um, would feel better if Hope was with Eli or me. I'd never forgive myself if something happened to her because Jasmine got distracted or too busy."

"She's very capable," Dominique said. "Or I wouldn't have hired her."

"Oh, I know that," I said. "Believe me, I know. I'll be back."

She pulled her phone out of her pocket and waved it. "Why don't I just call her? Find out what she's doing, where they are."

"No, that's okay. I don't want to make a big deal out of it. You know, make it seem like I don't trust her."

"You don't trust her," she said. "That's obvious. She happens to be really good with kids. Actually, she's good with everyone. I don't understand why you're acting so negative about her."

"I guess I'm just an overly protective aunt. Humor me this time, okay? I'll find them myself."

Dominique shrugged, annoyance flashing across her face. "I could use a little help here, you know. It is your vineyard."

"I know that. I'll be back as soon as I can. And there's nobody more capable in the world than you are. I've seen you handle bigger events with your eyes closed."

I started toward my car.

"You're just saying that because you know you're leaving me between a rock and the deep blue sea," she called after me.

"I would never do that and I promise not to be gone long," I yelled back. "See you soon."

I got in the Mini and earned another disgusted look as I drove by. As long as Dominique didn't call Jasmine and warn her I was planning to show up, I could still get Hope away from her before she realized I knew anything. Then I'd go to Bobby Noland.

But Jasmine hadn't dropped Hope off at the house, because Eli was nowhere to be found. I shouted his name up the spiral staircase and listened to my voice echo back.

"Lucie?" Pépé called. It sounded like he was in his bedroom. "*Qu'est-ce que tu fais?* What's going on?"

He came to the railing in the upstairs hall and looked down.

"What happened?" he asked. "You look dreadful."

If I was going to tell anyone, my grandfather was the only one I trusted right now. I waited until he came down the stairs.

"Jasmine Nouri is Maggie Hilliard's niece," I said. "She tracked down Stephen Falcone's sister, Elinor."

He went pale. "How do you know that?"

"Because I just visited Elinor Falcone in Washington and she told me. Jasmine was on her way to Paris to look up Vivian Kalman when she stopped in Washington. Maggie left a diary and Jasmine found it."

"*Mon Dieu.* What do you think she's doing here?"

"In the last six months since Jasmine visited Elinor," I said, "everyone in the Mandrake Society has died. Except Charles. And Jasmine is over at the Thiessmans' right now. With Hope."

"Let's go," he said. "I'll call Juliette."

"No. Don't do that. First we have to get Hope out of there. There'll still be time."

"How can you be so sure?" he said.

"I'm not," I said. "I'm just praying there is. Come on, let's go."

"Wait a minute."

My grandfather crossed the foyer to the library, which had once been Leland's office. He reached up and slid his hand along the top of the doorjamb. My heart started pounding in my chest. The key to my father's gun cabinet was up there; I'd never moved it from where he always kept it.

"My God, Pépé, you can't bring a gun. What are you thinking?"

Despite my father's legendary prowess as a hunter and a collection that could outfit a small militia, I avoided guns at all costs. Leland taught me to shoot when I was a teenager—he insisted since he kept weapons in the house—but I was way out of practice.

Pépé found the key and turned to face me. "If what you say is true, this young woman is capable of murder. I don't want to show up unprepared."

"Look, we're going to get Hope out of there and then call Bobby, okay? Leave the gun here. Please."

But he was already unlocking the door to the big glass cabinet and sliding open the drawer where Leland kept his small arms. I heard the click of a clip being loaded and then Pépé showed up in the doorway. My grandfather was a crack shot, just like Leland.

"I took the forty-five. Don't worry. I probably won't even need to draw it, but I like to be safe."

"You don't have a permit to carry concealed in Virginia."

"I have my *permis de chasser* from last year's *chasse*," he said. "It's in my wallet."

"Your hunting permit is only good for last year's *chasse*. In France," I said. "And you didn't hunt with a forty-five, so it's not even for the right gun."

"Obviously," he said. "But a permit will be the least of my problems if I end up using this, *n'est-ce pas*? Let's go."

On the drive over to Mon Abri, my grandfather grilled me about my visit with Elinor.

"Jasmine had a photograph of Stephen because it was in Maggie's diary?" he asked. "Do you think Vivian gave her the other picture of Maggie and Charles?"

"I guess so. Even Charles figured out that Vivian, who was the group photographer, took that shot. So it stands to reason Vivian still had it, don't you think?"

He nodded, looking thoughtful. "What makes you think Jasmine killed Vivian?"

"I'm not sure she did. But I think it's too much of a coincidence that all of them died within months of each other—beginning from the time Jasmine went to Paris. Who else could have done it?"

"Slow down or you'll miss the turn for Mon Abri," he said. "You almost passed the driveway."

I hit the brakes and put on my turn signal. "Sorry. My mind is in a million places. Here we go."

Pépé patted his suit jacket in the spot where the .45 sat on his hip.

"Yes," he said. "Here we go."

We drove up the long, shaded drive and pulled up to the front entrance.

"That's Charles's BMW," Pépé said as we got out of the car. "And Juliette's Lexus. Wait here a minute."

He disappeared around the side of the house. In a few minutes he returned. "There's another car. A Honda."

"That must be Jasmine's," I said. "What took you so long?"

"Just looking around. It's quiet. Everyone must be inside."

We climbed the stairs and Pépé rang the doorbell. The Westminster chime echoed inside the house.

"Luc? Lucie? What are you doing here?" Juliette opened the door, elegant in an electric blue jersey dress, a single strand of pearls, perfect makeup, hair upswept and regal.

"We were running errands in Middleburg so we stopped by to pick up Hope," I said. "Jasmine's babysitting her and Dominique said she came over here to get the flowers for tonight."

Juliette frowned. "Couldn't Jasmine have dropped her off at your home when she returned with the centerpieces?"

"Yes, of course," I said. "But it's nearly time for Hope's bath and her dinner. Eli called to say he was delayed. I told him we'd get her."

"Really?" Her frown deepened. "Eli called Jasmine a moment ago to say he'd be waiting for them both when she got back to the Ruins."

"Oh, gosh," I said. "We probably got our wires crossed. I've been gone all afternoon. As long as we're here, we'll bring her home with us. Could we come in?"

"It's not terribly convenient. Charles is having supper," she said. "He won't be at your dinner tonight. He's made other plans. I'll be there on my own."

"We need to have a word with Charles, Juliette." Pépé's voice was gentle. "It's important."

"Couldn't it wait?" Juliette fingered her pearls. "He's not in the best frame of mind tonight. Why don't you let Jasmine bring the child home and I'll see you both later? It'll be nice to spend some time with you, Luc."

"There's something Charles needs to know about Jasmine," Pépé said. "And you may as well hear it, too, though I know it will be distressing." He took her arm and stepped inside. "Please. Let's go see him."

"What about Jasmine?" she asked as we walked through the foyer. "I know about Charles's . . . girlfriends, if you're worried about that. I'm sure he's already tried to make a pass at her. Don't give it another thought. I'm used to it."

It was the first time I'd heard Juliette speak openly about Charles's infidelities. After what Pépé had said about how discreet and private she was about her marriage, the casual comment, as if she were discussing a routine household matter, surprised me.

Charles sat alone at the head of the table, eating a salad and drinking a glass of wine, in their dark, elegant dining room. The curtains had been drawn against the late-afternoon sun, making the lighting seem thick and cobwebby. Later I would remember that it had seemed as though we were all moving, talking, and thinking in slow motion or as though we were underwater.

Charles looked up as we entered the room, anger flashing in his dark eyes. He hadn't forgiven us for last evening's blowup at the Inn.

"We need to talk to you, Charles," Pépé said. "I'm sorry, but Juliette should know about this, too. It has to do with the matter we were discussing yesterday."

"Where is Jasmine?" I asked.

Juliette tugged on her pearls again. "What's this about? She's in the kitchen. What about Jasmine?"

I kept my voice low. "Jasmine Nouri is Maggie Hilliard's niece, Charles. Maggie left a diary, which Jasmine read. I'm pretty sure she tracked down Vivian Kalman in Paris, as well."

I left out Elinor on purpose, hoping he wouldn't ask how I'd found this out. We didn't have much time anyway.

Charles set down his fork on the edge of his plate and stared at it wordlessly. Finally he looked up. "Well, I'll be goddamned. All this time I thought it was Theo."

Though he sounded calm, his face gave him away. I knew as sure as if he'd said it what he was thinking: He'd let a beautiful girl insert herself into his life with the ease of the serpent slithering into the Garden of Eden and he'd missed it because he'd been too busy looking for a ghost in California. His worst fear had blossomed right here in his home.

"The little bitch," he said, an afterthought. "Every bit as devious as Maggie was."

Juliette's voice rose, a little bubble of hysteria. "*What* is going on? What are you talking about?"

"Charles will explain it to you later." I tried to reassure her. "Everything is going to be all right. But the most important thing right now is getting Hope away from Jasmine with as little drama as possible. Then I think we'd better call the sheriff's department. Everyone else in the Mandrake Society is dead but you, Charles. Why do you think Jasmine is here?"

"I didn't kill any of those people. Someone else did." Jasmine Nouri stood in the doorway to the kitchen, holding Hope in her arms. "I figured it was you, Charles. It was, wasn't it?"

She brushed a strand of hair off the face of my sweet, pink-cheeked niece who was chewing on her favorite toy pony. The gesture sent such a sharp pang of fear for Hope's safety through me that I gasped.

"Hope," I said, my voice cracking. "Come here, pumpkin. Beppy and I are going to take you home."

"Aunt Woozy."

Hope squirmed in Jasmine's arms but she held tight to the child. I heard her murmur, "In a minute, sweetie. We have to finish something first."

"No one's going anywhere." Juliette's eyes were hard. Something had changed in her and I'd missed it. All of a sudden she was in command, the feigned innocence and sweetness gone.

She exchanged looks with Jasmine, a coded understanding that passed between them. Jasmine nodded, but I thought she looked scared. Before anyone could speak or move, Juliette strode over to the sideboard and reached inside a large urn. When she turned around, she was holding a revolver.

"My God," Charles said. "Where'd you get that?"

She ignored him.

"Why did you have to come here now?" Her voice was full of sadness. It took a moment before I realized she was speaking to my grandfather. "I would have come to you."

"Juliette!" Charles's voice cracked like a whip. "Have you lost your mind? Give me that gun."

"No," she said. "I can't do that."

"*Qu'est-ce que tu fais, ma chère?*" Pépé asked. "Put the gun down, please. You don't want to hurt anyone."

Juliette closed her eyes like she was blinking back tears. "Luc, don't. Please don't make this any more difficult than you already have."

She turned to Charles. "I know, Charles. I know everything. Jasmine told me. The only remaining mystery is what happened that night at the beach forty years ago. You're the only one who knows because you were driving the car."

"No," he said. "No."

"You were," Jasmine said. "Vivian said you were. Maggie left the cottage on foot and you went after her. Somehow you persuaded her to get in your car. Then what?"

Charles's voice turned low and dangerous. "Viv told me when I saw her that someone had stirred up the past, brought it all back again. She let me believe it was Theo."

"You went to see Vivian when we were in Paris in February," Juliette said. "That's when you killed her."

"She died," Charles said, "of a heart attack."

"I wonder if she really did," Jasmine said. "The Préfecture de Police may want to investigate."

"*What happened at the beach?*" Juliette moved closer to Charles, the gun now trained on him. "What did you do?"

Out of the corner of my eye, I saw Pépé slowly lower his hands by his side. Juliette hadn't noticed, nor, it seemed, had Jasmine.

Charles picked up his napkin and wiped his mouth as though he had all the time in the world. "All right," he said like he was placating a child. "I'll tell you."

"Good." His wife gave him a heavy-lidded look. "We're all *dying* to know."

Hope squirmed again and Jasmine shushed her. "It's okay, angel. Just a few more minutes."

"I want Aunt Woozy."

"Soon," she said. "Get on with it, Charles. You heard what Juliette said."

He pushed his chair back, flashing a scornful look at the two of them as he crossed one leg over the other.

"What do all of you know? Nothing. You weren't there."

"If you don't start talking, I'll shoot you in the knee," Juliette said. "Maybe that will jog your memory."

Charles glared at her. "Don't be such a drama queen, darling. It doesn't suit you. You probably couldn't hit the broad side of the barn, anyway."

Juliette moved her finger over the trigger. "Would you like to find out?"

"All right." He held up a hand. "Point that thing somewhere else before you hurt someone. I said, do it."

She lowered her arm, a contemptuous look on her face. But Charles had won that small round.

"It was an accident," he said. "It just happened. A dark night with no moon, heavy clouds. Pitch-black. We'd all been drinking. Maggie wanted to talk about Stephen and there was a huge fight among all of them. She left, said she was going for a walk on the beach, so I went after her. She could hardly walk a straight line. I found her, persuaded her to get in the car. I figured we'd get away from the cottage, find a motel for the night, and work it out. Theo had already taken off in a fit of rage. God, he could be so complicated sometimes."

He shrugged. "To be honest, the next thing I remember was the car hitting the water. Obviously I drove off the bridge. In my condition . . ."

No one said a word. In another room, a clock chimed five.

"Somehow I got out. Got my door open and made it to the surface. Neither of us was wearing a seat belt. I figured Maggie got out, too; she was a good swimmer. But when I couldn't find her—I kept shouting her name but it was so goddamned dark—I started diving. Six, seven times, ten, I don't know. I knew it was too late." Another shrug, but I noticed that he avoided looking at Jasmine. "So I walked back to the cottage and told the others. Everyone was scared out of their minds. I told them we all needed to stick to the same story or we'd hang together. Maggie took my car and drove it off the bridge. The cops knew she didn't have a license and she was drunk. They couldn't prove anything different, no evidence to the contrary. We were four witnesses who could all alibi each other."

"In return you covered up Stephen's death and protected their careers."

"They were brilliant scientists," he said. "Their country needed them, all that they could offer. Science is research and sometimes things go wrong. It happens."

" 'Things go wrong'?" Juliette said. "My God, Charles. You're inhuman."

The tension in the room escalated with an almost audible click as she raised her arm again.

"Juliette," I said, "please put the gun down. There's a child—"

She gave me a scornful look. "That time has passed, Chantal."

Pépé caught my eye. Don't correct her.

"Before you shoot me, I have a question for Jasmine," Charles said in a conversational tone. "Did Vivian give you the photo of Maggie and me? Then you mailed it to all of us, along with the photo of Stephen Falcone, didn't you?"

She nodded. "I wanted you all to know that somebody still remembered. But I never thought you'd kill the others." Her voice rose. "Except maybe for Paul. I think he must have been the one Maggie called Chicken Little in her diary. The timid one. He hanged himself rather than face what was coming."

"What a bastard you are, Charles." Juliette's voice was cold. "I've never told you that, but you always have been. You let that innocent girl die, and you covered up the death of a disabled man who had no idea what he got into. Then you hunted down your former colleagues and killed them to finally silence everyone who knew what happened, to save your own skin."

She aimed the gun.

"No!" I shouted. "Don't!"

Jasmine's hand cradled Hope's head and as she turned my niece's face so she couldn't see what was happening.

"You will suffer," Juliette screamed at Charles. "Just like that poor boy suffered."

"You're out of your mind. What are you talking about?" He

threw up his hands like a shield, knocking his wedding ring against his wineglass.

I flinched at the sharp little *clink* as Juliette's words jackhammered inside my head. *Just like that poor boy suffered.*

Stephen died of anthrax poisoning.

I stared at Charles's wineglass and his dinner plate. He'd been eating a salad whose contents had probably come from Juliette's garden and drinking a bottle of his own wine. A clever scientist, Noah had said, could change a harmless pesticide like Bt into something that had the genetic makeup of anthrax. Spray it over crops and who would know . . . until someone ate the deadly meal or drank the poisoned cup. Even then, the reaction wasn't instantaneous.

Juliette had poisoned Charles. She didn't need the gun.

"Which is it, Juliette, the wine or the salad? Or both?" I asked. "Where did you get anthrax-laced Bt?"

Charles turned pale. "My God, Juliette, what did you do? Are you *insane*?" He, too, stared at the remnants of his meal. "It couldn't be the wine . . . but the salad—"

"You have no one to blame but yourself," she said in a cool voice. "Because my gardener was so busy ferrying your little concubines home at night, he didn't have time to tend to his duties. So I did my own spraying. With a new pesticide."

"Christ Almighty, you brought Theo here? Right into my own home?" Charles's voice rose to a screech. "When? How? He's dead."

"So you heard," she said. "A pity the way it happened, a shoot-out during a drug deal. And no, he never came here, Charles. I wouldn't be that stupid."

"Then how—?" He stared at Jasmine. "*You.* You got it for her. Theo gave it to you."

Jasmine shrugged. "Does it really matter where it came from?"

"Juliette," Pépé interrupted. "He needs to go to the hospital. You can't let him die like this."

"Sorry, but he's not going anywhere," she said. "If he tries to leave, I'll shoot him. One way or another, he'll die."

"Don't be an ass, Juliette." For the first time Charles sounded scared. "You won't get away with this unless you kill everyone in this room."

Juliette turned to Pépé and me. "Your timing is really appalling, you know? No one ever would have suspected the real cause of death, even when they did an autopsy. There are hardly any cases in the United States of death by ingesting anthrax, so it probably would have been attributed to something else. A sad but tragic natural death. Why do you want to save him when you know what he has done? Go away and leave us alone. He ought to die . . . he deserves to die."

"No," I said. "No one deserves to die this way. Not even for what he did."

"Luc," Juliette's voice beseeched him. "We could be together finally, after he's gone. Begin again, the two of us."

"No," he said, "we couldn't."

"Please . . ." Her eyes filled with tears.

"Put the gun down, Juliette." Pépé raised his arm and pointed Leland's .45 at her as she gasped. "You know I'm an excellent marksman. If I have to pull the trigger, you'll lose that hand. You'll never get your shot off in time."

"You won't," she said. "You wouldn't. You'd never hurt me."

"I would if you go through with this."

It will be a long time before I forget the anguished look that passed between the two of them. Then Juliette took a deep breath, almost a sigh, and squared her shoulders.

"Ah, Luc, my darling, then you must forgive me." She smiled at him and suddenly I saw a shadow of the young, beautiful girl she'd been in that beguiling portrait in Charles's study.

I knew, then, that Pépé had been there when she sat for that painting. The teasing, provocative look had been meant for him. I caught a glimpse of Charles's face. He knew, too.

Juliette aimed the gun, but her hand shook as though the weapon had become too heavy to hold.

"Don't," Pépé said.

Jasmine whirled around with Hope and ran into the kitchen. Hope started to wail.

"May you rot in hell, Charles."

Juliette steadied the revolver, this time with both hands. My grandfather flinched, but he kept the .45 trained on her as she tilted her head almost flirtatiously at him.

"*Adieu, mon amour,*" she said.

"No!" Pépé sounded panicked and I glanced at him in surprise.

Juliette took a step toward Pépé, and for a wrenching moment I thought she was going to shoot him before she killed Charles.

"Pépé, look out!"

"*Je t'aime, Luc.*" With one fluid movement Juliette brought the gun to her heart and fired.

She moaned and dropped to the ground like a rag doll, the gun bouncing off the carpet with a dull thud and skidding under the table.

My grandfather was at her side instantly, murmuring her name, pleading with her to respond. He looked up.

"Lucie, call 911. Now! *Vite!*"

I nodded. "Yes, of course. There's only a little blood . . . is she still alive?"

He bent his head so his ear was next to her mouth. "Barely."

In the kitchen, Hope's jagged crying had become hysterical as Jasmine frantically tried to calm her down.

"What about me, goddammit?" Charles asked. "I'm dying, too."

Pépé said, with some contempt, "Don't worry, Charles. We won't forget you. I can see how moved you are that your wife just shot herself."

"Don't talk to me about how I should feel." Charles was equally contemptuous. "You of all people. She married me after you exiled her to Washington and left for Belgium. She never stopped loving you. Don't think I didn't know it all these years. You're as responsible as I am for this."

My grandfather's face went pale but his voice stayed firm. "Lucie—an ambulance. Call now."

I started to dial as a door slammed in the kitchen. "Jasmine's leaving and she has Hope."

"Don't worry," he said. "They won't go far. I took the liberty of disabling her car when we got here—just in case."

I threw Pépé the phone. "Here. You give them directions. I'm going after Hope."

In the kitchen, my niece's cries grew louder as she called my name. A weight rolled off my chest.

"She's here. She's still here. Jasmine took off by herself."

"Go stay with her," my grandfather said. "Don't let her see this."

I nodded and pushed open the kitchen door. The last thing I saw before I left the room was the tableau of my grandfather cradling Juliette's head in his arms, an expression of unspeakable grief on his face, as her husband watched them both with the cold dispassion of a spectator. Charles must have felt my stare because he looked over at me one last time, with eyes as empty and vacant as dead planets.

I shut the door and went to comfort Hope.

CHAPTER 25

The expression of terror and gratitude on Eli's face when he picked up Hope at the Thiessmans' house was the same look you see on every television report or newspaper photo when parents get a reprieve from nearly losing a child to someone they thought they could trust and shouldn't have done. He looked wrecked, choking back sobs as we stood there with our arms twined around each other, crushing Hope between us. We were outside by the kitchen door, the exact spot where Dominique and I had chatted only a week earlier as she sneaked a smoke.

The grounds around the house were overflowing with cruisers, vans, EMTs, sheriff's department officers, crime scene investigators, ambulances, search dogs, even a fire truck. My head ached. It would be hours before I could go home.

I'd already called Dominique and warned her she'd have to make do at the dinner without Jasmine or me.

"What about the flowers?" she asked.

"You'll have to make do without them, too."

"What's going on? Someone who just got here said she saw ambulances and sheriff's department cruisers with their lights and sirens on making a beehive for the Thiessmans' house," she said.

"I'll explain everything when I can."

"Lucie?"

"I promise. I gotta go."

Bobby showed up right behind the first responders, letting Eli leave with Hope but sequestering me in the kitchen and putting Pépé in, of all places, the library with Juliette's portrait, until he could take our statements. Jasmine had vanished on foot since her silver Honda was still parked next to the back door.

"We're looking for her. We'll find her eventually," Bobby said. "And, uh, Juliette Thiessman . . ."

"Yes?"

"Bullet went straight to her heart. She didn't have a prayer."

"Does Pépé know?"

"Yup."

By the time he finished with us, it was nearly ten o'clock.

He came into the kitchen. "You two are free to go," he said. "I could confiscate that gun of your father's since Luc was carrying concealed without a permit. A French hunting license. Nice try."

"I'm sorry."

"Ah, forget it." He rubbed his tired eyes with both hands. "You and I are going to be talking again."

"I understand."

Bobby stopped rubbing and looked at me, fatigue and worry making canyonlike furrows that creased his forehead and deepening the marionette lines on his face.

"Jesus," he said, "isn't this a hell of a mess?"

Pépé stayed in town for Juliette's funeral. The press had a field day with the story; it was sensational, all the necessary elements—a secret society, murder, lust, greed, corruption, sex, and steeped in decades of lies and deception—that made it perfect for the tabloids. The Fauquier County police came out in force to keep the scrum of reporters and photographers away from what had turned into a major national media event as Pépé and I joined the other mourners at the old Episcopal church near Upperville.

The only person not in attendance was Charles, who was still in the hospital and expected to recover. Ironically, I heard from Kit that he was on a suicide watch. She had picked up the story for the *Trib* and kept me up-to-date on everything that happened in the weeks to come—that the police in Half Moon Bay were reinvestigating the death of Mel Racine, and in Maryland, the case involving Maggie Hilliard's accidental death was being reopened. The Loudoun County Sheriff's Department had also been in touch with French authorities concerning Vivian Kalman.

The day after Juliette's funeral, Kit interviewed Elinor Falcone and broke the story about Stephen, precipitating the national firestorm of moral outrage and shocked incredulity that Charles had predicted. She kept my name out of it and I was grateful.

Jasmine Nouri turned up in a motel in Charlottesville. Bobby told me the charges against her, which included being an accessory to attempted murder, would probably be reduced. She might even get away with a suspended sentence by cooperating with the police in putting together their case against Charles.

After the funeral, Mick Dunne cornered me and led me outside to the cloisters, where we stood as the rain poured down around us in the swirling gray mist. I told him then that it wasn't going to work between us.

"Because of Quinn?" he asked. "You got back together in California, didn't you?"

"No," I said, "we didn't. You were right, Mick. He'll be back for harvest this year, but that's it."

He put a hand on my shoulder. "I'm sorry, Lucie."

"It's all right," I said. "I'm over it."

CHAPTER 26

———— ∽∽∞∽∽ ————

I drove Pépé to the airport on a gray rainy morning, the day after the funeral. The depressing weather matched our moods.

"Are you going to be okay?" I asked.

"Of course."

"You mustn't blame yourself for what happened," I said. We had driven most of the route in silence. In another ten minutes we'd be at Dulles Airport yet again. "You didn't believe what Charles said, did you?"

"I should have realized how depressed she was. Maybe I could have prevented her death." He'd ignored the question.

"No. You couldn't." I was adamant. "Look, she thought she was going to be able to commit murder and escape a husband she loathed. When she got caught, she couldn't face the consequences, so she took her own life. It has nothing to do with you."

"I believe it does." He sounded so melancholy that my heart ached for him.

"I'm sure Jasmine had no idea the powder keg she set off when she sent Charles those pictures and that it would result in the deaths of three people. By the time she met Juliette and discovered she had a willing accomplice who wanted Charles killed off—plus she'd found Theo, who was also eager to go along—all the wheels were in motion for their little conspiracy. No one could have stopped anything," I said. "It played out the way it had to—including bringing you and me into it."

The highway billboards listing which airlines were located at which concourse began flashing by. I put on my turn signal when I spotted Air France.

"I'll come to Paris to visit you," I said. "This year when harvest is over, after you get back from Morocco. Maybe around the end of October?"

"It's about time. I'd like that." He smiled and brushed my cheek with a finger. "Don't park, *chérie*. Just drop me at the entrance near the Air France ticket counter. I have my boarding pass, so I can go straight to security after I check my bag."

I didn't argue with him, but I did wait after he exited the car until I could no longer see him and he'd disappeared in a maze of glass and steel. Though I hoped he'd turn around to wave goodbye, he never did.

I sat there, lost in my thoughts and worrying about him, until a security guard finally chased me away. Afterward, I drove slowly home in the rain, taking the long way on the back roads.

By October when we saw each other again, we'd be okay. Pépé'd bounce back to his old self and I would have finished the last harvest with Quinn.

Ready to move on, write the next chapter.

The next day I told Frankie I planned to advertise for a new winemaker. She looked at me the way a mother looks at a child who is about to do something she'll regret forever.

"Quinn will be back for harvest in a few weeks," she said. "Why can't you wait and talk to him about this? Maybe he'll change his mind and stay for good."

"We've done all the talking we need to do," I said. "Look, I need to clear my head. I'm going over to the cemetery to tidy up the graves. That wind and rain yesterday probably brought down some leaves and branches."

"Give yourself a break. You don't have to take care of that today." She paused and studied my face. "Never mind. I shouldn't be sticking my nose in your business, but I can't bear to see you looking so sad."

"I'll be okay," I said. "The Montgomery women are tough. I'll get through this."

She nodded. "I know."

★ ★ ★

When I was done cleaning what little debris there was among the headstones, I sat with my back against my mother's marker until the sun became a fireball and began to slip behind the mountains. A vehicle—the engine sounded like the old Superman blue truck that Antonio used—came down Sycamore Lane while the flame-colored sky was at its fiercest and most intense. It stopped at the bottom of the hill near the mulberry trees and a door slammed. Frankie obviously told Antonio where to find me.

He came through the gate, backlit by slanting gold light so he was completely in silhouette, but I knew right away it wasn't Antonio.

"How come you haven't returned a single one of my calls?" Quinn asked. He sprinted across the cemetery, threading his way between the graves before I could answer, and pulled me to my feet. "I called you every day for a week until I finally wised up and got my news from Frankie."

"There wasn't anything else to say," I said.

"What are you talking about?"

"Especially after you spent the night with Brooke right after we stayed together on the houseboat."

"What the hell—you think I did *what*?" He looked up and rolled his eyes. "*That's* what this has been about? You think Brooke and I—"

"What was I supposed to think when I called and you were right there while she was getting dressed?"

He put his hands on my shoulders. "Listen to me," he said. "Brooke is like a daughter to me. That's it. There is nothing—and I mean that—going on between us. I slept on her couch so I wouldn't have to drive back to Sausalito."

"Why are you here?"

"Because you're so damn stubborn, that's why. We could have sorted this out sooner and a whole lot cheaper," he said, "than a one-way plane ticket."

My heart skipped a few beats. "One-way?"

"I heard you're looking for a winemaker and I'd like to know why, when you've already got one."

"Do I?"

He nodded. "Unless you're firing me."

"No," I said. "I'm not."

"Good. Glad that's settled. Though I would like to make a few changes about the way we do things."

"Oh God, you want a raise. I should have figured."

"A raise would be good," he said, "but I was thinking more along the lines of a change of accommodations. Maybe we could try living together. You know, I could leave a few things at your place, see if it works. That is, if you'd be willing?"

I felt suspended, breathless. "I suppose you could do that. Eli and Hope are living with me now, too."

"I know," he said. "You'd be okay with me being part of your family?"

"Yes," I said. "I would."

"Me, too," he said. "Because you're part of mine."

I took a deep breath. "Then if we're family, you need to move in completely. No half measures, Quinn. It has to be all the way."

He grinned and kissed me. "All right," he said. "That's how we'll do it. All the way."

THE SILVERADO SQUATTERS

"The wine is bottled poetry," Robert Louis Stevenson wrote in *The Silverado Squatters*, describing the Napa Valley wines the Scottish author and poet drank on his two-month honeymoon in an abandoned shack on Mount St. Helena in 1880. Today Robert Louis Stevenson State Park encompasses the region where Stevenson, his new wife, Fanny, and her son Lloyd Osbourne stayed in a three-story bunkhouse located in Silverado, a defunct mining town in the Mayacamas Mountains a few miles north of Calistoga. In August 2010, the California State Senate named a stretch of Route 29, the main north-south route through the Napa Valley, in honor of Stevenson, who wrote such well-known classics as *Treasure Island, Kidnapped, A Child's Garden of Verses,* and *Dr. Jekyll and Mr. Hyde.*

Robert Louis Stevenson was born in Edinburgh in 1850 and, as a child, developed a series of medical problems from the damp Scottish weather that would plague him for the rest of his life. By the time he was an adult, he began traveling to warmer climates— particularly the south of France—for health reasons. On an 1876 canoe trip through Belgium and France, he met Fanny Van de Grift Osbourne, a married American woman more than ten years his senior. Though there were apparently no sparks between them at this first meeting, the following year they became lovers in Paris where Fanny had moved with her children to study art and escape a philandering husband who resided in San Francisco.

In 1878, Fanny left Europe and returned to California to settle matters with her husband; the following year Stevenson journeyed to America to join her. He took a second-class passage on a steamship that arrived in New York, and from there traveled by train to California, writing about his experience in *The Amateur Emigrant.* Penniless by the time he arrived in Monterey where Fanny was now staying with the children, the trip all but destroyed his fragile health. Later he moved to San Francisco where Fanny had gone to finalize her divorce, but poor health and great poverty continued to plague him.

In April 1880, Stevenson got word from Scotland that his family, which had been set against his proposed marriage to an American divorcée, had relented and now planned to send him an annual allowance. In May, Stevenson and Fanny Osbourne were finally married in San Francisco.

Determined to get her new husband away from the damp and fog of that city, Fanny decided the family should travel to Napa to stay at the home of an old friend. When the plans fell through, they moved instead to a cottage on the grounds of the Hot Springs Hotel in Calistoga. Unable to afford the ten-dollars-a-week rent, a local storekeeper directed them to the abandoned, run-down house in Silverado. After cleaning and fixing up the somewhat open-air place, they spent an unconventional honeymoon two thousand feet above Calistoga, which commanded breathtaking views of the valley. There, in the fresh air and warm sunshine, a contented Stevenson recuperated and regained his health.

During his stay in Silverado, he kept a meticulous diary, describing his adventures, mishaps, and encounters with the colorful local inhabitants; the memoir later became *The Silverado Squatters,* written in 1883 after he returned to England. Stevenson also used his notes about the beautiful and somewhat primitive scenery as the model for Spyglass Hill in *Treasure Island.*

In addition to Robert Louis Stevenson State Park, where a trail leads to the place the poet and his family once camped—the site is marked by a memorial in the form of an open book—visitors can learn more about Stevenson's life and works at the Silverado Museum located in the St. Helena Public Library.

ACKNOWLEDGMENTS

I had bicoastal help with this book, and there are many people to thank. The usual rule applies: It's not their fault if it's wrong; that's on me.

In Virginia, thanks to Rick Tagg, winemaker at Barrel Oak Winery in Delaplane; Brian Roeder, owner of Barrel Oak Winery (and native Santa Cruzan); Christine Ilich of Heirloom Kitchen in Front Royal; Dr. Christopher Burns, associate professor of medical education, Department of Microbiology, University of Virginia, Charlottesville; Detective Jim Smith, Crime Scene Section, Fairfax County Police Department; and Terri Cofer Beirne, eastern counsel, the Wine Institute.

In California, thanks to my family for their hospitality, support, endless driving, and patient fact-checking: especially Larry and Balen Crosby in Cupertino and Matt and Kristin de Nesnera in Santa Cruz. Annie Bones, state relations coordinator at the Wine Institute in San Francisco, answered questions and set up meetings for me in Napa. Thanks to my friend and fellow author Katherine Neville for introducing me to Michael and Jacque Martini of the legendary Louis M. Martini Winery. Jacque and Michael (he is the third generation of Martini winemakers) not only gave me the best insider tour of Napa Valley anyone could ask for but also graciously took in total strangers, offering me and my family their charming guest cottage as a place to stay. Thanks especially to Jacque (and

Larkin), for the driving, the tea, the restaurants, and for introducing me to their good friends Ed Sbragia of Sbragia Family Vineyards in Geyserville (Ed was formerly head winemaker at Beringer Vineyards) and Laura Zahtila, owner of Zahtila Vineyards in Calistoga. My favorite part, of course, was drinking truly amazing wine made by some of Napa's top winemakers; it isn't every day you get to drink a vintage from the year you were born.

Thanks for advice, comments, and reading drafts of the manuscript to Donna Andrews, Glen Gage, John Gilstrap, Catherine Reid Kennedy, John Lamb, André de Nesnera, Peter de Nesnera, Alan Orloff, and Art Taylor.

At Scribner, thanks to my wonderful editor Anna deVries, as well as to Fiona Brown, Rex Bonomelli, Katie Rizzo, and everyone else who does so much behind the scenes. Thank you to Cynthia Merman for copyediting.

Finally thanks and love to Dominick Abel, who makes it all happen.

ABOUT THE AUTHOR

Ellen Crosby is the author of six books in the Virginia wine country mystery series and *Moscow Nights*, a stand-alone mystery published in the United Kingdom. She is a former freelance regional reporter for *The Washington Post* and was the Moscow correspondent for ABC News Radio during the waning years of the Soviet Union. Crosby lives in Virginia with her family.

Printed in the United States
By Bookmasters